sticks + stones

A RANDY CRAIG MYSTERY

BY
Janice MacDonald

RaveN
STONE

Sticks and Stones
copyright © 2001 Janice MacDonald

published by Ravenstone
an imprint of Turnstone Press
607–100 Arthur Street
Artspace Building
Winnipeg, Manitoba
Canada R3B 1H3
www.TurnstonePress.com

Turnstone Press gratefully acknowledges the assistance of the Canada Council for the Arts, the Manitoba Arts Council and the Government of Canada through the Book Publishing Industry Development Program for our publishing activities.

The Canada Council | Le Conseil des Arts
for the Arts | du Canada

Canadä

Cover design: Doowah Design
Author photograph: Randy Williams

This book was printed and bound in Canada
by Friesens for Turnstone Press.

Canadian Cataloguing in Publication Data

MacDonald, Janice, E. (Janice Elva), 1959–
Sticks and stones

ISBN 0-88801-256-X

I. Title.

PS8575.D6324S74 2001   C813'.54   C2001-910050-7
PR9199.3.M31132S74 2001

Acknowledgements

First, thanks to Marni Stanley, friend, colleague and great conversationalist, who mentioned what was to be the kernel of inspiration for this story to me in a phone call. Thanks to The Canada Council for the Arts, The Alberta Foundation for the Arts and Joyce MacDonald for funding the time it took to write the first draft.

Thanks to Cora Taylor, Martina Purdon and Randy Williams for reading drafts; to Jennifer Glossop for tightening the manuscript and stretching me; to Manuela Dias and Jeff Eyamie for making the non-writing parts of this fun; to Madeleine and Jocelyn Mant for their patience and support; to the folks of both Biz and Brainstorms who cheered it on; and for my mom, who never got to read the final version.

Edmonton is definitely more than a state of mind. The University of Alberta is a real place, as are most of the places mentioned. None of the events depicted actually took place there, though. None of the people really exist, either, although some of the names are borrowed from people I like.

This is for Randy—the real one.

I WASN'T SURE IF IT WAS THIS PARTICULAR CROP of students or this year's freshmen in general, or, God forbid, me, but I was finding it tough to inspire in my morning class an appreciation of English literature. Granted, English 101 is the required course for those who hate reading, culture and aesthetic experiences on principle, but in past years I had usually been able to jolly them into a semi-sullen respect for what they were studying by late September. It was almost a month past that, and these folks still weren't buying it.

I suspect that most of them had made some sort of deal with each other to share notes and texts and to alternate attending lectures. Those who approached me after missing two lectures to ask if we had taken up anything "important" while they were away were the ones I really adored. "No," I would coo, "I noticed you weren't here so we just marked time doing shadow pictures on the overhead projector." A few had the grace to blush.

Not that all of them were lackadaisical. I had some keeners, and thank the lord for mature students. Other sessionals remarked that lecturing to people older than themselves intimidated them, but I'd found that students who returned to school after a break in the real world were thrilled to be studying anything. As well, they had a fund of life experience to add to discussions of literature. There were two older women in my morning class, and one older guy and one woman about my age had transferred into my afternoon class.

This was my third year as a part-time sessional lecturer in the English department of the University of Alberta, in Edmonton, or what one professor had jokingly called the University of the Southern Yukon. Two classes of thirty-four students each, a small overheated office in a condemned house on university property, and year-long library privileges. All in all, not a bad part-time job. When I wasn't marking essays and exams, I tried to keep my hand in the freelancing game by writing reviews and articles. Anything longer, like the Great Canadian Novel, was just going to have to wait.

At the moment I was standing in the general office, reading my paltry mail and waiting in line to use the photocopier.

"How's it going, Randy?" came a voice close to my left ear. It startled me, absorbed as I was in the list of new acquisitions to the department reading room. I turned to look at Denise Wolff, a full-time sessional who also had an office in the House, a former campus house now condemned for residential use and designated as overspill offices. As usual, she looked genuinely interested in my response. I find it a source of never-ending sorrow when incredibly attractive people are also incredibly nice. It would be so much easier to hate them and have done with it.

"I'm just doing a little mourning in advance, Denise."

"Why? What's wrong?"

"Today's the day I start Shakespeare with my 101s."

"Oh, God. " She sighed. " I know; it's not easy to lead the greatest poet the world has ever known to slaughter, is it?"

"Exactly. This year I chose *Twelfth Night* because I couldn't bear to hear one more eighteen-year-old dismiss *Hamlet* with an airy 'We did it in high school.' "

"Right." Denise's dissertation had been on Shakespeare's tragedies. She nodded and her glistening sixty-dollar haircut bounced vigorously. "I've seen seven productions and studied it intensely for about nine or ten years, and they figure they've got it aced because they did a line-reading in grade twelve and saw Mel Gibson or Kenneth Branagh strut about at the Cineplex. It's enough to make you weep."

I was just warming up into a good heated discussion when the copier came free. I smiled goodbye to Denise and settled in to figure out the intricacies of copying sonnets onto a transparency. The anthology we were using had chosen four, but only one was a favorite of mine. Thank goodness Shakespeare was beyond the regulations of copyright infringement.

I got to class with just enough time to write the day's journal topic on the board before the clock buzzed. I could have predicted the groans from the class as they read it. My morning class was politer, but they too had been slightly dismayed.

"Why is poetry considered the language of love?"

I glanced at their bowed heads as they began their daily exercise in writing to prescribed topics. Journals were a particular hobbyhorse of mine. They weighed a ton whenever I called them in for grading, but a year of journal-writing improved skills like nothing else I'd tried. It also got them into a literary mode, of sorts, at the top of the class. It cleared their minds of the business stratagems and amino acids they'd been pondering in the previous class, and focused them on rhetoric and ideas.

The rest of the eighty minutes was taken up with a lecture on Shakespeare's sonnets. I examined their order, the young man, the dark lady, and the argument of whether or not they were autobiographical. The young man seemed to excite the homophobes, while the mathematicians got a kick out of sonnet structure. Nobody seemed interested in the old Wordsworth/Browning argument of "with this key Shakespeare unlocked his heart" versus "if so, the less Shakespeare he." One person wanted to know whether they'd

3

have to be responsible for the sonnets on the transparency for the exam. I smiled and nodded. They groaned.

"Have a good weekend," I chirped as they loaded their backpacks and pulled on their jackets. Some of them looked resentful, and I recalled that I was the only one who worked a Tuesday/Thursday schedule. They likely had classes tomorrow.

I glanced outside at the late fall beauty. It was weather like this that made me think of old university days movies. I had an inordinate desire to go out and win one for the gipper. Maybe there was some truth to that adage that these would be the best years of my students' lives. At any rate, this was bound to be a fine weekend for those who could struggle through *Twelfth Night* in one sitting, I thought. What I didn't realize was that it would be the beginning of a living hell for some others.

SINCE I HAD NOTHING TO MARK, I SPENT the weekend relaxing. Edmonton in the fall is a glorious experience. If the winds hold off, the river valley, which bisects the city, is literally ablaze in autumn hues you couldn't get away with on canvas. We had been lucky this year; it had been a mild October, and the trees had been tenacious with their leaves. After stocking up provisions for the week, I'd spent most of my time on the endless bike trails in the river valley.

My bicycle is an old-fashioned ladies' one-speed with coaster brakes and a wire basket in front suitable for carrying extra-terrestrials should the need arise. My helmet, on the other hand, is made of a glossy space-age polymer over Styrofoam, which makes me feel like one of the flowerpot men from the old kids' TV program. I gamely pedaled past power walkers and some runners, and moved over for the in-line skaters. Everyone, it seemed, was out enjoying the weather. Edmontonians know better than to look gift weather in the mouth. My students wear shorts till well into November and begin to sport them again in March if the snow deigns to melt.

I was feeling pretty rested and at ease with the world by Monday. Even though I rarely head to campus when I'm not scheduled to teach, I popped into the Humanities Building to pick up my mail and kibitz with anyone who had time for a coffee.

Denise and Julian Lang were already in the coffee lounge. Denise's eyes were flashing—a sure sign that she had an opinion about something—and even Julian's rather phlegmatic features showed signs of animation. They turned to me in unison.

"Randy, where have you been? Have you heard?" Denise's voice was shaking with what I assumed (correctly as it turned out) was rage.

"Heard what? I just got in."

"Denise just came out of her 101 class." Julian wasn't teaching this year; he'd got a SSHRC grant to complete his dissertation. Unfortunately, the reduced pressure that steady money provided was playing havoc with his work schedule. He always seemed to be coffeeing or generally hanging out. I think he missed the teaching, too. From what I'd heard, he really came to life in front of a class. He'd have had to.

Denise wasn't going to let Julian scoop her.

"I couldn't get them to settle down at all. Half of them live in residence this year, anyhow, so most of them were in situ for the events."

"What events? Back up, Denise. What the hell are you talking about?"

Denise took a deep breath to steady herself. "Apparently, on Friday night a group of Fraser residents took it into their heads to invite some women from Rundle to a party."

"Fraser, that's the co-ed residence, right?"

"Yep, and Rundle's for women only, and Simpson's the men's only," interjected Julian. Denise glared at the interruption.

"So anyway, they drank a few cases of beer and penned personal notes to every woman on three floors, and then, before their testosterone deserted them, they sneaked in and slipped them under all the doors."

I was in awe, trying to imagine first-year students able to write more than a hundred letters. Something in Denise's tone of voice told me this wasn't the issue, though.

"When those poor women woke up, they were treated to

the knowledge that only one slim door had been between them and those cretins. Can you imagine how vulnerable they must have felt?"

"I'll bet some of them thought they were singled out, too. How could they know right off that they weren't the only ones getting an 'invitation'?" added Julian.

I knew there was something missing from this story. I still wasn't getting the point.

"Sorry, Denise, I don't quite make the connection between invitations to a party and your outrage."

Denise shuddered. "That's because you haven't heard the context of the invitations. They all began with some 'I would like to invite you to our party blah blah blah,' and then turned into 'if you don't come we will dot, dot, dot.' "

"What kinds of threats were they making?"

"I heard only two verbatim. One said they would find her and rape her until her cervix bled. Another was sent to a student of mine who's confined to a wheelchair. It said, 'we know you can't run from us.' "

"Apparently some verged on death threats, but all promised some form of sexual assault," Julian added.

"Does anyone know about this?" I was stunned.

"I would think so. Some of the girls are pressing charges."

Julian and Denise went on to decry the mentality of male residence dwellers in general, combined with the primal urges of post-adolescent hormones mixed with alcohol. Julian, while making sure not to condone anything, tried half-heartedly to defend his half of the species in vague generalities. Denise just snorted.

I poured myself a cup of coffee and sank into one of the understuffed chairs. I wondered what the fallout was going to be. How many of my students had been involved in this fiasco? Were any of my female students targets of such wrath? Had any of my male students been the authors? How in hell would I be able to look any of them in the eye tomorrow?

B Y THE TIME MY FIRST CLASS MET ON TUESDAY morning, all
hell had broken loose about the poison pen party
letters. Tearful girls had been interviewed on the local
television news, and solemn-faced university spokesmen had
been interviewed on the CBC National. The abrasively ener-
getic morning anchor of the radio station had asked the question that was on everyone's minds: "What is the university
going to do about the boys who had penned these letters?"

I groaned over my Shredded Wheat when I heard the subject noun. The media, regardless of whether or not it thought
it was pursuing truth and justice, had already bought into the
myth that I knew was going to undermine any positive action.
Punishment might have been meted out to "men," but didn't
we all know that "boys will be boys"?

Denise, it turned out, had also been quick to pounce on
the underlying message. She was in the grad lounge when I
popped in between classes, and as close to frothing at the
mouth as I'd ever seen her.

"Any minute now they're going to start equating this with
placing Volkswagen Beetles in bus shelters during Engineering
Week, and that's the last we'll hear about justice for these poor
girls."

"Don't you mean *women*, Denise?"

This came from Professor Dalgren, a misogynistic old poop

who had probably never been breast-fed as an infant. Why he bothered with the grad lounge was beyond any of us, but he always managed to be around long enough to find some sort of quibble. Denise looked over at him with a look that held less than her usual contempt for his hatred-masked-as-banter.

"No, Dr. Dalgren, I mean girls. Unsuspecting, naïve, neophytes to a system that isn't going to pay attention to the fact that they have just been victimized in an unconscionable manner."

Dalgren almost grinned at what he could foresee as an easy argument. "But you've just elaborated that the media is at fault by considering the perpetrators of this gag as boys. Surely you can't have it both ways?"

The few of us in the lounge were quiet, waiting for Denise to rise to the challenge of the wizened old fart.

"I think we're at cross purposes here, Dr. Dalgren. I too think of the fellows responsible for what you call a 'gag' as boys. I certainly think of them as too immature to be housed in an establishment of higher learning. Perhaps you are right: they are too young for university. In that case, it would be in everyone's best interest if they were sent home to do their growing up. What I am objecting to is not that they are called boys, but to the fact that much is overlooked by society at large when actions are labeled the works of boys. The phrase 'boys will be boys' is not something of which our society should be proud, don't you agree?"

To give him the benefit of the doubt, maybe Dr. Dalgren was late for a tutorial, but those of us in the room he scuttled from felt that the round had definitely gone to Denise. In fact, even Arno Maltzan, a young professor who had been sitting next to Dalgren, seemed a bit uncomfortable, as if his position on the couch had somehow compromised his own integrity.

Of course, I wasn't too sure what a comfortable Arno Maltzan might look like, as I hardly ever saw him in the grad lounge. He hadn't been a grad student here, and rarely came in of his own accord. He must have been entrapped by Dalgren in the mail room prior, or something. Or perhaps he was aspiring to move beyond being what my friend Leo Derocher would call a UTOF, or Untenured Old Fart, and was getting pointers from Dalgren, who was the quintessential TOF. Arno Maltzan wasn't old, mind you; I figured he was about my age, give or take five years either way. He wasn't much taller than Dalgren, though, which was likely why the old poop had zoned in on him. I've noticed that short men seem even more intimidated by tall men than tall women, although they don't care all that much for us, either.

Poor Maltzan obviously had no wish to continue the discussion and made a big production of reading the local theater playbills left on the coffee table. His sandy hair fell forward and hid his eyes. I didn't blame him. I couldn't imagine him flogging the same dead horse that Dalgren rode constantly. Of course, I'd been raised by feminists; I assumed that everyone of my generation thought much the same way I did. That sort of assumption had got me into trouble in the past.

The conversation, which was stalled into silence for a few minutes in the vacuum left by Dalgren, eventually resumed.

"A couple of reporters have been wandering the building." Denise rolled her eyes.

"Here in Humanities?" I asked. "You'd think they'd be scouring the Engineering Building or something. Not to make wild generalizations," I hurried on, making wild generalizations.

"It is odd, though. What do you think they want here?" Arno asked. "What faculty are the boys, er, students responsible from?"

Denise shook her head. "It's hard to gauge. From the looks of things, it was a wing of one floor of the residences, and they are mixed in terms of majors to provide a cross-mingling of people as a better university experience."

"Well," observed Arno wryly, "it looks as if the wrong people mingled."

Denise looked at him and laughed. "I'll say. Something poisonous sprouted in that gang, for sure. I refuse to believe that, coincidentally, twenty or thirty misogynistic psychopaths just happened to move onto the same floor in residence!"

"You've obviously never lived in residence, Denise," I quipped, and we all chuckled. The laughter was out of proportion to the level of the humor, but it was probably a pressure release.

I poured another cup of coffee before gathering up my briefcase and papers. Arno and Denise were still chatting, and I had a feeling Denise would have yet another admirer to add to her metaphorical coup stick. Poor girl, she couldn't help men falling head over heels for her. Just as the rest of us couldn't avoid lint.

I was leery of entering my class, but it didn't seem any different from the previous Thursday. None of the fellows was wearing a mark of Cain on his forehead; none of the girls looked shell-shocked. In fact, they all looked perfectly ordinary—a little bored, perhaps a bit hungry. I turned my back on them to write the journal topic on the board.

I'd been ready with a topic on unrequited love, but something, maybe a residue of Denise's anger, gave the chalk in my hand a will of its own.

"Sticks and stones may break my bones but words will never hurt me. True or false?"

There was a hush, and as I turned back to my students I saw the look in a few faces that made me realize my class hadn't gone unmarked by the weekend's events. I had been halfway hoping that this wouldn't have to be one of my battles, that I could just go along supporting Denise in righteous indignation and be done with it. Now I knew that I would either have to deal with the poison pen incident or spend the rest of the year skirting the issue.

"You've got ten minutes," I told my class.

EVERY ONCE IN A WHILE IT OCCURS TO ME that life doesn't
imitate art, nor does it occur merely to be a catalyst for
literature. It's not an easy concept for me to admit,
especially when I watch kitchen sink drama, or read some
post-modernist work that insists on listing the contents of
Aunt Betsy's medicine cabinet as an exercise in verbal futility.
In fact, I have entire days where I walk about in a dreamy haze
that makes me think magic realism might be how the world
really works.

I like to think of myself as a woman of the world, but who
would I be kidding? I am so caught up in the ivory tower
world of academe that I'm not even able to name all the pre-
senters at the Academy Awards. I still think they shouldn't
have done away with the self-deprecating little introductions.
Suppose someone from the Amazon Basin, or me, for
instance, happened to be watching?

What I'm getting at is that given half a chance, I will liken
real life events to situations in fiction. That's why it was so
eerily right that we were studying *Twelfth Night* as all this
hoohaw unfolded.

I've always maintained a sort of sneaking sympathy for old
Malvolio, even though he is such a stickler for the status quo.
Although I know I'm supposed to side with Maria and Sir
Toby and the rest of the merry denizens of Illyria, the tricks

they pull on Malvolio seem beyond the pale. And, of course, the trick itself is in the form of an anonymous letter. Anonymous letters were beginning to get on my last good nerve.

There had been quite a lot happening in the last week and a half. The university had come out with a statement that the perpetrators of the so-called "invitations" had been taken to task, and that two demerits had been placed on their records. Some reporter had dug up the information that it would take three demerits to kick someone out of the university residence. Since demerits were invoked only for fairly major things, it seemed likely that the writers of the notes could keep their noses clean and stay in residence through graduate school. When the news came out that the boys weren't being expelled, most of the girls involved withdrew their charges. I could understand why. It would be hard enough going through a court case, let alone having to see the offenders over breakfast every morning. Apparently some of the fellows involved tried to show their better sides by signing on as volunteer security walkers for lone women leaving the library at night. I made a mental note to leave the library before sundown.

So nothing was going to happen. Maybe the administrators were right; if nothing much was made of it, maybe everything would die down and we could all pretend that the ivory tower was a safe haven for mind and body. Of course, the media didn't see it that way.

The local papers came out with printed excerpts of the offending invitations, and laid out the page with a massive reproduction of one of the worst: a death threat.

It read :

Dear Gwen:

We would like to invite you to a party in your honor on 7th B. Dress is casual, and there will be refreshments.

If you choose not to come, we must warn you of the consequences. Sodomy is an equal opportunities punishment, but don't make a sound, or the floor monitor might give you a warning. You wouldn't want that now, would you?

Any hey, since you threw away your kids you won't be needing your breasts anymore, will you? Remember . . . shhhhhh! We can't disturb anyone else's studying. Or the knife at your throat might dig too deep. That might be a bummer as well.

> *Yours sincerely,*
> *The Party Animals of 7th B*

R.S.V.P.

I suppose it would be only natural for the press to make hay out of that one. Although I'd almost convinced myself that leaving bad enough alone was the better part of valor, part of me agreed with their exposure of what was beginning to be spoken of as "boyish pranks." To call this sort of thing boyish was to think of Jeffrey Dahmer as being an eccentric gourmet.

On the other hand, I was shocked that the university would allow the letter to be published with the given name of the girl addressed. This wasn't Wales. Gwen wasn't the sort of name you have three of in any given class. In fact, I couldn't remember ever having had a Gwen in my class. Until this year.

GWEN DEVLIN WAS ONE OF THOSE STUDENTS instructors long for. She was a bit older than the rest, maybe twenty-eight, if I had to guess. She always had the assigned reading done in time for class; her questions were thoughtful; she jumped in to initiate discussion but never monopolized.

She was interesting to look at, too. Some of my students have turned up with nose rings and teased green hair, startling fashion statements difficult to ignore when delivering a lecture on *Pride and Prejudice*. In mid-sentence I stop thinking about Elizabeth and D'Arcy and wonder how those nose rings would feel when you have the flu.

Gwen, on the other hand, dressed well but simply, and wore interesting earrings. Not gaudy numbers, but colorful beads and intricate symbols worked in metal. Her hair was reddish-brown, not quite auburn, and dropped to her shoulders. Sometimes she held it back with combs, which made the earrings easier to admire.

She'd come to see me in my office after the third week of lectures, when she'd transferred into my class, in order to discuss a couple of the essay topics. She was returning to school after a long time away and seemed a little taken aback by all the writing required. That's what I liked about mature students; they looked upon university as work rather than a four-year bunny hop into the work force.

She was pretty forthcoming about herself during our visit. She had recently left her husband and two children (boys, I think) up in some oil-patch town. She had found herself yearning for fulfillment, or words to that effect without the woman's magazine slant. She'd decided to go to university, a step she'd missed by getting married in grade twelve.

I was impressed, despite the initial shock at hearing she'd left her children. I'm not sure whether it was the gumption to break away, or the undisguised delight with learning for learning's sake that got to me the most. Gwen wanted to be at university more than anyone I'd ever met.

She'd got a partial scholarship to return as a mature student, and was earning her room and board by acting as a floor manager for one of the residence halls. I knew that because it was the reason she had transferred into my class. The English class she'd been assigned to had several students from her floor in it, and she was concerned that they'd feel overwhelmed and spied on if she seemed to be everywhere in their lives, so she'd asked to move to another class. My gain. She had done some admirable research on two topics on my sketchy list of essay topics. And that was the third week of classes! I wanted to clone her.

We had discussed both topics; she leaned towards one and then we had left it at that. So far she hadn't been back to see me, so I had no idea how the first two months had affected her outlook. I was intrigued to read her class journal, to see what she had to say about the more personalized topics I'd assigned.

And now she was up to her ears in this mess. It had to be her. How many Gwens lived in residence? That bit about the floor monitor had to be aimed at her. Part of me was grateful to think that the horrific piece of garbage I'd read in the paper hadn't been shoved under the door of some seventeen-year-old naïf, but mostly I grieved for the disruption to the joy that was university for this gutsy woman.

The lurid spread had appeared in the Thursday paper, but I hadn't caught up with it till that afternoon, well after the class that Gwen attended. They had all seemed so calm in class, except for the few who had forgotten I was collecting journals and left theirs at home. Either none of them had seen the paper yet, or she didn't mind her letter being used. I was suspecting the former. It never failed to amaze me how out of touch with current events students could allow themselves to get. Whatever the case, I resolved to speak with her on Tuesday morning. Maybe I could take her for a coffee.

I was spending the weekend helping a fellow grad student move, so I decided not to haul my two boxes of journals home and left them on the closet floor of my office. Most of my students wouldn't mind a break from writing for a week or so.

Having shot my weekend, I stayed at home Monday catching up on laundry and apartment cleaning. I lived in a cozy apartment building two blocks from campus. It had no security door, which drove my parents crazy the time they came to visit, but it made up for that and other deficiencies in sheer charm.

A dim hallway bisected the building. At either end a staircase led to the upper floor. Six apartments were situated on each floor, mine being the small one at the back. I had a lovely view of the garbage bins from my kitchen window, and an envious view of the neighbor's lawn from the living room.

I cleaned both sets of windows as well as the one in the bedroom. The bedroom was just big enough for a twin bed and a highboy dresser. A small closet hid behind the bedroom door, but most of my clothes hung off of hooks on the three doors—bathroom, bedroom and closet.

The kitchen was divided from the dining area by a glass-doored cupboard, which I suppose was intended for dishes, but which housed the books that didn't fit into the five bookcases I had lining the living room walls. The kitchen itself was rudimentary, with an old, low porcelain sink and shallow counters. The cupboards were plentiful for the size of the room, but I was still waging a battle with flour beetles the last tenant had invited in, so everything was stored in jars, and all my dishes had to be turned rim down on the shelves.

The best part of my haven was that it was small (easy to keep habitable), close to campus, and above ground. I had sworn off basement suites three years ago, and I had no intention of ever moving out. Most of the other tenants felt the same way. There was an old man in number 7 who had lived there for twenty years and counting; an opera singer friend who played Scrabble and other assorted word games with me whenever we had time; a jazz musician and his wife who threw great parties in their bigger front apartment; a movie director in the other upstairs big suite; a lawyer friend who would look over my freelance contracts for a meal; and a librarian and her husband who handed over their key once a year for me to water their plants when they left to do volunteer work in Nicaragua. I didn't really know the folks in the other five apartments, but we smiled when we met at the mailboxes, and nodded to each other at the local Safeway.

I often brought marking home to the apartment, but I usually left most of my textbooks in my office, which was, after all, only a few blocks away. I liked the ability to shut out the university. Not that I minded the work; in fact, I thought it was great. Although, in the grand scheme of things, sessionals are overworked and underpaid, it was still a great way to make a living, and I didn't need all that much to survive. You don't need a power suit to lecture about Alice Munro. I suppose it would help with Gore Vidal, but he wasn't on the 101 curriculum.

On Monday night I sank into a well-earned bubble bath in the abnormally large bathtub for such a small room. My apartment glowed; even the old venetian blinds were shining. I'd sorted through my summer clothes and packed them away in the suitcase under my bed. Fiona the opera singer and I had shared a meal of "prostitute spaghetti" (a joke of Fiona's I'd never really understood, but the dish was always tasty) and a quick game of Scrabble, and then I'd cracked the latest Jane Urquhart, which was so full of water imagery that a bath seemed inevitable.

No goose walked over my grave. No chill went down my spine at approximately ten forty-five p.m. Instead, I cuddled into a flannel nightshirt and slept the last good sleep I would have for some time to come.

TUESDAY MORNING I WAS FEELING MIGHTY self-righteous that I was the first to arrive at the House. I started the communal coffeepot going and trudged upstairs to my office, which was once a very small bedroom. The living room downstairs had the best view, but Leo and Greg had to share it, so I really didn't mind the cramped conditions in my private space. My students couldn't tell whether I was there or not in daytime, since I kept the drapes drawn against the winter sun, which seemed to get in my eyes no matter where it was in the sky. In Edmonton, one spent the winter either squinting or completely in the dark, once Daylight Savings Time came off. Pitch black at four-thirty p.m. Of course, summer nights were bright and sunny, but somehow that just didn't register in November.

Regular office hours didn't start till the afternoon, so I had left the front door locked. Everyone who worked in the House had his or her own key. I left my office door ajar to listen for Denise and Leo—Denise, because I wanted to talk with her about Gwen's name being used in the paper and how I was going to talk with her, and Leo because he owed me five bucks.

Leo Derocher was a wildly flamboyant poetic type, who reminded me a bit of Kenneth Branagh the actor and more of an old boyfriend who was now doing post-doctoral work at U of Toronto. I missed Guy whenever I saw Leo, which is odd in that Leo is devotedly gay. He lives by the code that nothing succeeds like excess, and postures uncontrollably whenever it might embarrass the faint of heart. He's working on the Romantic poets, and is only ever really serious when discussing his dissertation. He holds the record for writing the longest comprehensive exams ever seen in the department, and can chat with authority about almost everything, including most contemporary writers, which is amazing when you consider the concentration required by his own topic. He always has a Gatsby scarf trailing around his neck, thousands of papers shoved into his satchel, and never-matching gloves.

Part of my admiration for Leo is that I secretly wish I could be that comfortable in limelight. I skulk through life, hoping no one spots me and assigns me yet another task, while Leo jumps into everything with absolute joy. Mind you, he is always broke, and usually embroiled in something shocking, or so he would have you believe. He sponges off his friends all the time, but if it weren't for Leo coming to dinner, I'd eat alone a lot more often than I do.

I was still listening with half an ear for my friends to show up, nursing my first cup of Colombian, and sorting through my notes for class when I heard the banging on the front door. My first reaction was to ignore it. Surely even first-year students could read the office hours notice attached to the door. When the banging continued, I drifted toward the stairs, assuming that Leo had misplaced his keys again. I'd got halfway down when I realized that Leo would be hammering out the beat of a Broadway tune instead of the persistent staccato, but by that time I could see the uniformed man through the glass window of the front door.

When I opened the door to the policeman, I noted with mild curiosity that he was City of Edmonton, not Campus Security.

"Can I help you, Officer?"

"I'm looking for M. Craig," he said, consulting his notebook. He actually had a notebook, just like in detective novels.

"That's me, Randy Craig." I stuck out my hand, then wavered. Did one shake hands with the police? He solved my dilemma by shaking it and smiling slightly. "'The M is short for Miranda," I said. I never reveal that. Just goes to show how a uniform can make you talk.

"Steve Browning."

"Any relation to Kurt?" What was I doing chatting as if this was a social call? Later on, I figured that maybe my subconscious was trying to keep me from jumping to the panic stage. After all, how many times do the police show up to tell you you've won the lottery?

"Afraid not, but I wouldn't mind." He smiled a little more broadly, and I realized that Officer Steve was a very good-looking fellow. Well, they didn't call them Edmonton's finest for nothing. I guess I was staring, because he coughed politely, and I gave a start.

"Uh, come in," I spluttered, wondering if I should take him upstairs to my office or take him through to the kitchen. He decided for me.

"Could we speak in your office? You do have an office here, don't you?" He seemed to be just now taking in the fact that this had once been a rather splendid private house.

"Sure, it's upstairs. Uh, would you like a cup of coffee?"

He thought that would be nice and took it black, which is something I have never been able to do, and I let him carry his own cup upstairs. It was hard enough walking upstairs in front of him. I hate having my back to anyone, especially at close quarters. Not that I'm particularly ashamed of my body, it's just that bits of it seem to have a will of their own.

We got upstairs. I cleared off the student chair for him, throwing my jacket into the closet behind my desk, and tried to look professional.

"What can I do for you?" I was racking my brains to figure out what a policeman would want with me. Not that I'm perfect, but I am incredibly law-abiding. I don't even jaywalk. I don't own a car, and I wouldn't dream of littering. My foibles, as far as I knew, were all legal, unless using too much hot water in the shower had recently been put on the books.

Officer Steve took an appreciative swig of coffee and put on his official face. A very serious official face. I had a premonition that I wouldn't like what I was about to hear.

"You are the professor of English 101, Section C5?"

"Sessional lecturer."

"I beg your pardon?"

"I'm not a professor, I'm a sessional lecturer. I have an eight-month contract to teach freshman English. But, yes, I teach Section C5."

Officer Steve noted down my distinction, although he didn't seem to make much of it.

"You have a student in Section C5 by the name of Gwen Devlin?"

The penny dropped. This had something to do with the printing of Gwen's letter in the paper.

"Yes, Gwen's a student of mine. Is that why you're here? Is she pressing charges against the Party Animals, or the newspaper?"

"I gather you saw the letter to her reprinted in the *Journal*, Ms Craig." Officer Steve's voice seemed to drop an octave, but it might just have been the dark pressure behind my ears, which began to mount as I listened to his next words. "No, Ms Devlin is not pressing charges. I'm here because last night Ms Devlin was murdered. If you've read that letter, you will also know how she was killed."

I F I COULD RELIVE MY LIFE, I THINK I WOULD choose not to throw up fifteen minutes after meeting the handsomest man I'd ever known, but you can't have everything. At least I'd managed to get to the bathroom across the hall, and it was, for once, in working order. Police officers must be used to this sort of thing, because Officer Steve seemed unperturbed as he handed me wet paper towels, and was quite gentle leading me back to my office.

I don't think it was the knowledge that Gwen had been killed, so much as the vivid picture those horrific words in the letter had painted. It had hurt me to read them and to think of Gwen having read them; to know that she had been made to endure them was too much to assimilate.

The closest I'd ever come before to reading anything even remotely pornographic had been *Myra Breckinridge*, and that had only been mildly revolting. The letter I'd read in the paper had been vile; the words had practically steamed off the page with their hatred. But who could have hated Gwen so much? Had those fellows writing that note even known her? They must have; the note had made reference to her kids and her job as hall monitor. Maybe she had busted up one of their parties, put someone's nose out of joint. But, sheesh, it was only November; how could anyone work up that strong a hatred for anyone in two months?

It seemed that Steve—he told me to call him that—was checking into Gwen's life on campus, questioning her professors and the women living on her floor in residence. All together, it seemed that my class was the smallest in class size and the most concentrated in in-class and written assignments. Steve, I think, was hoping I could paint a clearer picture of Gwen Devlin than her other profs might. I doubted it, but I was willing to try. I told him the meager facts I knew. He pressed me for my impressions of her both as a student and a person. He cut in on me while I was describing her earrings.

"I gather you liked her," he said.

"She was easy to like. She had standards and integrity. She had something to offer the class, and she absorbed what I said in class. That's enough to make any lecturer love someone. But, yes, I think Gwen was a lovely person. Aside from leaving her children, which I must admit I have some problem with . . ."

"Did she say anything to you about her ex-husband?"

"No, I don't think she even mentioned his name to me. Mind you, it's not as if we had any real gossip sessions. We just talked about literature and essay construction." I searched my brain for anything else I could think of, willing this gorgeous man to stay longer, then immediately felt awful when the full circumstances dawned again.

Steve was getting up to go. Maybe it was my imagination, but he too seemed to want to linger a bit.

"If you think of anything else, call me. Here's my card. If I'm not there, a message will reach me."

"Are you in charge of Gwen's murder?" I asked, out of curiosity. I'd always wondered how police investigations really worked. They couldn't all be like Ed McBain novels.

"There are several of us at work on it now, but it will likely fall to me if it isn't sorted out immediately."

"Because you took the call?" I hazarded.

Steve smiled at my attempt at Hill Street Blues vernacular.

25

"No, I am usually assigned to crimes with a university connection. I'm thought to have an insider's understanding of the campus, in that I have a Master's in Sociology. Thank you for your time, Randy. I'll be in touch."

Steve let himself out of the building, leaving me to who had murdered my star pupil. Mind you, he had cleared up one mystery for me.

I now knew what you could do with a sociology degree.

DENISE WAS AS SWACKED OUT BY THE NEWS of Gwen's death as I had been, but she obviously had a stronger stomach. She didn't seem as fascinated as I was about the police investigation, but then she hadn't laid eyes on Officer Steve. Thank goodness. All I needed was for another man to go dancing attendance on Denise only to need patching up after a bout of her feminist put-downs. I think the only person who resented Denise's good looks more than me was Denise herself. Not that she chose to dress dowdily to mask her attributes; she just seemed leery of male attention and forced them to respond intellectually before she would take them seriously.

I, on the other hand, always knew men were talking to me rather than my cleavage. For one thing, I had no cleavage. This had depressed me in high school, but it made life easier on the whole. Aside from one Yeats scholar who had declared he would like to "skinny dip in my chestnut hair," of which I have a lot, most of the time I felt undistracted communication was achieved with the opposite sex. Not that I am as plain as a hedge or anything. I'm probably quite attractive in an ordinary sort of way. I'm tall, slim enough to get good deals on clothes, with clear skin and hazel eyes. It's just that I'm the sort of woman that people's mothers love, and to me that reads as unexciting and unthreatening.

My fleeting moment of jealousy alarmed me, but I put it down to having been solo for so long. Writing a thesis is an all-consuming passion, and I had needed no other at the time, but it had been a couple of years since my master's defense, and I was starting to feel a bit itchy, if that's not too indecorous a way of putting it. I probably would have fancied Steve even if his eyes hadn't been quite so green, his lashes so unfairly curly, and his muscles so pronounced under his shirt.

I put my libido on hold to concentrate on what Denise was saying.

"So it takes an actual murder to get anyone to do anything about the letters, does it? That's bloody typical."

"But, Denise, do you think the letter had anything to do with it, really?"

"Didn't you say that's what the policeman said? She'd been killed according to the tenets of the letter. That's horrible to think about. I mean, did you read that letter?"

"That's what I mean. Think about it, Denise. Who didn't read that letter?"

Denise stared at me. "What are you saying? That the letter-writer made good on his promise, or that someone used the letter in the newspaper as a recipe?"

"Which is worse?"

Denise banged down her reusable thermal coffee cup. "You know, if the university had done something about those letters, this might never have happened. If those women had received some justice right away, the press wouldn't have got so eager, and . . ."

"And Gwen might not have died," I finished.

"Yes," said Denise.

"Unless . . ."

"Unless what?" demanded Denise.

"Unless someone was planning to kill her anyway, and the letter business made a good cover for their actions."

Denise looked thoughtful. "Still, without those Party

Animal jerks, and the complacent university administration, and the muck-raking press, she needn't have died that way."

"How many people do you want to jail, Denise?"

"All of them! Let's start civilization over, and get it right this time." She smiled with the weary grace of a professional pugilist. "But I'd settle for the bastard who did the deed."

So would I. The bigger ethical questions would have to wait. As usual.

E VERY ONCE IN A WHILE I AM LED TO A GREATER than usual belief in Jung's theory of the collective unconscious and synchronicity. It most often happens when I'm looking in the Yellow Pages for something. I'll spy the name of a business like "Retreads," one I'd never heard of, while searching for Chinese take-out menus. The next day I'll spot the neon sign "Retreads" from the bus, then someone will recommend I take my skates there to get them sharpened for cheap. So maybe my putting *Twelfth Night* on my syllabus this year was some form of synchronicity.

Or maybe the term I was searching for was serendipity, if you could call anything linked to murder and poison pen letters serendipitous. Whatever it was, my Tuesday afternoon class was one of those you dream about as a lecturer, where everyone has an opinion, and the material seems to be pertinent to world events and touches people where they live.

I'm not so callous that I would have wished a student dead to get this sort of discussion going. In fact, it would have been a thousand times better if Gwen had been there to participate. Mind you, in an eerie way she was. Although the lecture theater was just three rows of tables rising one behind the other to the back wall, with no assigned desk space, the chair where Gwen had sat in the middle of the front row was empty. The rear line was just as cramped as ever. None of them had moved down to avail themselves of the newly open area. I wondered how long it would take the class to adjust to her absence.

Last Thursday I hadn't been able to get anyone talking about the trick played on Malvolio by Maria and Sir Toby. Today I couldn't seem to stop them. One side, populated mainly by men, but with a couple of camp followers among the women, maintained that practical jokes are just that, and that people who don't find them humorous are lacking in the funny bone department.

The other faction, surprisingly led by a girl who until now had said little in class, maintained that the letter sent to Malvolio was malicious in intent.

Sharon had the floor. "When you consider he was nearly committed to a mental institution, and you think of the condition of Bedlam and other institutions of Shakespeare's time, the outcome of that letter could have been fatal."

There was an impenetrable silence following her last word. She looked the way one does when uttering an inanity like "Couldn't you just die?" to the recently bereaved.

"As it was," she bravely filled the void, "it still ended unhappily for him."

"But he deserved it," interjected Dennis, one of the first group.

"How do you determine that?" I said, mainly to preserve the fiction that I was still in charge of the discussion.

"He was asking for it, being all straitlaced and sober, cramping Sir Toby's style," Dennis continued.

"But that was his job." This was from Carmen, a solid B student, if mid-terms were anything to go by.

"Yeah, but Shakespeare is trying to get everyone to have fun and be silly," said Dawn. I was impressed with her interpretation. She had struck me till now as a line reader rather than an absorber. Her alliance with the guys wasn't a shock, however. I'll admit that I was judging book covers, but I'd have laid odds her designer dust jackets were aimed at snaring her M.R.S.

"But is that really what he's promoting? After all, the only ones who are having any fun are the drunks." Myron was the other older student in this class. I had pegged him at about twenty-five. His written work struck me as thoughtful, and I had been wishing he'd speak out more. Some of the fellows of the pro-party party looked scandalized that Myron would take the "woman's" position. An impassioned argument about the relative merits of Illyria followed.

I was about to break in when Myron spoke again.

"Not that I think it exonerates Maria and Sir Toby, but Malvolio was not obliged to act on the message."

Now we were getting somewhere, I thought. I gave Myron my "Yes, go on" look, honed from years of practise.

"After all, the letter wasn't addressed to Malvolio personally. He just leapt to the conclusion that it was for him from Olivia," Myron continued, with a musing tone in his voice, as if he was just thinking through his thoughts as he heard them in the air before him.

"Good point," I said. "In other words, we as audience realize the culpability of the jokers, but Malvolio brings about his downfall by placing himself in a position of ridicule through his own hubris."

That last bit must have sounded like an exam question, because all heads bowed in unison to scribble in their binders. The bell rang, and I found myself wondering whether Gwen had somehow brought her fate upon her. Had she been a faceless victim, or was she an actual target?

I had to find out more about Gwen's situation. I didn't think I was being ghoulish; the bottom line was that if Gwen had been the actual target, then that was that. If, however, she had merely been convenient, then maybe the danger was just beginning for all of us.

I managed to shout out a reminder that papers were due in

the next class. As the lecture hall emptied, I sighed. As much as I had enjoyed hearing their brains working, the impassioned discussion had put us a class behind on *Twelfth Night*, which meant I wouldn't get started on poetry until next week. While I try to build some leeway into my syllabus for this sort of occasion, it would mean hurrying through Marvell. That was a shame, since "To His Coy Mistress" always seemed to energize them for the more modern stuff. I looked at my watch as I always do when I feel the pressure of time. If the papers were coming in Thursday, I'd have to get cracking on their journals. I'd just give them a cursory read-through to see how their thesis statement creation was progressing. I vowed to stay late and mark journals, and finish the rest throughout the day on Wednesday. Then I would have the weekend for the papers. Whoopee. Maybe I'd schedule a massage for Monday as a reward. Some reward. After eighty-odd journals and eighty odder papers, I would require a massage just to walk erect.

IT WAS WEDNESDAY AFTERNOON BEFORE I CAME TO Gwen's journal in the box (which didn't seem to get any emptier no matter how long I drudged). I had tried to goose myself along by treating myself to a bowl of *bibimbap* at the Korean restaurant in HUB mall, but I'd been accosted by a student asking questions about thesis statements, which had me depressed. I wondered how many of them had even started their essays yet. After all, they had all of fourteen hours before it was time to hand it in, why rush greatness? I decided that being in HUB, which was part apartment residence and part food court, was a hazardous place to be. The acronym might be short for *Housing Unit Building* but it felt like the hub of the entire university.

Soon I was back in my office, with some Java Jive coffee steaming out of the wee hole in the top of my covered mug, trying to slog my way through the final thirty journals. I must have been on autopilot, because I had the spiral-bound notebook open before I realized what I was about to read.

You can't study English literature for six years while harboring an aversion for dead people's writing, but I wasn't sure I was up to reading something so freshly posthumous. I felt morbid as I pulled the notebook toward me, tossing my red pen on my desk. There would, after all, be no point in correcting grammar or making comments in the margins of this journal.

Gwen's writing was like her, easy to read and distinctive without being flowery. It wasn't as neat as that of some of my students—notably my Chinese students whose penmanship seemed like art—but it was head and shoulders over the rounded, childish writing or flattened, right-slanting scrawl of most Canadian-born eighteen-year-olds. Gwen's writing was full of controlled little spikes upward and tight loops under the line. She rarely crossed anything out; she double-spaced throughout; and she delineated paragraph breaks with both an inch and a half indent and one extra line space. The presentation was determined. As I began to read, I realized the thoughts were also.

Gwen hadn't needed the journal as exercise, but she seemed to have reveled in it. She poured herself into coming to grips with my topics, which I had to admit were occasionally off the wall. I tried for a mixture of topical arguments thrown into syllabus-based questions. Every once in a while I would allow an open-ended topic to gauge their ability to create an argument extemporaneously. While Gwen dealt with the course-dictated topics well, it was on the topical and freestyle issues that she soared. I found myself enjoying the read, which couldn't be said for most of my day prior to this.

It was the entry dated two weeks before her murder that caught my attention, pulling me out of an interesting read into the world in which policemen came to call.

I had been rushed that day, I remembered, and I'd slapped up "Admit what's been eating at you" on the board to gain myself some time to review my notes on Gatsby.

Gwen's entry began with: *"I lied to my therapist yesterday."*

Now if that wasn't a grabber, I couldn't name one. I read on, captivated.

I was talking to my therapist about my study group with two girls from my geology class, and how we alternated bringing a big Thermos of coffee. Jane seemed to pounce on the fact that this showed I had a positive relationship with compatible people who shared nurturing and all that crap she's always on about, when she's trying to make me see what I'd been missing before. As if bringing a Thermos of coffee was equal to caring for a child or listening to your desires. Anyhow, although I'm not sure why I said we alternated the coffee bringing in the first place, I felt as if I couldn't really correct her.

We don't alternate bringing coffee. I'm the one who always remembers. Maybe I'm the only one with a Thermos. Maybe it's because I'm ten years older than they are and they figure it's up to me. Maybe Jane is right and I am trying to buy love with good deeds.

Perhaps it's the way I was brought up, but it seems like selfishness to want something just for yourself. Jane is one of those "happy me, happy others" sermonizers. Maybe she's right. But right now, here, where it's all for me, "happy me" doesn't seem to be surfacing.

It makes me wonder if any of it is worthwhile. I'm paying what I think of as an enormous price to be here, and not just money-wise. Is it worth it?

It has got to be. It hurts too much to be for nothing.

I sat back, a little bit shocked by the honesty on the page. Had Gwen been so wrapped up in her thoughts she'd forgotten this was an open journal? Or was this a message to me personally? Had she seen me as someone she thought she could to talk to?

The phone rang just then, but it was a pre-recorded announcement listing the locations of the blood donor drive the following week. While I jotted down the dates, I skimmed through the few remaining pages of Gwen's journal, finding only the breezy voice of the earlier entries. Not sure what to do with it, and unwilling to put it back in with the other journals, as if somehow it might contaminate those belonging to living people, I pulled out some old thesis notes and phone directories and stuck the journal beneath them in the second drawer of my desk.

The rest of the afternoon was eaten up by journals, but around six o'clock I was finished and ready to head home. I set the box of journals on top of my desk in order to remember to haul them back to their owners. I sighed as I recalled that I would only be trading them for similarly uninspired essays, then I shrugged into my duffel coat.

It was pitch black in the hallway outside my office. I hated being alone in the building in the dark. The trouble was, I'd got used to working till eleven during the summer with the sun just setting as I walked home. Now, it was only early evening and I was spooked. I inched my way down the stairs and let myself out the back door, pulling it firmly behind me.

November in Edmonton. Real Edgar Allan Poe weather. Oh well, at least the snow was holding off.

THE RADIO ANNOUNCER WOKE ME UP WITH THE cheery message that the snow storm had begun around 2:00 a.m. I rolled over and lifted my rice paper blind two inches, causing my phone, which I keep on the windowsill, to fall on my head. I was off to a great day.

I used my entire share and half of Mr. McGregor's share of hot water in my shower, threw on my rose-dotted Stanfields long underwear and fuzzy slippers and schlepped out to heat water for my cereal. From the looks of things outside the window, there was already about a foot of snow on the ground, the big fluffy variety, puffed up like a down comforter. One thing, it did make the world outside a lot brighter.

I flipped on the radio in the kitchen. The morning show hosts on CBC One seemed to be trying to get as sappy as the private station jocks. I wasn't sure why they thought this would boost their ratings. At least the weekend and FM hosts retained some dignity, maybe because they were resigned to their ratings. I don't know why they bothered. Everyone I knew listened to CBC during the day, and had CJSR, the campus station on in the evening. Mind you, since leaving high school, I'd run with a tonier crowd. I no longer could count as personal acquaintances people who opened beer bottles with their eye sockets.

The kettle sang and I filled the cup with instant coffee and the bowl with expanding fiber, drained the water off the cereal, and took the two to my small kitchen table. Milk in both, sugar on cereal. I listened with semi-somnolent ears to the morning's "Commentary." Some woman down east was speaking about the irony of violence outside abortion clinics. I'd wondered about that myself. I'd always figured I'd have more respect for the pro-lifers if they were seen fostering children and baby-sitting so that teenaged mothers could finish high school. I wondered how much the CBC paid for the "Commentary" spots, as if I could come up with a cogent opinion on anything topical at the moment. I knew I was just hungering for freelance gigs because the Damoclean sword of marking papers hung over my weekend. And I had to get through two classes before I could even get on with them.

I hate teaching on the days that essays are due. No one wants to listen. If they're keeners, they're still hung up on their papers' topics and want instant feedback. If they're drones, they figure that getting the paper in gave them immunity against thinking for at least a week.

So, all in all, I was pleasantly surprised to see Officer Steve waiting for me on the steps of my office when I'd trudged through three blocks of unshovelled snow. Anything that could take my mind off my job and the weather would be welcome, I figured, and this diversion came so well wrapped.

He smiled at my mock salute.

"They told me your teaching schedule at the main office; I was hoping you'd have time to talk before your first class."

I thought of the buzz his request would have created in the office. Let them talk; my life was so pristinely boring that any innuendo could only enhance my image.

"Is there something more I can help you with?" I asked, letting him in the front door. We stamped our boots in unison, and he followed me into the kitchen. First one in has to start the coffee was the rule in the House, so Steve waited as I did the necessaries.

"It'll take about five minutes. Come on up. I'll run down and get us a cup in a minute."

I backed Steve out of the kitchen and he led the way up the stairs this time. I pulled my huge ring of keys out of my coat pocket, along with a wad of fuzzy Kleenex and two old gum wrappers.

When Steve and I were settled in my office, with the space heater blasting at our feet, he got down to business.

"Things are pretty much still up in the air with the Devlin case, although I'd rather you didn't spread that about. The powers that be here on campus would like things cleared up as soon as possible. They're getting a lot of heat from parents of the other girls who received the so-called invitations, as well as the fact that any murder on campus doesn't look good to potential students or investors."

"I can imagine." I bit my tongue on the thought that things might have gone a lot easier on them if they'd been just as quick to deal with the letter business in the first place. I wasn't quite sure where Steve stood on feminist issues, and I have to admit, the uniform did its required bit to cow me.

"So, to facilitate matters, I suggested to my superiors that we ask you to aid us in our investigations."

"Isn't that what they say in the detective novels just before they book someone?"

Steve laughed. It was a nice laugh. "I wouldn't know. I'm more into speculative fiction, myself."

This guy was looking better and better all the time. I checked my yellow wall clock. I was due in front of the first class in about an hour. Too bad. The coffee would be ready by now, too. I excused myself to run down and get us some, glad that Steve took his black, since the milk in the decrepit fridge smelled suspicious.

"How do you think I can help you?" I asked as soon as I was back in my office. "I thought I'd told you everything last time."

"Well, although the crime replicated the words of the letter published in the newspaper, we're thinking beyond one of the poison pen writers or a copy cat crazy, although we're not ruling them out."

I liked the fact that he hadn't called them "boys." I leaned forward on my desk, thinking he was telling me an awful lot more than policemen in novels ever seem to divulge and wondering where I'd fit in to all this.

Steve continued.

"We're checking on Ms Devlin's family and friends as well, to see if any motive appears. What I'd like you to do is to look through her notebooks and school work, to see if anything jumps out at you as out of the ordinary."

"I thought you were the campus expert."

"That doesn't mean I'm going to catch something in her English papers or her margin notes."

"And you think I will?"

Steve pulled a sheaf of papers from his briefcase.

"We found these in her room. They appear to be the rough drafts and a finished copy of her essay for your class. I was wondering if you could look them over and see if anything might reflect her state of mind when she was writing them."

"You're not implying she committed suicide?"

Steve looked grim. "I don't think that's physically possible."

Maybe I started to look a little green around the gills again, because he hurried on.

"No, it's just that it's been a long time since I read *The Great Gatsby*, but the Valley of Ashes part doesn't ring a bell with me at all."

I was intrigued. I wondered just what slant Gwen had taken on the essay.

"The Valley of Ashes would probably appeal if you were coming out of a rotten marriage," I said.

"And you're sure she was?"

Just then I remembered the journal sitting in my drawer.

"Well, I know Gwen was separated from her husband, and that she was seeing a therapist."

I'm not sure why I didn't just hand Steve the journal right there and then, except that his pager went off, and that that distracted me. Oh heck, my whole life could be said to have been guided by random non-occurrences, sort of Odysseus in reverse.

"Sorry about that, I have to be somewhere. You wouldn't know the therapist's name, would you?"

"Jane; that's all I know. Maybe you can find her in Gwen's address book or something."

Steve made a note of it.

"Well, if that's all you want . . ."

"Right," he said as he rose. "I know you have to prepare for a class so I won't keep you any longer. I appreciate your aid on this."

"Oh, that's okay, it'll be like marking one more essay, that's all. When do you need my opinions by?"

"As soon as possible." Steve stood in my doorway, with his empty cup of coffee in one hand and briefcase in another. No rings on either hand.

I made an amazing jump of audacity and found myself saying: "Well, if you want to come by my place for dinner tomorrow night, I could give you my impressions then."

Steve raised one eyebrow slightly, in a manner I'd practiced in a mirror to no avail one summer when I was twelve, and smiled.

"That would be nice. I'd like that," he said.

I hurriedly pulled open my middle desk drawer and hunted out one of the business cards I use for freelancing.

"Six-thirty all right?" I asked.

"I'll be there."

I stood, barking my thigh on the still open drawer. I am so damned graceful sometimes it's a wonder I didn't spend my childhood at the National Ballet School. Avoiding a curse, but wincing a bit, I took his coffee cup and followed him down the stairs. Then I hobbled back up for my coat, notes and the first box of journals to return. I had just enough time to detour to the main office for my mail, if I hurried.

Stomping through the snow with the cardboard box held the way one of the little Wise Men would hold the myrrh in a children's church pageant, I mentally kicked myself for forgetting to give Steve Gwen's journal. It wasn't as though I was her therapist holding confidential files, and I had told him what I figured was the most important element of its contents. I resolved to take the journal home with me tonight and give it to Steve when he came over for dinner.

Dinner with a cop. What the heck would I serve? You can't base an entire menu around doughnuts.

I'D FORGOTTEN ALL THE SIDE BENEFITS THAT COME with having a new person over for dinner. For one thing, the apartment was sparkling. It looked almost as good as it had during the final draft of my thesis, when I would cheerfully defrost the fridge rather than get to work. This time I'd alternated one hour of cleaning for every hour of marking, and managed to fold the last load of laundry and put it away with only three papers left to mark. I'd decided on lasagna for the meal, since the dishes could all be cleaned up after I'd built it and shoved it in the oven in the afternoon.

Steve had arrived on time with a moderately priced bottle of Okanagan white and no uniform. Instead he looked great in a brown leather jacket over a Cosby-styled sweater and dark wide-wale cords. I was impressed. My father had always looked better in his Air Force dress uniform than in any casual clothes or even a tux, but Steve was one of those people who make the uniform rather than the other way around.

I was surprised at how easy conversation came to us. Somehow we made a tacit agreement not to talk shop during dinner, and even over coffee we were casual about getting into the deep stuff. He asked me questions about sessional work, but they seemed motivated by just your average curiosity. I didn't have the sense I was being probed, if you know what I mean.

He soon had me off on one of my favorite subjects, the *faux pas* and malapropisms I collected from freshman essays. My winner from this last batch had been the one where one of my students had referred to Jay Gatsby as a "Flin Flon man."

Steve laughed.

"Obviously not a native of Manitoba," he said.

"You never know."

"Is it really as bad as they say? I mean, are the schools producing illiterates who are entering university?"

"The best way to answer that would be yes and no." I was off on another favorite topic, but Steve had asked for it. "My feeling is that students are probably no better or worse than ever before, even with 'whole language' rather than phonics and with no grammar being hammered into them. It's just that the concept of the university seems to have changed in the last ten or fifteen years. While the term *elite* has taken a beating lately, it's probably a useful one for the classic concept of a university. Not that many years ago, there were perfectly acceptable routes for the average person without a degree to follow toward a career. But now there is an insistence that universities be available for anyone. It never used to be a sin not to go to university; now you're a failure if you don't. In addition there's less government money for institutions, so universities need more students and more tuition. Pressure gets put on the university to lower its standards and admit more students. The five percent who would have been there in the first place thrive, and the others play catch up or sink; and then feel like they've been tricked when there're no jobs for them at the end of the rainbow."

"Is that the ratio of good students in your classes? Five percent?"

"I usually manage a fair crop of sixes with a few eights and one or two failures."

"You're still marking on the stanine system?"

I nodded and poured him another cup of coffee.

"Can you explain it? I never did understand a marking system of nine."

"No I can't explain it, and few universities use it. Most are on a four-point system. Here goes, though. Nine is the ultimate mark, four is a pass, often conditional, and six is a solid mark. Most good students see a lot of eights and maybe two or three nines in their entire university career. Nines are easier to get at the grad level, but that's just because you get booted out if you get lower than a seven, and the department doesn't like to admit they made a misjudgment in accepting you in the first place."

I wrapped my fingers around my coffee cup. It was my favorite, a large mug with an impressionist view of Boston on the side. My neighbor Fiona had brought it back for me after a summer at the Music Conservatory.

"Do you give out many nines?" Steve asked.

"I once heard a prof say that he'd give out a nine only if he wished he'd written the paper himself. I got the feeling he was never going to admit that, so I suppose he didn't give out many. I liked what he said though, and I follow his rule to a point. I give out nines when I wish that I'd written a paper like that when I was in first year university."

"You strike me as a fair marker, Professor Craig." Steve smiled.

"Oh, I hope so." I felt myself blushing. "I'm probably a bit too easy. I'm trying so hard to make them like the subject that I find myself giving them credit for simply appreciating what they've read."

Steve shifted at the table. I'd already cleared away the dishes, but we'd been lingering over the social aspect of the evening. I realized that I'd wanted to linger. Steve was very easy to be around, and I'd been alone far longer than most hermits would deem necessary. Mind you, I still hadn't come upon any amazing truths.

We both knew there was business to get down to. Steve said, "So what sort of student was Gwen Devlin?" just as I rose to get her paper off my desk behind his chair.

"Gwen was a nine student, by anybody's standards. This is a fascinating interpretation of *The Great Gatsby* in terms of metaphorical place. She comes to terms with the Valley of Ashes, the town where Daisy's husband visits his mistress, in a really personal way. You see, if Daisy is meant to personify the American Dream, the unattainable goal someone like Gatsby is striving for, then why on earth would her husband require a mistress, and what must the mistress represent? Well, what the mistress represents, according to Gwen, is the true American Dream, vulgar and tarty and common and commercial. We want what we don't have. Jay could have a hundred mistresses like Myrtle, but he wants some ethereal projection from his youthful fantasies, a meta-Daisy. The man who actually has Daisy wants a flesh and blood woman, but he can't really have Myrtle either, because she's already someone else's wife. Whether he would want her if she was single is another question."

"Gwen's paper said all that?" Steve sounded skeptical.

"Not in so many words, but she's on the right track. Most of my students get lost in the simplistic structure of the novel and forget to read it as a fairy tale gone wrong. Maybe you need to have lived a bit before you read Fitzgerald. Maybe you have to know that there are precious few *'happily ever afters'* out there in the real world."

"And you think Gwen knew that?"

"I think she was projecting her interpretation of the novel from her own unhappy marriage. We're talking *Cinderella Complex*: spend your life waiting for Prince Charming without realizing that all fairy tales end at the start of marriage." I stopped short. This wasn't exactly first-date conversational fodder, and I had to admit I wouldn't have minded calling this a date. I shifted my train of thought a bit, trying not to look as though I'd lost my place, a skill I have had great practice with during 101 lectures.

"Although she misses the symbolic relationship between the names Daisy and Myrtle and, in fact, in a couple of places transposes their names, she does pick up on the affair as the underlying rot of the American Dream." I stopped. "Was Gwen's husband having an affair?"

Steve looked disconcerted in that way the fraternity of men does when having to rat on a member. "So far, we have a very sketchy interview with Rod Devlin from the RCMP who contacted him. He lives in Fort McMurray with his two sons. I'm expecting to hear from him this coming week, since he'll be coming down to clear up his wife's effects."

"Why?" I couldn't imagine an ex-husband being so concerned, but then again, I'd never had one.

"Apparently they had separated on only a trial basis, while his wife 'tried to find herself' at university. From the sound of it, he expected her to realize she was out of her depth and be back with her tail between her legs by Reading Week."

"If that's what he really thought, he didn't have much of a line on his wife. Gwen was born to go to university. She might have been short on the classics, but her command of contemporary literature was pretty sound. Surely he must have noticed she was reading Atwood and Findley, not the *National Enquirer*."

Steve shrugged. "People see what they want to see, Randy."

I looked at him, puzzled by the tone of voice. He was looking at me in a decidedly first date sort of way, which caused a warm feeling in me down somewhere near the lasagna. I wondered what Steve Browning was wanting to see while looking at me. With any luck, it was the same thing I was seeing.

By tacit agreement, Steve went off duty as we moved into the living room with another cup of coffee. It didn't seem too contrived to find ourselves together on the couch, since the other living room chair is a ratty little wicker job which looks like a summer cottage reject.

After a suitable interval—to borrow a coy phrase from Victorian novels—Steve left, with the promise to phone about tickets to a concert at the Yardbird Suite, the local jazz temple. As I waltzed my way dreamily to bed, sated on romance, it occurred to me that I still hadn't told Steve about Gwen's journal.

Oh well, it's not as though I wouldn't be seeing him again. Tra la.

I F SOMEONE HAD ASKED ME PRIOR TO MEETING the two men, I would have expected to take a shine to Mark Paulson and want to hiss when Rod Devlin walked into the room. After all, Paulson was a reporter with the local daily, and I would imagine we'd have something in common. Devlin, on the other hand, was a murder suspect and the ex-husband of a woman I had liked a lot, and chances were he'd be behind my social eight-ball from the start. It just goes to show you that I am not as in touch with my inner social convenor as I thought I was, because the reverse proved to be the case. Of course, it was possible that my first impressions were skewed by the fact that I met them both on the same day as the graffiti artist struck the English Department.

Denise had called me at home at eight-thirty on the Monday after my marking weekend. I'd been hoping to get all the marks recorded before doing my laundry. The plan had been to reward myself then with a stroll through Old Strathcona, the nifty boutique and bookstore haven of Edmonton. I had been thinking of a visit to Greenwoods to buy a book, and maybe a browse through Southside Sound or Sam the Record Man.

But, no, instead of whiling away a day with cafe lattes and fiction, I was aiming my 35 millimeter lens at venomous prose on office doors. It had been Denise's idea to call me, since I lived the closest to campus, and she knew I had a camera. She had arrived at seven to prepare for her early class. About a half hour later, she'd gone across to the building to run off some handouts and deliver a paper to Grace Tarrant for her quarterly. She'd found *Lepine had the right idea* scrawled in red felt marker on Grace's door. On her way to the office to report it, she noted several other doors marked with equally abhorrent messages: *PhD = Phrustrated Dyke; Montreal was a good start; Ballbreaker; Get back to the kitchen; Die, bitch;* all in blood red upper case letters.

The police arrived just as I was inserting another roll of film. Steve was with them, and came straight to me, which probably did not endear me to Dr. McNeely, chairman of the English Department, who was standing next to Denise.

"What's going on?" Steve asked. He sounded out of breath, as if he'd run all the way from the station.

I explained what I was doing, getting recorded evidence for Denise before the maintenance people came to clean the doors. Steve abruptly turned away and spoke to one of the other officers, who hurried away.

Seeing my puzzlement, Steve explained. "I've sent him downstairs for the evidence kit. We'll try to hurry our procedure so that this can get cleaned up as soon as possible. Can I get your film developed as well?"

"Are you sure I'm going to get it back?"

"Randy, we're the Edmonton Police Department, not the KGB. I would just rather this sort of thing wasn't sent out to a private firm for development. I take it you wouldn't want to see one of your pictures on the front page of the *Sun*?"

I got the point and dropped the film into his outstretched hand. "It's not all graffiti shots," I warned him. Come to think of it, I wasn't sure what was on the top of the roll. At the speed I shot pictures, there might even be some shots of the bison that Guy and I had seen on our picnic last summer to Elk Island.

"Don't worry, I'll get it back to you, no charge." He smiled, somewhat grimly.

I belatedly remembered who buttered my bread, and referred him to Dr. McNeely. McNeely had been fired up by Denise already, but he was already on record as being a proactive feminist, so I knew his blood would be boiling over this spectacle.

Steve asked me to wait around, saying that he'd like me to walk him through the hall after he'd spoken with Dr. McNeely. Denise and I sat on one of the low benches near the elevator and I reloaded my camera while we waited. It gave Denise enough time to fill me in on what had occurred before I was called in.

She had counted eight defaced doors on her way down to the office, but found four others after patrolling the other corridors, waiting for me to get there. The "scribe" had confined himself to the English Department. Religious Studies and Philosophy hadn't been hit, and the offices of the Classics Department were locked behind their general office.

She'd then phoned Fine Arts and Engineering, to see if they'd been attacked in the same way. With all the references to the shootist Marc Lepine, and what's now known as the Montreal Massacre at L'Ecole Polytechnique, Engineering would have been a safe bet, but apparently the Lepine fan was only angry with the women of the English Department. Why?

I was startled out of my reverie by a voice close by, to my left.

"So you think this has a connection to the Montreal Massacre? What about something closer to home, like the Co-ed Murder?"

Denise was startled, too. We were clearly both feeling jumpy, sitting down the same hallway that had so recently been walked by someone full of hate for women. I waited for Denise to lambaste him for eavesdropping on us. I was too tired. It seemed she was, too, because she listened semi-politely to his introduction.

"I'm sorry," he said. "My name is Mark Paulson and I'm with the *Edmonton Journal*."

Denise deigned to shake his hand. I managed to avoid it by standing up and moving a few paces from the bench, supposedly to look out for Steve.

"Why do you think there is a connection to something else, Mr. Paulson?" Denise seemed calculatedly curious. Perhaps she was toying with him.

Mark Paulson shook his head.

"All I know is that they didn't like me writing about the Poison Pen Plot, and I doubt they'll be happy to see me here now. Do you feel safe here at the university?"

It was my turn to shake my head, metaphorically. It was as if the guy was talking in 20-point headlines. Poison Pen Plot. Co-ed Murder. I just love the names the press comes up with for grisly events. What would we do without all the various Stranglers and Rippers and Grabbers? Might we just absorb the details of the story without the lurid headline? Or would we just unwittingly flip through to the horoscope and cross-word puzzle, never knowing what we were missing? And who in Canada has ever heard of a co-ed anyhow? As I sighed in exasperation at the words echoing in my head, it hit me. This was the guy who had printed the letter about Gwen in the paper. Regardless of whether it was logical or not, I realized I had been holding him responsible for what had transpired. It was just as well that he was such a creep; I had taken an instant dislike to him, and now I had a good reason. I couldn't understand why Denise hadn't let fly at him, herself.

Steve came back just then, and after gracing Paulson with a curt "No comment" and a withering look, he motioned for me to join him. I said my goodbyes to Denise and grabbed my camera. She could fend for herself with a mere reporter, I was sure. Steve and I walked through corridors that last week had seemed benign to me. Today they made me feel like a twelve-point buck in hunting season. Hate seemed to scream from the doors we passed. Steve said very little, sensing my distress.

He walked with me to the House, supposedly to check our doors, but mostly to see me safely to my office. I hesitated as we climbed the stairs, afraid to see what might be printed on my door. It hadn't occurred to me till then that I too might be a target for the scribbler's rage.

I must have been holding my breath, because it all came out in a gasp when I saw that my door was untouched by red pen. Steve looked at me.

"Did you think your door would be marked too?"

"I wasn't sure what to think." I unlocked the office and ushered him inside. "I'm relieved, though. I'm not sure if I wouldn't have taken it personally."

"Do you think the others should be taking it personally?" Steve was in detective mode. I could tell it wasn't an idle question.

"I'm not sure. I was so shocked by it all, that I really couldn't tell you whose doors got hit, besides Grace's."

Steve took out his notebook and started to read from it. "Grace is G. Tarrant?"

I nodded.

"Is Grace outspoken about her feminism?"

I laughed, but it came out sounding shakier than I would have liked.

"Grace's outspoken about everything, but yes, I guess you'd know she was a feminist within a moment or two. Grace is the co-editor of *HYSTERICAL*, after all." I saw the look of incomprehension on Steve's face. "It's a quarterly journal of feminist theory. Hysteria, or tremulous mental incapacity, was thought to be a 'woman's disease,' which is why you get it using the same root as 'hysterectomy.' The latter, in fact, was often used to cure the former. So, if you told someone that they were being 'hysterical,' what you actually meant was 'stop that, you're acting like a woman.' Grace and her editorial board are playing with reclaiming the term. The same way queer theory is reclaiming the word 'queer.'" I stopped with the etymology lesson and got back to business.

"What about D. McLaughlin?"

"Dr. Deborah's a nun. I don't know if you'd call her a feminist or not. I've never heard her speak one way or the other."

"How about S. Tanner?"

"Sylvia is a medievalist. She's married with twins and a nanny. I'm sure she believes in equal rights for all, but it's not her field."

"Okay, what about H. Claridge?"

"Are you sure you copied that right?"

"H. Claridge? 3-17. *Burn, Baby, Burn.*"

"There's got to be a mistake on your list, Steve. H. Claridge is Professor Howard Claridge, the Melville specialist."

"A man?"

"Last time anyone looked. Read the rest of the list."

"N. Hocking."

"Nancy."

"T. Bevingson."

"Ted."

"J. Guthrie."

"Joyce."

"M. Arnese."

"Marlene."

"E. McCloud."

"Elizabeth."

"D. Bamvanni."

"Dharma. Male."

"C. Trainor."

"Christina."

"F. McWhirter."

"Fred. Are you sure you got the right names?"

Steve looked a bit put out at my question.

"Okay, so you got it right. I told you, I wasn't even looking at the names; all I saw was the red writing. So, why wasn't it only on the doors of female professors? I assumed that we were the targets of the hate."

"So did I. Can you think of any sort of pattern to account for it?" Steve checked his notebook again, making some sort of fast calculations. "There were eight doors on the north hallway, and one on the south corridor on the third floor. Then three more on the fourth floor."

I shook my head.

"I just don't see it."

Steve asked to use my phone. I felt uncomfortable being privy to a police call, so excused myself to get us some coffee. I looked around the kitchen of the House as I reached into the antiquated, round-shouldered refrigerator for the 1% milk. I'd always bitched about not being in the same building as my classes, my mailbox and the department office, especially in January when the snow was higher than my boot tops. But today I was glad to be away from the Humanities Building and the ugly red writing that had poisoned the third and fourth floors. The old Formica table piled high with outdated magazines and academic journals, and the institutional orange chairs had never looked so comforting. Maybe Denise and I could get a couple of the plants from the grad lounge moved over here, I mused, and then felt a little ashamed. I was thinking of hiding from the horror, and Denise was not the sort of person who would go along with that. She'd be rallying the troops even now and crying for blood.

I turned to go back upstairs with the two cups of coffee I'd poured and doctored with milk for me and nothing for him (I figured it was a positive sign that I remembered how Steve took his coffee) and was at the bottom of the stairs when the front door opened. I looked over my shoulder, half-expecting to see Denise. Instead, there stood a huge man in a nylon team jacket and blue jeans. He wasn't one of my students, and I knew Leo and Greg didn't schedule office hours on Mondays, but he could have been one of Thora's or Denise's. For once, I felt as if there were entirely too many students allowed access to my office. I wondered how some of the women with the painted doors were feeling, if this was how the fallout was affecting me.

The man-mountain looked unsure of himself, but some students never do come to office hours, so it wasn't unusual to see a newcomer to the House even in November. Most students couldn't believe they were talking seriously about university topics with their professor in what had been someone's bedroom. They spent their first fifteen minutes gawking at the molding on the ceiling. Chantal Dupuis, a post-doctoral student in the back office, had a chandelier for a lighting fixture; her office had once been the House's dining room.

"Can I help you?" I asked. In my fragile state, I didn't feel like having strangers roaming around. If he was here to see someone, I'd make sure he got to their door.

"I hope so. They told me at the English Department office that I could find Professor Randy Craig here. Am I in the right place? Do you know if his office is in this, this place?"

Well, we were evenly matched. I had no idea who he was, and he thought he was looking for a man. I figured that gave me the upper hand.

"I'm Randy Craig, and yes, my office is in this building, but I am in conference right now, so ..."

I hoped Steve wouldn't mind being used as an excuse, but there was something about this mystery man that felt odd. It could be the sheer size of him. I'm not petite, but big men tend to scare me a bit. A friend of mine had dated a football player, and once, when he came to pick her up at my place I was sure he was going to break things just moving through the room. I avoid Schwarzenegger films for the same reason;

I spend the whole time worrying about breakage that isn't plot-related. Even though this man couldn't have been more than six-four, he seemed to fill up the doorway. I mean it; I couldn't see daylight around him.

"You're Professor Craig?"

Maybe I was just ultra-sensitive this morning, but there seemed to be a shift in his demeanor. I wasn't sure but I thought he seemed relieved that I had turned out to be a woman.

"Yes, can I help you with something?"

He recovered his equilibrium and stuck out his hand, then drew it back when he noticed that my hands were full.

"My name is Rod Devlin. They told me my wife, uh, Gwen, was a student in your English class."

So this was Gwen's former husband. I still wasn't sure what he wanted with me.

"Yes, that's right. I'm sorry." My words sounded wrong somehow. What was I sorry about? Perhaps they were the right words, after all, though, as I saw him nodding in agreement. We were all sorry, in some way or other.

"Well, I was here picking up her things, and I figured I'd try to talk to people who knew her, and maybe pick up anything of hers you still had."

"I'm not sure what I could tell you, except that she was a good student. I didn't really get too much of a chance to get to know her. It's a lecture course, not a seminar." This didn't seem to register with him, but then again why should it? I tried to find something to say that would help this bear of a man. He just seemed so out of place and lost. "The police have her papers, I think."

He nodded, but I wasn't sure whether it meant that he knew the police had Gwen's effects or that he had assumed as much. He looked at me, and his eyes were like fog lights, trying to cut through everything to get to some clarity. I shivered and slopped coffee onto my thumb, causing me to wince.

"You don't have any idea who could have done it, do you? I mean, did she hang out with any weirdos in your class?"

Steve had asked pretty much the same things of me, although couched in much more diplomatic language. Answers, we all needed some sort of answers, or we were never going to get to any form of closure. I grimaced and shook my head, wishing I had something I could tell Rod Devlin. It was odd, even knowing that Gwen had left him and that he had presumed university would be too much for her, I couldn't automatically dislike this man. He just looked wounded. Besides, he was so big, he seemed more like a force of nature than a human being.

"Mr. Devlin, I'm not aware of who Gwen spent her time with. I really don't know what I could tell you that could be of any help. It was a terrible tragedy, and I'm very sorry for your loss."

"Well, I'll be in town for a couple more days. If you think of anything else, I'm staying in the Varscona Hotel on Whyte." He turned and swung the door wide, letting it slam behind him as he clomped down the stairs.

Steve was off the phone when I got up to the office.

"They're sending your photos and copies of ours over to me here, if that's okay with you. They should be ready in half an hour. I want you to go over them with me. Meanwhile I'm having someone go through the files on the five men who had their doors defaced. Maybe they're closet feminists or something."

"So you want to camp out in my office all morning? I'll never get to Greenwoods at this rate."

"I'll drive you there afterwards."

"Will you put on the siren? Will I have to sit in the back?"

Steve laughed. "It's an unmarked car. Sorry about commandeering your office. You didn't have to leave, you know." He took a slurp of his coffee. "You could have come back sooner, too."

"I had to talk to someone at the door."

"Oh?" He didn't sound interested. Probably he thought I meant a student.

"Yeah. Rod Devlin paid me a visit."

Now he looked interested. "I wonder who guided him your way?"

I told him the gist of Devlin's talk with me. Steve didn't look happy. "It makes you wonder, his showing up on campus this morning of all mornings."

"Steve, you don't think Devlin defaced the doors, do you?"

Steve looked alarmed. "I shouldn't have said that. Forget I even said anything."

I felt insulted. While even I could see that knowing someone enough to spend an evening necking wasn't necessarily a guarantee of their utter discretion, I had hoped that Steve would know me a bit better than he was implying. I never said logic was my strong suit, though.

"I'm not about to go spreading rumors and wrecking investigations," I retorted, archer than even I realized.

To my surprise, Steve laughed. "You look like a porcupine with its prickles up. Sorry, I overreacted."

He reached out his hand. I took it, meaning to shake it, but he pulled me close, sending my heart going far faster than it ever had on a cold Monday morning in my spartan little office. I was beginning to think there were better things in this world than coffee and chocolate after all.

THERE WAS A LOUD RAPPING AT THE MAIN DOOR of the House about ten minutes later. Steve checked his uniform for uniformity and ran down the stairs. He was right in assuming it was for him. I think they must teach door knocking in the police academy. Even I knew it had to be the law at the door.

Steve returned with two packets of pictures in plastic bags. Without opening them, he handed me one.

"Here are your pictures."

I admired his delicacy. For all he knew I might have umpteen shots of old boyfriends on the roll, but even if there were, I had the feeling that, at the moment, I wouldn't be able to remember their names. He was looking through his photos, so I shook off the urge to crawl onto his lap and opened my own plastic bag.

I whipped through nine or ten shots of my summer trip to the Tyrrell Dinosaur Museum in Drumheller, and came to the morning's pictures. Denise had made me take two of each door, which was just as well, since the flash had reflected off a couple of the nameplates, creating a paler version of the bloody lettering. Even so, I could read each malignant message.

I laid them out like a solitaire game, with the best shot on top of each pair. Steve did the same on his side of my desk.

Even upside down, I could see that his prints were better. Feeling competitive, I searched my pictures for something revealing.

It was Steve who noticed it.

"Randy?"

"Yeah?"

"Do all the office doors have peepholes?"

"No. I asked about that once. Apparently a few years ago there was some problem with some guy harassing profs and students studying at night in the building, so Campus Security installed them in the office doors of female staff. There was a bit of a ruckus about it, because instead of making women safer, it just highlighted which doors belonged to female professors. We figured it must have been a cost-saving measure."

"How often do people change offices?"

"Well, the north-facing offices are more prized because of the view of the river valley, so when someone retires from one of those offices, the next person in line jumps to one of them. New professors get inner offices or south-facing offices with a glorious view of the parking lot and Law Building. Grad students who are teaching share inner offices." I thought a minute. "I'd say there's a bit of a shuffle every year, but no one moves from the north-facing offices, unless they turn Emeritus."

"Why aren't you in one of the offices in the Humanities Building?"

"We're the peons of the department. We have to have office space, since we need to have somewhere to see our students, but since we're not taking classes we are more dispensable. Actually, some people working on their dissertations prefer the House for the quiet. Not as many students want to trek over here to argue their marks, and people aren't always dropping by to lure you to HUB for coffee."

I realized I was speaking to the crown of Steve's head; he

was once again staring at the photos in front of him. I looked down at my set. The answer was suddenly just as clear to me.

"All the doors here have peepholes."

Steve grinned. "You got it, Sherlock."

"So that means whoever did this didn't know the professors by name, and thought that he was targeting women because of the peepholes."

Steve shook his head. "I'm not sure about that. Would someone who didn't know who was who in the English Department know about the peephole business in the first place?"

"What do you mean?"

"What about this: the perpetrator knew at least one of the names on the doors, and extrapolated from the presence of a peephole on her door and not on all doors, that peepholes represented women's offices."

"Are you saying that one person is the target, and the others were done on impulse?"

"I don't know what I'm saying yet. Let me drive you to Greenwoods, and then I've got to get back to work." Steve swept his pictures into a deck, knocked them into order and slid them back into their bag. He stood up and shrugged his jacket on.

"You don't really have to drive me. I should go by my place to drop off my camera, anyway, and I'd hate to stand in the way of an official investigation." I could imagine McNeely wouldn't be too happy about it either.

Steve and I walked downstairs and left by the front door. I locked it behind me since no one else seemed to be in the building. Steve touched my arm on the steps. I was hoping for a kiss with that adolescent belief that public displays of affection somehow cement the seriousness of a relationship, but Steve seemed more maturely aware of the public nature of where we stood. Not that anyone was around to watch, but what the hell. We agreed to meet for dinner on Wednesday, since Saturday's jazz concert seemed a long way off.

He was halfway across the street when I called to him.

"Do you want to take my pictures, too?"

"Don't worry, we've got another set of them still at the lab." He waved, and headed back to Humanities.

So much for my earlier theories about his discretion. I headed for home, thinking I really didn't mind how far he saw into my personal life. I shivered, not sure whether it was the weather or the unusual sense of vulnerability I was allowing into my cloistered little life.

THE GRAFFITI HAD BEEN EXPUNGED BY MONDAY noon, but the words might as well have been carved in the stone facing of the Tory Building. Everyone, including the coffee servers in HUB Mall, seemed to have heard about the event. Three students came to my office before class with feeble reasons to see me. I figured they had just come to see if my door too showed recent signs of scrubbing.

The air was electric in my Tuesday morning class. I thought I might as well hit it head on, or we'd never get any work done. If they'd been a grade two class, I would have had them do the Bunny Hop around the room for five minutes. Instead, I thumped down my briefcase and hoisted myself onto the edge of the table at the front of the lecture hall.

"I gather you all have heard of the graffiti on the English Department doors."

Vigorous nods all around.

"It occurs to me that this is something worth discussing, in that it makes a case for the importance of the written word in our increasingly visual and electronic lifestyle."

A few of them looked as if they'd have rolled their eyes at me if I weren't in a position to fail them. I could read their faces: typical English prof, take some juicy gossip and turn it into an essay topic. I soldiered on, thankful for my status as suzerain. The best way for them to forget all about the incident would be to make them responsible for it on a future exam.

"There are theorists who believe that the novel is dead, and that indeed, nothing useful can any longer be written since people have become too sophisticated to be swayed by the rhetoric of fiction. This theory doesn't explain certain things, though. It neglects the aspect of human nature that makes us listen to and believe campaign promises; it eliminates from its viewpoint those members of society who subscribe to tabloid newspapers; and it forgets the activities of literary terrorists. To me, graffiti falls into this category."

I jumped off the table and turned to the blackboard. Leo had once told me, after observing one of my classes, that I didn't use the blackboard enough. I didn't admit to him that I had a phobia about writing on the blackboard when students were in the room, since I figured that, of all my muscles, my gluts were the least likely to obey and probably jiggled to their own drummer as I scribbled. Instead, I tried to make the most of the "ultimate teaching tool," as he called it, on days when I was either wearing a long jacket or control-top pantyhose. Today it was a combination of oversized pullover and leggings.

Blessing the inventor of Lycra, I wrote a modified timeline across the length of the board, starting with: WRITER with an arrow pointing left toward (AGENT) and then another arrow to EDITOR. Another arrow led to PUBLISHER with another to REVIEWER, with yet another to (TEACHER) and a last arrow to READER. As I turned to say, "You don't really have to write this down," I saw I was too late. Forty-three heads were bowed in obeisance, scribbling furiously in their notebooks. I bit off my words. Writing notes used to keep me awake in undergrad, too.

"This is the path any contemporary work of fiction will follow before it comes into your hands. The factors in brackets are possibles rather than essentials, but I'm putting them in there to show you how many gates there are between you and the approved written word. Now, I'm not saying that everything you read is destined to be of classical value, or that everything that gets stopped at any of these junctures would be harmful to you. What I am trying to say is that a great deal of thought, some of it mercenary, some of it aesthetic, goes into the publishing of written material.

"That doesn't hold true for the writing on bathroom walls, anonymous letters, chain letters, Internet homepages, self-publishing or vanity press, promotional pamphlets or hate mail. Technically, of course, the same holds true for your journal entries to me. Those things accost you straight from writer to reader, with no quality control checks along the way. Sometimes they're innocuous, harmless or funny. Sometimes they're provocative, insightful and philosophical. Sometimes they're corrosive."

I went back to the table and leaned against it, rubbing the chalk dust off my fingers.

"Words are the most powerful tool ever invented by mankind. Forget the pulley, never mind the microchip. Without words, ideas cannot be transmitted efficiently. The question is, do we have a right not to receive those ideas? I'm not talking censorship, although that"—I gestured back at the blackboard—"publication path effectively censors most unnecessary, ineffectual or downright bad writing for you already. I mean hatred. There are actual laws against the transmission of hate-mongering material through the postal system. There are laws against the defacement of public property. Laws of slander and libel protect against defamation of character. Whenever anyone tells you that literature doesn't matter, that the written word doesn't stand a chance in the twenty-first century, think again. If the written word wasn't so powerful, do you think a death warrant would have been taken out against Salman Rushdie?"

I was winging it, and the little editor in my brain was

tsking away, telling me that any hopes of turning them on to the cavalier poets was shot if I didn't get back on schedule, but I was on a roll.

"One of the reasons that fiction is, to me, so much mightier than didactic prose is that it insinuates its message rather than preaches it. Our minds, if we keep them open and educated, are able to detect the hidden agenda behind a politician's speech or an evangelist's sermon. We can take in what they say and hold it up for reasoning, accepting it only once it has passed through our critical scanners.

"Literature, on the other hand, pulls us into a false reality, and we read what is written through that lens, the lens the writer has pre-determined through his choices of voice, point of view and environment. We are easier prey, since we read with our emotions rather than with our critical minds. In a nutshell, that is what a literature course is trying to impart to you: a way of reading literature with both your emotional and your critical faculties at work. Yes?"

Myron looked thoughtful. "I take your meaning for literature, but how does that relate to graffiti? Are you suggesting it is like fiction?"

"Good question. No, I wouldn't liken graffiti to literature, because literature, of course, has that filtering system I was speaking about." I motioned to the board behind me. "In a way, though, I would claim graffiti as akin to advertising. Commercials, too, have an insidious way of working on us. The object is to lodge a product name into our brains. Persuasion is often used, attempts to convince us that the product is the best of its kind. Jingles are created to ring in our heads. Downright bombast is used by the used car ad approach, where the pitchman just shouts the name of the store or product over and over. The overall effect is the same, whatever the means. Graffiti plays on that same tendency for our minds to absorb even that upon which we're not concentrating. It bothers us more, in the sense that it is an anarchic act, but that is societal conditioning rather than brain patterns, I think. Most of us were brought up to color on the paper, not on the walls. Some of us rebel against that authority, if we feel we don't have the aptitude to rebel against authority in any other way."

I glanced at the clock on the wall, and realized I'd better start wrapping up this diatribe. Most of the time I managed to get my class up and out with a few minutes to spare before the class change. I was running right to the dot today. A couple of students with back-to-back classes somewhere across campus were already discreetly packing up and edging out of the back of the class.

"We haven't examined the content of the messages scribbled on the department doors. I choose not to, and I don't want you to think it's because they are too disturbing to deal with. Let's just say I probably won't be discussing *Mad Magazine* with you either, and we'll leave it at that. The doors are washed, class is almost over, and the mid-session exam is looming. Thursday, I promise we will be dealing with Andrew Marvell and Robert Herrick's reply. Please have them read, and your texts with you. If you want to comment further on the happenings around here and how they've affected you, feel free to record them in your journals. That's all."

A couple of people wanted to talk about their extensions on the essays, but most of them left quietly. Students for the next class began to pour in as mine left the room, and I mouthed a silent apology to Arno as I ushered the remaining students into the hall. I hadn't known he had the classroom after me. I wondered briefly if he'd heard anything of what I'd been discussing. It wasn't exactly on topic, although sometimes you have to go where the class leads you instead of being locked into a syllabus. I just hoped Arno wasn't going to score points with some stickler for rules by turning me in. Besides, I wasn't sure if I'd defused the tension or not. I felt winded but tingly, the way I used to after a five-kilometre race.

Pontificating will do that to you. The same small voice in my head muttered that I shouldn't be feeling so cocky. I'd taken a stand and supported my argument, but maybe making a shot across the bows wasn't such a bright idea when there was a loony loose. The thought made me look up sharply, but all I could see was a hall filled with ennui-laden students.

No psychotic eyes trained on me. I felt no menace from the third row. I shivered and giggled slightly at the same time. The situation was really getting to me if it could make me believe freshmen had anything more on their minds than beer and essays, in that order.

WEDNESDAY BROUGHT FRESH SNOW AND A blindingly bright afternoon, the sort of day on which I'd like to go crunching down the walking trail in my clompy white moon boots with sunglasses on and bird seed in my pocket. Instead I was cleaning my apartment madly and deliberating about what to wear for my dinner with Steve. I was holding off on cleaning the tub till I'd washed my hair and shaved my legs.

The *hausfrau* efforts and the combined tension of the last few days kept me in the shower far longer than my neighbors would have liked had they been home to hear the pipes thrumming. I let the hot water pound out the iron bar that seemed to be wedged between my shoulder blades. After slathering on some hair conditioner, I leaned down to tackle my legs.

Carl Reiner and Mel Brooks were wrong when they did the skit about the two-thousand-year-old man. The greatest invention known to man is not Saran Wrap; the greatest invention I'd come across was shaving gel. After squirting the pink goop onto my leg, I rubbed it up into a thick foam and pulled the razor through, confident that no nicks would occur. Some oil in the potion made my denuded limb feel soft and silken. I could understand now why men hardly ever complained about daily shaving. This little ritual had such immediate and positive results.

71

I tend not to shave my legs once I've packed away my summer clothes, relying on opaque tights to see me through any formal occasions. This change of habit brought back a conversation I'd had with my mother when I was about fifteen. I'd asked her about shaving then, since my legs were beginning to show my direct lineage back to Leakey's Lucy.

"A woman needs to shave her legs only if she intends to go to bed with a man." My mother had smiled. I think she meant this to be one of those complicit mother-daughter moments we would look back on fondly as we sipped our International Blend coffee over old photo albums. Instead, it had the reaction of making me feel vaguely guilty about the act of depilation, something to be done clandestinely, if ever.

Remembering the moment now made me giggle, wondering if Steve would take my silken legs as a sign of premeditation. Thinking about what it was I was premeditating made my stomach clench. I was definitely out of practice in the seduction department. Did this qualify as our second or our third date? Should I have made preparations for safe sex? Should I ask for a blood test? How did one go about having a romance any more?

I thought about calling Denise to get a crash course, but decided against it. Talking to Denise these days was like inviting Betty Friedan to tea. You know it'll be good for you, but you're not sure how much fun it'll be. Denise was planning a vigil near the memorial garden the university had planted to honor the slain women in Montreal. Every year on the anniversary of the massacre a ceremony was held there in the morning, with readings and speeches. I'd been to a couple of them and had been very moved.

This year Denise was planning a candlelight vigil to go through the night before and into the evening of the anniversary. She was going to beat a small gong once every ten minutes to signify how often women are beaten, abused, harassed and killed in our supposedly enlightened and advanced society. From what I knew of Denise, it would make a tremendously powerful statement. Whether or not it would change the minds of those who weren't already converted, I couldn't say.

In any case, Denise was probably not up to giving me tips on how to get a man into bed. I'd have to figure this one out on my own.

"Don't worry, Randy. It'll be like falling off a bicycle," I said out loud, startling myself. I wasn't sure which to be more worried about, the talking out loud or the screwing up of metaphors. At this rate, I'd probably drop my plate of curried chicken in my lap and all of this premeditation would be academic.

That was the one unbeatable aspect of the night ahead. We'd be eating at the High Level Diner, the best restaurant in Edmonton as far as I was concerned. I spent most of my "eating out allowance" there, since it was just down the block from my apartment. During the summer, there was nothing nicer than sitting on the outdoor terrace and starting a day with a bowl of their multigrain porridge. Summer evenings with a banana frappa out there were a close second.

We wouldn't be eating on the terrace tonight, but the interior was lovely as well, especially the tables that looked out on the river valley through the denuded branches of the bordering trees. Local artists hung their work in the Diner, changing often enough to make me feel that I was keeping abreast of the scene. The menu changed from time to time as well, but the curried chicken stayed on by popular demand. I regretted the loss of the Diner's chocolate eclair, a sinful platter of hot fudge and cool whipped cream over a pastry filled with vanilla custard, but my waistline probably couldn't have taken one more year of them. Lots of university folks frequented the place, but so did business types and people from around the area, so there was always a healthy mix of humanity. If there was one thing I could get sick of in a hurry, it was homogeneity.

I was on a greeting acquaintance with most of the staff,

who looked Steve over pretty carefully as Sheila showed us to our table. I hoped they liked what they saw; I certainly did.

Steve looked around, admiring the casual comfort of the place, the friendly bustle of the staff and the buzz of happy patrons. It was crowded, but thankfully we hadn't had to wait.

"You know, I've never been here, even though I meant to—especially after the first write-up they got."

"It's great. I've been eating here for about three years and have never been disappointed."

"You look great, Randy." Steve smiled, and I was glad I'd shaved my legs.

"You too." I felt a bit embarrassed, not really used to this part of the mating dance any more. I took a gulp of water and felt an ice cube escape and land on the table. Great.

Steve sensed that it was not appropriate to laugh. He busied himself with his napkin.

So much for breaking the ice. I grabbed the menu I already knew by heart.

Steve suggested we order wine, and asked if white was all right with me. I admitted that was all I drank.

"Because of the histamines in red wine?"

"Partly, though somebody told me that there were red wines that didn't give you such awful hangovers. Actually, though, I think it had more to do with signing my first damage deposit than with my health. White wine spilled on the carpet just isn't half the headache, if you know what I mean."

We segued from wine into our meal without spilling anything. Steve ordered the tostada, but begged a bite of my curried chicken. This was another check mark in his favor. I've never understood couples who both order the same meal at restaurants. They might as well just stay home and eat out of the same pot.

Part of me didn't want to talk shop, and I could sense that Steve had somehow decided that since we had become an item, as it were, it was no longer proper to discuss the case with me. However, there was something I had to tell him. I waited until Jody, our waitress, brought our coffee.

"I've been meaning to tell you—" I started.

"That I have beautiful eyes?"

"Well, there is that, but actually it has to do with Gwen."

Steve's beautiful eyes looked a bit somber suddenly. "Randy, I don't think we should be discussing things any more. It just isn't kosher, and if my superiors ever got wind of it—"

It was my turn to interrupt. "I don't want to discuss it. I just want to say that there's something you should see, although I don't think it's of much importance, but anyhow—" I found myself taking a deeper than needed breath—"it's come to my attention that Gwen's journal is in my possession."

"Her what?" Steve spluttered. "You've got her diary and you haven't said anything?"

Steve's voice was carrying, and I looked around the restaurant, hoping that we weren't causing a scene. No one seemed to be looking our way. Maybe the jazz background music had muffled his yelp. Jody, the waitress, saw my look and reached for the coffeepot, heading our way. I admired the way she threaded her way through the crowd of tables, like some sort of Gauguinesque water bearer. She slid, without causing a frond to shiver, between a palm tree and a table for two with one man sitting at it, his back to us. The back looked familiar. It's that sort of a restaurant; no one minds coming in alone to eat, and eventually you begin to nod at other regulars.

Steve didn't say anything while Jody was pouring coffee and reaching for our cream pitcher to take it in for a refill. After she'd left, he resumed in a quieter tone.

"I can't believe you'd withhold this. What did you think we were after when I first asked for anything you had of hers?"

"It's not a diary," I muttered back at him. "The journals are a writing assignment I have my classes do to warm up for the class. I put a topic on the board and they write for about ten minutes, that's all. They're only worth ten percent of their mark, so most of them don't take them too seriously. I haul them in a couple of times a year to check how their extemporaneous writing is coming. I think it makes them better at writing exam essays. It's not as though they're writing anything personal in them."

"And you read this journal?" Steve seemed to have calmed down a bit.

"Sure, that's how I knew to tell you about the therapist."

That was the wrong thing to say.

"She's writing about her therapist in it and you don't think it's anything personal?"

I winced.

"Steve, I'm sorry. I read it, and then put it away and forgot about it. I only remember it when you aren't around." I shut up then. I could hear the slight edge come in to my voice that indicated there would be tears soon if I didn't get a grip. I didn't want this man mad at me. Especially not tonight. Heck, I'd shaved my legs! As soon as the thought entered my mind, I was mortified. Steve was concerned with finding a killer and all I was thinking about was my own gratification. Luckily, the lights in the Diner were gentle, and my flush might not be too noticeable. The appropriate penance came to mind immediately.

"We could go to my office after this and I'll give you the journal."

Steve looked a bit startled. "Now?" Maybe he'd shaved his legs too.

"Well, if you think it's so important . . ." I trailed off. Penance was penance, but I wasn't about to be a martyr. I'd let him decide.

He took a moment and a long swig of water.

"Oh, hell, I can just as easily pick it up tomorrow. As you say, it's not likely that relevant. And, after all, they say one of the first elements of a good investigation is not to mix business with pleasure." He grinned, a bit like the wolf does in old-fashioned fairy tale illustrations.

Honest to god, my toes curled.

S TEVE HAD PARKED ON THE STREET IN FRONT OF my apartment, so we strolled back from the Diner. The back door to my place was more than a stone's throw from the parking lot reserved for Diner patrons, but a good ball player might have nicked it. We were almost out of the lot when a car pulling out and spinning gravel made Steve draw me close to him. A dark Taurus whipped past us and down the alley to the stop sign. As it waited momentarily under the alley light, I caught sight of the man driving.

"Steve! See that guy?" I nudged him furtively, although the driver probably couldn't see us.

"Who, the guy that almost ran us down? Yeah, when I'm on foot I really hate drivers. But then, you should hear what I say about pedestrians from behind the wheel."

"Yes, him. I think that was that reporter. Paulson. Do you know him?"

Steve released the grip he had on my shoulder, but not by much. He glanced after the now receding car.

"Oh really? That's quite a coincidence."

"Maybe. I'm pretty sure he was in the Diner while we were. I thought there was something familiar about his back, but I didn't place him till now."

"I wonder which one of us he was keeping an eye on," Steve said as we reached my door and he held it open for me.

I was waiting for a lecture on non-secure buildings, but I guess he had other things on his mind. The reporter, and whether or not I felt my personal life infringed upon, melted out of my mind like the snow slipping off the toes of my boots onto the door mat in the warm interior.

Steve riffled through my record collection while I put the kettle on for tea. I came back to the melancholy Dougie Maclean singing "Silently Sad," which I usually reserved for long bubble baths, but seemed suddenly appropriate for a cozy evening in a warm place with a warm man. Hell, "Seventy-Six Trombones" probably would have done the trick at that point. Steve was sitting on a floor cushion, propped against the couch with his arm draped over the seat cushion. I placed our mugs of tea on my coffee table, a shellacked backgammon board on legs, and lay down on the couch so that my head rested on his upper arm. He stroked my hair with his hand, and sipped his tea. It felt like a romantic scene from a ski movie. I just wished the old gas fireplace in the hearth actually worked. Still, for a budget picture, it was pretty good.

I shared my film vision of the moment with Steve, who laughed.

"You know, Randy, there are people out there who just live their lives, instead of always analyzing the scenes they're in."

"There's more than one historic example of life imitating art, you know. There just doesn't appear to be one handy for me to wound you with at the moment."

Steve laughed again and I smiled. I tried to hold the mock hauteur by sniffing in my best Victorian fashion. I took a deep breath and felt my nose tingle with the scent of Steve, a subtle aftershave mixed with heat and a freshly laundered shirt. Thank goodness for the sense of smell; until they came up with a Scratch 'n Sniff version of the World's Classics, I could anchor myself in the real world. I giggled as I imagined that edition of *Moby Dick*.

Steve looked at me with a half-quizzical smile, as if it would be okay to share the joke if I wanted to but not really necessary. I decided not to break the mood. I leaned into him and we kissed.

A long time after that I realized the record was over and my tea was cold. I straightened up to get more, but Steve beat me to the cups.

"You pick the music this time."

I thought for just a moment before pulling out Joni Mitchell's *Blue*, figuring not to argue with a successful mood. The cover picture made me think again of seeing Mark Paulson in the light from the alley.

As Steve rounded the corner from the kitchen, I said, "You know, if this were a movie, Mark Paulson would have to be the villain of the piece."

Steve set down the tea and moved toward me, taking me in his arms and swaying me to the beat of "My Old Man."

"I'm willing to dump the press into it any old time. But what is your reasoning for this, my dear Spielberg?"

"Elementary, my dear Lucas. He was sitting in the smoking section of the Diner."

"Your logic escapes me."

"Haven't you noticed that these days only the bad guys smoke? You really notice it when you catch an old TV show and all the protagonists are lighting up. Now you only see Jack Palance or some Mafia hitman puffing away."

"Hmmm," Steve murmured into my hair. "Maybe this isn't a modern picture, though."

"No?"

"Maybe it's one of those old-fashioned shipboard romances where two people meet through strangely cosmic circumstances and realize they're made for each other."

"Hmmm."

ON THURSDAY MORNING I SAILED THROUGH "To His Coy Mistress." I was in the mood to seize the day all right. Some of my enthusiasm must have worn off on the class because they almost seemed interested. Mind you, I could have been cheerfully teaching the phone book. Steve had left my place at about five in order to get home and report to work at some ungodly hour. I felt like Scarlett O'Hara after the trip up the staircase, and let the rosy mood carry me through both classes and on into office hours.

Leo and Greg were into some sort of harangue about Mary Shelley, and Denise was clearing away her work when I popped down to the main floor. Leo tried to get Denise and me to trek off for Thai food, but Denise was bushed and on her way home, and I still had some notes to go over before I left.

"What are you doing out of your hutch then?" Leo demanded.

"The upstairs toilet is on the fritz again. I'm heading down to the basement."

"Will you lock up then?"

"Sure," I called back to him as I trooped through the kitchen to the basement door. Greg was still in his office, but Denise and Leo headed out as I switched on the light for the stairwell to the bowels of the House.

Bathrooms aren't pleasant getaways at the best of times, but the basement loo in the House wouldn't even qualify as a cell in Alcatraz. It was a small room with a small cracked porcelain wall sink and a very old toilet. Three rolls of toilet paper were lined up on the reservoir, and a small mirror hung crookedly over the sink. Some former occupant of the House had put up a sign to the effect that one's mother would not be by later to clean up. Someone else, presumably Leo, had left a three-year-old copy of *Books in Canada* on the floor beside the throne. I leafed through it for lack of anything better to occupy my mind. This was not the place to think about romance.

After a few moments, I heard footsteps on the stairs. I turned down the corner of the page on the article about Maggie Siggins and shouted, "I'll be right out, Greg."

Instead of Greg's reply, I heard some scraping outside the door. It couldn't be Greg; he was too well mannered to stand outside a bathroom door. There was someone out there, though. The noises weren't the usual house-settling noises. It sounded like something was being dragged across the floor. Right, and I was cast as Jamie Leigh Curtis in one of her earlier roles. I had a sneaky suspicion who the casting director was.

"Leo?" I wasn't going to rise to his sophomoric attempt to scare me. I flushed the toilet and washed my hands before I spoke again. "Ready or not, here I come." I turned the doorknob.

It wouldn't budge.

"Leo," I brayed, "this is not funny. Let go of the knob."

The knob suddenly moved under my grip, but it still did nothing to get the door open. I heard footsteps going quickly up the stairs.

"Leo, damn you. Let me out of here!"

No answer, but the footsteps sounded farther away, and then there were other muffled noises I couldn't place.

I was fuming. I kept trying the doorknob, as if it would

suddenly allow me egress, and when I realized how futile that was I began to pace in a small oval. I couldn't even sit down, seeing as how the toilet was institutional with a black half-seat rather than lidded.

After a few minutes of pacing I sat down on it anyway. I was so frustrated I began to cry, which only served to awaken fear. Someone had locked me into the basement toilet. No one I knew would actually do this sort of thing as a joke, not even Leo.

So this was very likely someone I didn't know. Or someone I didn't want to know.

I searched the small room, inventorying my surroundings for some sort of exit plan. I had just picked up the toilet brush tucked behind the commode in an old cut down bleach bottle, when the lights went out.

The dark was absolute, and I heard myself whimper. I was locked in the dark, and there might be a murderer at the controls. I hunched over, in what was likely some psychological attempt to make myself small and unnoticeable. As if he didn't know exactly where I was.

It wasn't until I heard the front door slam that I allowed myself to breathe.

I HAD NEVER CONSIDERED FEAR OF DARKNESS to be one of my phobias, but this was an inky blackness with no residual light. I held my hand in front of my face and succeeded in hitting my head with the toilet brush.

Long ago, as a teenager, I'd been on a hike with others at the summer camp at Naramata Centre out in the Okanagan. The leaders had taken us to an abandoned U-shaped railway tunnel to experience total blackout. We linked arms and walked to the center of the tunnel, using the rails as our guides. Some of the others had expressed fear of the blackness, but I was more concerned about the snakes sunning themselves on the rocks at the other end, and was happy to return the way we'd come. This experience felt the same. I was deprived of sight, but I was pretty sure I didn't want to be seeing what lay beyond in the light.

They say losing one sense heightens the remaining four. I strained to hear noises from upstairs, but I guess heightened senses don't immediately get bestowed. Either that or there was nothing to hear. I liked that thought. For a while.

Darkness does seem to throw off one's sense of time. I couldn't tell how long I'd been locked in, and cursed the fashionable big-faced watch on my wrist. What I wouldn't give, right about now for the old Timex I'd worn through high school, with its sickly green glow, or even one of those three-dollar digitals with the button light. I must have been sitting on the toilet for about half an hour or so, because my knee was starting to seize up on me, something it did after long stints in one position.

I stretched out my legs and just about fell into the open toilet. Wouldn't that be great? To look as though I'd wet myself when I was found. I giggled, and stopped myself when I heard the noise I made. I wasn't sure if it was the dark, the solitude, or my psyche, but my laugh sounded a trifle manic. I didn't want to turn into a drooling mess; what would V.I. Warshawski think of me? I wondered if a working knowledge of crime fiction would help me out of this. Could anything Sara Paretsky had written be relevant to this situation? One of her books had seen her heroine crawling through sewer tunnels, pursued by bad guys. Thoughts of crawling through the toilet to escape made me want to laugh again, but I controlled it. Norman Cousins might have approved, but hearing my own laughter was spooking me.

I tried to take stock, but all I could come up with was a blocked door, and a small black room. How was I going to get out with only a toilet brush and an old issue of *Books in Canada*? I briefly considered breaking the mirror, but couldn't think of a good reason to bring bad luck and a nasty cut upon myself. I settled well back onto the black toilet seat, and tried to recall the various schedules of the other occupants of the building. Would any of them be likely to come in on a Thursday after five p.m.? I couldn't think of a good reason, so with a depressing shift, I started to concentrate on Friday timetables. I was shakier here, since I myself never came near the place on Fridays.

Greg was always in, but usually didn't come in till nine-thirty or ten. Denise had a morning class on Friday, and would come into the office prior to that for her notes, but that could be anytime from eight-thirty till ten. Leo, like me, didn't teach on Fridays. Chantal was a wild card, and I couldn't recall if I'd ever seen Thora on the Monday/ Wednesday/Friday shift. Chris and Lana taught evening courses, and not even the English Department slated evening courses on Friday. I couldn't remember if either of them had a Thursday evening class this term, which wasn't so unusual since I hardly ever saw them. The only other occupant of the House was Jeremy, and he spent most of his time at home.

My best bet was Denise, some fifteen hours from now. How on earth was I going to keep from going crazy in the meantime? I thought about stories of prisoners reciting poems to keep them going in solitary confinement. The only poem that sprang to mind was "Hey Diddle Diddle." Lousy advertising for an English Lit. education. I tried for something more befitting of my station in life. Rejecting Marvell as too limiting for a long stretch, I searched my mind for Shakespeare, as if quoting the bard would somehow bring Denise in quicker.

Even though I'd just spent almost a month on *Twelfth Night*, I couldn't for the life of me bring one line of it to memory. What sprang up instead was the Prologue to *Romeo and Juliet*, "Two houses, both alike in dignity, in fair Verona where we lay our scene . . ."

Half a lifetime ago, when I'd been a stage-struck teenager, I had been the understudy to everyone in our high school's production of *R & J*. It had something to do with the fact that I had been the only girl to sign up for stage fencing who had a pageboy haircut, and more to do with a besottedness with theater and a desire to be at every rehearsal. I spent every show as a kinswoman of the Capulets praying that Tybalt would really break a leg. All the grade twelves got the speaking roles, and I fed them their lines. Ironically, when I got to grade twelve, I was cast as the lead in all three shows, but it was *Romeo and Juliet* that stayed with me.

I was halfway through Mercutio's Queen Mab speech when I heard the upstairs door crash open.

F OR ALL THE FEAR OF BEING ALONE IN THE DARK, I almost wet myself thinking my captor had returned. It didn't help to think I was in the right room for the job. I could feel my ears straining out of my scalp to hear what was happening upstairs. The next thing I heard nearly made me weep with happiness. It was Denise. Maybe darkness makes the time really go faster, even though you think it's slower. Was it morning already?

"You are such an asshole, Leo," I could hear Denise griping. "There is a bubble bath turning into soap scum on the sides of my tub at home right this minute."

"Darling, I will buy you a hundred white candles and you can have your very own Streisand moment. You are saving my life and I love you from the bottom of my heart."

"Why you don't just put your keys on a string around your neck, I will never know. What is this, the sixth time this term?"

"I know where they are, they're right here by the coffee maker. I put them down to throw out the grounds. By the way, you should always use an odd number in hyperbole. Even numbers are simply too plebeian, and for some reason odd numbers are funnier."

They were thumping about above my head in the kitchen. I began to shout at them. It took them a while to hear me over

Denise's tirade and Leo's rambling semi-obsequiousness. Then it took them a couple of minutes to figure out where my calls of "Help me, I'm locked in the basement bathroom" were coming from. And these were members of the top five percentile.

They looked so shocked to see me tumble out of the doorway they had cleared of the tilted chair under the doorknob that I began to laugh.

"Randy? What the hell are you doing down here?"

"I haven't the faintest idea, but I have never been so glad to see anyone in my life."

I told them my version of what had happened, which was that I had been locked in the loo by persons unknown who then turned out the light switch and closed the basement door.

"I heard some more movement after that, but I'm not sure how long it took, or when he left."

Leo was about to begin on a theory of time but Denise cut him off with the suggestion that we search the House for more signs of mischief.

"Mischief?" I rebelled against the word. "To lock a slightly claustrophobic person into a dark bathroom is not mischief, it's diabolical."

Denise conceded my point and again urged us to look over the House. There was nothing untoward in the kitchen, but we had to remind Leo once again to pick up his keys. Denise didn't budge until he put them in his pocket. It seems he had been to dinner and had got all the way home when he realized his keys were missing. He had called Denise from a phone booth to ask her to drive him back to the House to get them.

Both Denise's and Leo's office doors were locked, and a glance inside each showed nothing out of place. We climbed the stairs together. Light spilled into the upper hall from my office. Denise got to the door first, with Leo right behind her.

They stopped in the open doorway and then silently let me through between them.

It was a disaster. Papers had been pulled out of my filing cabinet and strewn about the floor. My desk drawers were all yanked out, and it looked as though badgers had been snuffling through the contents. All the books had been pulled off their shelves, and several older Penguins had lost the will to be bound and had come undone in a drift across the room. The contents of my coffee cup were spilled across the papers on my desk. I heard a little moan, a diminutive version of Peter Cook's coal miner's sound when the great lump of coal falls on his foot, and realized I had made the noise.

"I take it you didn't leave it like this," ventured Leo. Denise hit him, but his feeble attempt made me laugh. It was just as well, for if I'd started to cry, I don't think I could have stopped anytime soon.

"Let's go downstairs and call the police," said Denise with a bit of starch in her voice.

"The police?" said Leo at the same time as I said, "Downstairs?"

"It's a crime scene, isn't it? Don't touch anything. You never know, it might have something to do with the rest of the stuff that's been happening."

"Why, Denise, you sound so knowledgeable. Could it be you also read something less noble than the Elizabethans?" Leo queried.

"Well, you don't think *King Lear* could put me to sleep at night, do you?" replied Denise archly.

And with that, we trooped down the stairs to phone the cavalry.

I was too shook up to care that Leo and Denise would now know of my involvement with Steve. I pulled out his card from my wallet and dialed his pager number directly. I checked Denise's wall clock, and was amazed to discover it was only nine-thirty. It had seemed as though I had passed more than four hours in the dark. I found myself yawning as the phone rang. I left Denise's office number and sat in her student chair while Leo went off to start the coffeepot going. I wasn't sure whether it was shock from my "ordeal" or the sight of my office, or sheer nervous exhaustion, but I was nodding in my chair when Leo popped back in with fresh coffee that he'd dripped directly into cups.

"Here you are," he announced, handing me his favorite cup, on which was printed "So what if I haven't written much lately? Neither has Shakespeare." The fact that he was letting me use it was, I realized, a mark of concern.

"A hot cup of sustenance, like my Aunt Jessie always said. Although I think she was referring to gin at the time." Leo took a slurp of coffee as punctuation. I followed suit and almost gagged on the amount of sugar he'd put in my cup. "What is this made of, treacle?"

"It's good for you; you've had a shock to the system. In a better world we'd be giving you brandy right now."

"A better world," echoed Denise. I looked up at her. The weary and slightly frightened look on her face did more to make the situation sink in than anything else. I'd been operating on instinct till now. As I sat back in the safety of her office with my friends around me, I started to see the big picture. Someone had locked me up and ransacked my office. At any time I'd have probably felt violated. In the wake of a murder on campus and the defacement of the doors in the department, I began to feel truly frightened. Gloria Steinem would not have been proud of me. All I wanted right then was for my man to ride up and save me.

THE PHONE ON DENISE'S DESK RANG AND WE ALL jumped. Leo and I giggled as Denise answered. She passed the receiver to me, and I felt my shoulders unwind a bit as I heard Steve's voice on the other end.

I told him as succinctly as possible what had happened. He told me that he'd call in a crime scene unit and meet them at the House.

"Can your friends stay with you till I'm there?"

"Sure, I guess. You'll be needing to talk to them, anyhow, won't you?"

"I suppose. Right now, I just want to make sure you won't be alone."

I smiled, then saw Leo leaning toward me, trying to catch the disembodied voice through the receiver. I made a face at him, and replied to Steve, "I don't think you'll have to worry about them sticking around."

Leo gave me a look of mock hurt as I replaced the receiver on the cradle.

"Miranda, you don't think we're in this just for vicarious pleasure, do you? We care about your safety, darling."

"Give it a rest, Leo," said Denise wearily.

Leo gave her the same hurt look I'd received. Then he sniffed a Lady Bracknell sniff, and got back to business. "And just how well do we know this policeman, Miranda?"

"What's that supposed to mean?"

"Well, not only do you have his private number, he obviously has a personal stake in this as well. If we're not intrinsic to the investigation, we're here to keep you safe until he arrives. He cares about you."

He looked to Denise for verification. She nodded.

"I can't believe it. With all that has gone on tonight, you are more interested in my personal life?"

"We're your friends. We're supposed to gossip about you."

"Don't let him get to you, Randy," Denise overrode my comeback to Leo. "Leo's archness can be a bit too much at times, especially when you're exhausted. And if you're not, you should be. I know I am."

I looked her over. She did look tired, but she probably would look better than me after three days stranded by an avalanche in a mountain cabin. I hoped Steve wouldn't have too many questions for her.

We saw lights reflected on Denise's wall and looked out to see a police car all ablaze pull up in front of the House. Steve's car pulled in behind just as the first car cut its lights. He met two men at the base of the walk, and all three trooped up to the steps. Leo had bounced into the hall to open the door. I started to get up, but sank back, bone weary. I hadn't done anything wrong. Let them come to me.

Part of my mind, the editor that stands on guard for me, was considering how Steve was going to play this. It wasn't as if we had anything to hide, but he was a policeman in front of other policemen, and my friends were hovering too. As I listened to the treads of large male feet on the front steps, I decided that I wouldn't really be too bothered if he retained some professional aloofness. I would understand.

Steve pushed past Leo in the doorway and knelt in front of my chair, bundling me into his arms.

"How are you?"

So much for aloofness, and I was relieved. Steve's hug was

91

exactly what I needed, and I'd have probably held it against him if it hadn't been there spontaneously. I hugged him back, and some of his strength seemed to flow into my fragile shell.

"I'm okay, just a little shook up."

With some help from Denise, whom, I noted, Steve seemed to glance at only cursorily, I managed to tell him what had happened. Steve ordered a dusting of the bathroom door and the chair that had been wedged in front of it. One of the uniformed policemen set off for the nether regions. The other, whom Steve introduced as Officer Trent, went with us up to my office.

It was even worse to see it a second time.

Steve whistled at the destruction.

"We haven't moved or touched a thing," Denise offered from behind.

Steve gave her a grim smile. "Thanks, that's something. Once we dust a few surfaces, do you think you'd be able to tell us if anything is missing?"

"Do you keep anything of value in your office?" This was from Officer Trent.

I tried to think. "Nothing like money or first editions, if that's what you mean. My mark book is in here, and my class notes, and, oh lord, my mid-term exam!"

"Give us a minute, Randy." Steve grabbed me before I could complete my spring forward. "The guy probably wore gloves, any movie would teach him that, but we want to check it anyway. Trent will take some pictures, and Michaels will be up soon with the fingerprint kit. Might as well get everything messy before you start redecorating."

Denise and Leo gave statements to Steve and hugs to me before they left. I went down to the front door with them, and then, for something to do, put on another pot of coffee. I washed out some cups and handed one to Officer Michaels on his way through the kitchen. I called upstairs to see how

Officer Trent liked his coffee and then slopped three cups up to the landing. Steve and I sat on the stairs while the crime scene boys made my door, desk, bookcases and filing cabinet even grubbier than before.

Who cleans up after the police? I wondered.

I must have spoken out loud, because Steve laughed.

"Be thankful it's just fingerprint powder, and not a corpse. We hunt down bad guys; we definitely don't do windows."

"I suppose I'd better bring in some cleaning supplies tomorrow; I can't imagine the cleaning staff touching this."

"Let them handle the basement. Don't worry, they won't be spraying the books on the floor. If there's anything to find, it'll be clearer on a hard surface."

Small comfort. I slurped my coffee and then yawned. The whole evening was catching up with me.

"I know it's getting late, but I'd appreciate it if you could look through for a few things. One, your mid-term. How many students would be sitting it?"

"About seventy-five. I made only one for both classes. I was going to haul in the exam sheets after the first sitting."

"Well, it's a possibility. How much is it worth?"

"Twenty-five percent of the full year mark. But it's mostly essay questions. Even a sneak preview would only let you in on about forty percent."

"Well, who knows, it might not be what's missing. There's something else I want you to look for."

I looked up at him. I'd been sitting one step down from him, using his legs as a side support. He looked grim, a look I'd only seen once before. Last night, when I'd told him about the . . . my jaw dropped along with the penny.

"Gwen's journal?" I squeaked.

Steve nodded.

"Oh, you don't think . . ."

"Randy, I hate to disillusion you, but I doubt if I could justify two crime scene guys for my girlfriend's tossed office. On the other hand, when there could be a tie-in to an unresolved homicide, the overtime comes cheap."

It was a good thing Officer Trent appeared in the hallway just then, because I could feel myself starting to shake. Words like "unresolved homicide" tend to do that to me. Words like "girlfriend" have the same effect.

"We're done here."

Steve stood up and helped me to my feet.

"Okay, it's showtime."

OFFICERS TRENT AND MICHAELS EXCUSED themselves, and Steve made arrangements to see them the following day. I braced myself in the doorway and then moved forward into the mess. Aside from the silvery powder smeared about in places, nothing had changed since Denise and Leo and I had first peered in. I waded through the detritus on the floor, and was halfway round my desk, when I stopped with a cry.

"Randy? What is it?" Steve was in the doorway.

I bent down to retrieve my autographed copy of *Medicine River*, which someone had trodden on open, and mashed open.

"Is nothing sacred?" I muttered, then almost immediately began to question my bitterness. Of course it felt real, but wasn't I somehow devaluing and dismissing the horror of events like what had happened to Gwen? Here there was no blood; this scene could be repaired and life could go on, even if I would never feel quite the same about this little sanctuary. Was I too cut off from reality?

Steve seemed to intuit what I was going through. He moved towards me.

"This isn't going to be easy, and yes, you have a right to grieve for your loss of safety. Don't feel guilty that you aren't the thing ripped apart on the floor tonight."

95

"How did you know?"

"I could pass it off as superior policing skills, or amazing sensitivity, but hasn't anyone warned you off playing poker before now?" He hugged my shoulders, and then got businesslike. "How's about if I sort through what's on the floor and pile it up into salvageable, important but ruined, and don't even bother? You tackle the desk."

We worked in silence for about half an hour. After clearing the surface of the desk with paper towels from the upstairs bathroom and trying to make sense of the confetti that had been my fall class notes, I started on my upper drawer. I piled up a batch of cue cards to take home to dry. They contained my jottings for the entire year's syllabus, and the coffee had drained through them. I could decipher some of it, and was glad I'd never had the urge to use a fountain pen.

Once I could close the first drawer, I was able to untangle the files sprouting out of the second. To my dismay, even the notes for my mid-term were missing. I had told Steve what the file would look like, and so far he hadn't turned up anything remotely like it on the floor. He was downstairs for a moment, getting the last of the coffee. It was heading on one-thirty.

It wasn't the fact that the mid-term was gone that caused me such problems. I could write another in the time I had before the exam date. Even the thought that one of my students was a thief wasn't too much to bear. I have a friend in Ontario who teaches English at the Kingston Penitentiary, and if she could handle it, so could I.

What worried me was the thought that Steve had brought out the big hitters for something that, in the big scheme of things, was so paltry. How the heck was he going to justify this to his bosses?

He returned just then, and I must have telegraphed my feelings again, because he tilted his head to one side and raised an eyebrow.

"Don't tell me you had an autographed Chaucer, too?"

I snorted, a truly attractive quality, which I list among my better features, and told him about the missing exam file.

"And this means a ton of repeat work for you?"

"No, not that much," and I explained my worries as I slid drawer number two back into its casement.

"Randy, if it makes you feel any better, I'd rather we found the journal and I faced the music about hauling out the scene team than losing Gwen's journal as well."

I looked up from rummaging through the final drawer. "Well, it actually makes me feel worse, because Gwen's journal is gone too."

re you sure?" he asked.

"Of course I'm sure. Believe it or not, there used to be some organization in this room. I put the journal in this drawer under last year's campus directory and the city phone books. They're still here."

Steve turned businesslike almost immediately. I was inclined to think brusque, but that could have been the hour talking.

"Well, now we know it's connected. Do you have much more to do? I want to get you home."

I looked ruefully around my office. It was still in a state of chaos, but resembled the middle of marking three sets of essays more than the effects of abject vandalism. Steve had made two piles of papers on the floor, and placed a large green garbage bag, almost full, by the door. What books he could rescue were piled neatly on the floor in front of the bookcase. He handed me a list of titles he had been unable to salvage. I put it on the now cleared-off desk, unable to focus on what I might have to replace. I was hoping that most of them would be complimentary volumes from sales reps, things I'd welcomed but not really wanted.

I scribbled a quick list of what I'd need to bring in tomorrow to clean the place and locked the door. Steve was standing halfway down the stairs, looking too distant for my mind.

We rode to my place in silence. He pulled in the back alley, and I turned to him as I opened the door, not wanting to wait to see if he wasn't going to kiss me goodnight.

"Steve," I started, hoping my voice wasn't going to break, "I'm really sorry. You've got to believe I wasn't holding out on you. I meant to give it to you . . ." My voice drifted away.

"I know, Randy." He gave me a ghost of a half-smile. "Anyhow, you're not the one who should be apologizing. You've been through a heck of a lot tonight. Do you want me to see you in?"

"And check under the bed for bogeymen? No, I think I can manage."

I swung my legs out the door, and the cold air hit me fully awake.

"Will I be seeing you soon?" I hated myself for asking, and prayed it didn't sound too pleading.

"Tomorrow, I figure."

"Oh?" Maybe it was the lateness of the night playing tricks on me after all. My heart leaped up a bit.

"We'll need you to come in and sign a statement as soon as you can. Take care."

It wasn't what I'd been hoping to hear, and the cold air felt good against my cheeks as I watched the car disappear around a curve in the alley. That's the trouble with opening up emotionally. It makes you so darned vulnerable. I closed the door quietly against the night and moved down the carpeted hall to my apartment, which seemed a lot less charming and a lot more insecure than it had twenty-four hours ago.

I SLEPT TILL NOON THE NEXT DAY AND WAS AWAKENED by the telephone. I stumbled into the dining alcove to answer the call, pushing matted hair back from my forehead. It was Denise, reporting on what was happening in the department. Apparently I was awaited by Dr. McNeely, and she thought I should get in there as soon as I could.

I was getting tired of being summoned in on my off days. I decided they could wait until I'd showered.

I braided my still damp hair and jammed a woolly toque over it, knowing I'd be sporting icicles if I tried to walk in without it. I had a turtleneck on under a cheerfully bright orange sweatshirt, and worn brown corduroys. My comfort clothes. Let McNeely realize I was coming in under duress.

The walk brightened my spirits, and I dumped my bag of cleaning supplies inside the door of my office, which looked a lot better than I remembered it from the night before. Sunshine will do that. I figured I had about two hours cleaning time to put in before it would be completely in order, but that would have to wait until my visit with the department chairman. I left my coat on, but threw my toque on the desk. My hair would have to hold its breath on the walk to the Humanities Building.

Marjorie, the chairman's secretary, smiled at me as I leaned in the open doorway and knocked on the jamb. She crooked her finger at me and spoke into the telephone, announcing my arrival.

"Dr. McNeely has been hoping to see you today," she said.

"So I hear."

She seemed about to say something more, which was unusual, since Marjorie is discretion itself. I'm sure she knows everything that goes on in the department, but she never gossips. Maybe that's why people tell her things. Anyhow, before she could break her code of silence, the inner door opened and there McNeely stood, ushering me in to the inner sanctum.

I'd never been inside the chairman's office before. It overlooked the river valley and thus had probably the best view on campus, although you used to be able to simulate it from the cafeteria on the fifth floor until they'd closed it as a cost-cutting measure. There was room for a huge desk, with a couple of nice chairs in front, and a couch and coffee table grouping as well. Low bookshelves stood at attention under the windows, with highboys on the opposite walls. Some nice art, which I assumed must belong to the university, hung on the walls, and various catalogues and brochures were on the coffee table, making me think that McNeely was aware that the trappings were a ruse to get people to stand for the job. I mean, who in their right mind would opt for bureaucracy after spending most of their life trying to get beyond it?

Not that McNeely wasn't suited to the job. Things ran smoothly and there was little dissent over the way the department was being run, from what I'd heard. In these days of cutbacks, most people saw any form of maintaining the status quo as a victory. McNeely was hot on status quo.

And it seemed I was not. After a few pleasantries and some tut-tutting about the desecration of my office, McNeely got down to business. As news leaked out about last night's business (Leo and his fat mouth, I assumed), the powers that be were outraged that procedure had not been followed. Had I memorized my policy manual when hired, I should have known enough to call Campus Security first, before the Edmonton city police.

I apologized, and explained the circumstances. I guess Denise had already covered this ground, because McNeely waved off my excuses.

"What I'm really concerned with is the detrimental value this sort of thing will have if the press makes a field day out of the tribulations of the English Department. I've already fielded several calls from this Mark Paulson, who wants to tie everything to the murder just because the young woman concerned took an English course. For heaven's sake, everyone has to take English, I told him. The trouble is, she did take English, you were her teacher, and now you seem to be involved even more. I want to stress to you the importance of retaining at least an outward calm in the face of all these events. The bottom line here is reputation, and if we can't hold on to that, our funding and our enrollment will suffer."

I hate people who say "bottom line." What was I supposed to do, stay in the basement bathroom? I took a deep breath and tried to reassure Dr. McNeely that I hadn't sold my story to the *National Enquirer*.

"Just as long as we have an understanding, Miranda." He smiled and stood up, letting me know the inquisition was at an end. I wasn't sure if he was using my given name because he had channeled my mother, who used it only when I'd broken something (a window, a vase, a moral imperative), or if he'd just looked at my file prior to my entry to make sure who I really was. Either way, I felt put in my place, as nothing like hearing that name can do.

Anyone considering dumping a Shakespearean name on their offspring should try something strong like Rosalind or Portia. We Ophelias and Mirandas are here to testify that the naïf label just doesn't cut it. That is, unless you want us living in your attic until we're sixty, wearing gauzy outfits while writing poetry and collecting cats. I've been Randy ever since I hit grade school and it suits me. I like the feeling it gives me of setting my own pace rather than having to live up to an image that can only be defined in sepia and lace.

I refused to let McNeely see he'd managed to get a rise out of me, and backed my way out of the office, doing the contemporary version of bowing and scraping. I'm not sure why I was apologizing for being victimized and vandalized, but needing a job will do that to you. If I didn't need the work, I probably would have considered suing the university. Unfortunately, it takes money to make money.

I N THE NEXT FEW DAYS I WENT DOWN TO THE police station, signed my statement, was interviewed by one of Steve's henchmen about what I could remember of the contents of the journal, tried to patch together a new mid-term, alerted Campus Security and the Faculty of Arts that my exam had been stolen, and tried to recall various questions I'd put on it. All this recall was lousy on the spirit; I felt as if everything I was doing was mired in the past.

Even working with Denise on the plans for the vigil wasn't helping much. It didn't take much to jump back to the days after the Montreal Massacre in 1989, when all of us were reeling from the news. Perfectly respectable men were trying to argue that it wasn't a misogynistic stand; it was the senseless act of one specific madman. While I could see what they were saying, I could only shake my head and move away from such conversations. If they couldn't understand how that specific act had made women feel, they never would.

Part of me was a little worried about what McNeely would think about my involvement with the vigil, but there were lots of others involved as well. The two leaders of course were Denise and Grace Tarrant, the editor of HYSTERICAL. She had taken the defacement of her door rather well, I'd thought, but then there's such a backlash stereotype of the pro-active feminist, that I suppose even I'd bought in to it a bit. Grace lived up to her name, shrugged it off with a toss-off line about "considering the source," and got on with things.

Julian and Leo were helping a bit with the fetching and carrying. Arno had managed to find a wholesaler willing to sell us candles and the foil tart cups that we were going to use as wax catchers around the candle bases. I hadn't been surprised to see Julian, since he was eager to be part of anything that would keep him from having to write his dissertation; and Leo was always where any action was. Arno's involvement surprised me a bit, especially when he refused acknowledgment in the list Grace was writing up for the program. I mused to Denise that maybe Arno was a little sweet on Grace.

Denise snorted and replied that it was more likely that Arno was keeping an eye on Grace given that they both might be sitting before the tenure committee in the spring. She had a point, though personally I was hoping for my theory. I had seen other folks get into major sycophant mode when tenure time came up, and it could get pretty ugly. It would be much nicer if there was romance brewing. Every now and then I get these really turgid matchmaking urges, especially when I've been touched in that department. I want everyone I like to be in love, too. Although I am calming down as I age, people I admire would do well to run and hide when I get into these moods. Of course, given my track record to date, love seemed to be a rather bittersweet thing to wish on people.

I really admire Grace. She sits on three committees, teaches a full load, edits and puts out four issues of *HYSTERICAL* every year, mainly from her office, has three grad students already, and she hasn't even got tenure yet. The best thing about her is that she treats sessionals as colleagues, when precious few others in the department even deign to recognize that we exist. She always hosts a Christmas party for the entire department on the Friday evening before the start of mid-term exams; usually only the younger members, sessionals and the heavy drinkers attend, but the parties are always a blast.

I was using the thought of that upcoming party to come to keep me focused through the last weeks of teaching. It wasn't easy. I'd known enough to schedule some short stories for pre-exam classes. My students would be too wired on caffeine to do justice to poetry, and discussions that could be contained within one class were more likely to be fruitful since most of them were cutting their more "expendable" classes every so often in order to study. There would be a three-day lull between the last class and first exam, but I suppose that's not enough for someone who has spent the first term drinking beer.

The Tuesday session on Flannery O'Connor's "A Good Man Is Hard to Find" went well. Mind you, I could teach that story in my sleep; it's so full of hooks on which to hang discussion. On the other hand, they hated Marquez's "A Very Old Man with Enormous Wings," a story I adore. It was with a heavy heart that I started into the last lecture's topic, which was "Boys and Girls," the only Alice Munro that ever seems to get anthologized.

It was like an early Christmas present. Most had caught the fact that the boy's name, Laird, was full of meaning, and that the girl had no name. A couple of the more chauvinistic tried to make the case that narrators can't call themselves by name realistically, but their arguments were quickly squashed by other members of the class. I was starting to have high hopes for the first work of the new year, which would be Louise Erdrich's *Love Medicine*.

I'd saved the last ten minutes of the class for a quickie talk about mid-session exam writing. They'd already written one for me, but my first term mid-term is usually ten short snappers and two small essays, and for some of them it was the only university exam they'd as yet encountered.

"Remember to bring more than one pen, and spend the first five minutes reading through the exam paper. There's a story, most likely apocryphal, that goes around this time of year about a prof who gave out an exam with 'PLEASE READ THROUGH THE ENTIRE EXAM FIRST' printed at the top. Then there were about a hundred furiously difficult questions. The final question said, 'Do not answer the above questions.'"

Lloyd in the back row raised his hand.

"Yes?"

"Any chance you'll be doing that?"

"In your dreams."

The class laughed.

"Two more things. I want *Love Medicine* read for the first class in January. Don't groan, it's a good read. I think you'll enjoy it. In fact, if you're in doubt, it makes a good present, too. Just don't give away your copy. And second, for those of you who care to participate, there will be a candlelight vigil held tomorrow evening starting at six p.m. at the memorial garden in front of the Administration Building. This is to commemorate the death of the fourteen students the École Polytechnique on December 6th, 1989. You might have seen posters up around campus."

I checked my wristwatch against the clock on the side wall.

"That's it. See you on the sixteenth at nine a.m. in this room. No books. No snacks. Drinks allowed as long as you don't intend to spill them on your exam booklet. Good luck with the studying."

The noise wall rose immediately. I had a feeling there was more discussion about last class blow-out parties than library study dates, but I could have been wrong. I've been wrong before.

I T WASN'T ONE OF OUR INFAMOUS COLD SNAPS, BUT I still think there is something intensely heroic about willingly standing out in minus 10 Celcius weather at six in the evening for an unspecified amount of time. I'd thought of quizzing Denise about how long things were going to be, but I didn't feel right asking after she'd been going to so much trouble to make things meaningful and poetic. She looked like what I've always imagined medieval saints must have looked prior to one of their ecstasies: tired, harassed, and driven.

She and Grace had planned everything. They had worried the consequences of each segment in the same way my aunt had planned my cousin's $10,000 wedding. I felt a bit guilty, as I'd just run errands. Of course, I'd done about as much as any of the fellows had. I looked around for them. I could spot Greg on the other side of the stairs, handing out candles. Julian, I figured, would be with the sound engineer, since he had an affinity for that sort of thing. I couldn't spot Arno anywhere, but it was a big crowd. So I had not contributed as much as Grace or Denise. That didn't make me less of a person.

The handbills around campus had done their stuff. The pavement in front of the Administration Building was filling up, mostly with young women in parkas and moon boots. A few young men were also in attendance, but not as many as I'd have wished.

Denise had mentioned that she'd contacted the media, but I was impressed with the turnout. Both newspapers were there, as well as a camera crew from the CBC and A-Channel. Denise came over with Mark Paulson, the *Edmonton Journal* reporter, in tow. She had apparently promised him an interview after the scripted portion of the vigil was over. She handed him over to me, then made her way up the stairs of the Administration Building, where the sound system was set up.

I could tell Mark Paulson was smitten with Denise from the way he kept his eyes on her even as he shook hands with me. What did I care? I'd already had the cold shoulder from Steve this week. Mr. Paulson could do his best to make me feel inadequate, but he couldn't compete.

"We can get a bit closer, if you'd like," I said. "Most of the presentation will come from the steps, but there's going to be something happening around the shrubbery garden after about ten minutes."

"I know we met before, but I never did catch your name," he said, his reporter's instincts conquering the cold.

"My name's Randy. I'm just helping out." I was remembering the chairman's warnings about keeping out of the picture.

"Randy?" His pen was poised over the ubiquitous notebook.

"Craig," I answered, checking his spelling. The universal quest for fame won out over my desire to keep a low profile to avoid risking McNeely's wrath. Caution won out and made me continue. "Honestly I'm just a friend of Denise's helping out. Denise and Grace are the real organizers. Dr. Grace Tarrant."

He gave me a look I recognized from my first-year students trying to remember trivial details like the name of the author of *Paradise Lost*. I had dubbed it the "mentally constipated countenance."

"Randy Craig. I know that name."

I wasn't about to help him out. "You're probably thinking of the hockey player. Gregg. It happens a lot."

"No, I know your name. Something to do with the Co-ed Murder? You were her prof, that's right. I covered that story and the Poison Pen Letters. No leads anymore. I've tried to get on to the policeman in charge, Browning, but he doesn't have the time of day for the fourth estate. Usually that's a sign of a no-hoper."

Just hearing Steve's name was enough to make my heart do a little flutter kick.

"So what do you think?"

I tuned back in to Mark Paulson, who had kept right on going, just like that annoying pink rabbit in the TV ads. How did he ever get any quotable quotes if he was always doing all the talking?

"I beg your pardon?"

"I said, what would you say to an interview, your impressions of the victim as a student? I could couple it with some family reminiscences."

My look of horror must have telegraphed itself to him. Maybe Steve was right and I did have a see-through face.

"Hey, it would be useful. Get an unsolved death back on the front burners where it belongs. It's not ghoulishness"— Steve had to be right, this guy was reading my mind—"it's a public service. You do want to see justice done, don't you, Dr. Craig?"

"It's just Randy."

Paulson looked unnerved, and I realized that it sounded friendlier than I'd intended.

"I don't have my Ph.D. I'm not Dr. Craig."

Just then, the ceremony began, and Mark Paulson's nose turned away from me and toward the news.

GRACE BEGAN BY WELCOMING ALL AND EXPLAINING the symbolism of the candles and the gong. She spoke about the memorial garden, and made a touching reference to its snowy, sleeping state. She ended with a short essay that I think came from Alice Walker's *In Search of Our Mothers' Gardens*, and then turned the microphone over to Denise. Even bundled up against the elements, she looked right out of *Vogue*. Mark Paulson edged closer though the sound system was more than adequate. Denise just has that effect on men.

"In 1989, fourteen women died, because they were women. Marc Lepine didn't know these women. He had nothing to fear from these women. These women had not snubbed him or scorned him. Yet, because these women believed that the world really meant what it said and that women were the equals of men, they had the temerity to choose to train as engineers. That is what Marc Lepine took to be their sin."

The tone from the gong sounded just as Denise paused to take a breath.

"We must remember these young women every day if we are ever to get beyond the boundaries of a world where women are afraid to walk alone at night, where women are shackled to abusive husbands, where women must strive beyond excellence to compete with the merely satisfactory work of their fellows.

"I am not suggesting that we claim these young women as martyrs. They did not wish to be martyred. They merely wished to live their lives as they chose to live them. This they were not allowed. Let us instead remember them with sadness, and pray for the day when all girls can sleep safely and dream whatever dreams they want."

The volunteers had silently passed through the crowd, handing out candles. Denise lit hers with the taper and turned to light Grace's. Grace moved down the stairs and in turn lit the candle of one of the front row students. Candles began to flicker throughout the crowd, like a wave of fireflies passing over the assembly. It was an incredibly moving gesture, and I found myself sniffling a bit as I leaned toward the girl in front of me to shield my own candle from the wind.

One of Grace's graduate students was reading the names of the Montreal students. Those lilting French Canadian names hit at my heart the same way they had every year at this time. The gong sounded its melancholy death knell for yet another Canadian woman. Mark Paulson had edged away from me toward Denise, and I felt a momentary bitterness against his lack of understanding of the sacredness of the moment. It was like getting up to leave church before the minister has passed your pew.

Just then someone touched my arm. Assuming it was another candlelighter, I cupped the flame and turned to see Steve, bundled in his EPS regulation parka.

"I couldn't find you at first. Who was that guy?"

I marveled that he sounded jealous.

"That was Denise's reporter. I think he's going to find it rough going if he interrupts her too soon, though. Have you been here long?"

"Yep, very nice ceremony."

I nodded my agreement. I wasn't sure I was up to a conversation yet, the moment was still upon me. Steve seemed to understand. He stood beside me, watching the lights bobble among the crowd.

After a few minutes, and another note from the gong, I turned back to him. "You're here officially?"

"In a manner of speaking. There are some regular officers assigned, just as for any organized gathering. I just thought I'd come along, since it seems so much a part of the other stuff."

"You think there'll be trouble?"

"Well, there hasn't been so far, and there's not much left is there?"

I tried to remember the agenda. "I think there's just the anthem in a couple of minutes. Mind you, there'll be people sticking around, holding vigil most of the night, I would guess."

"In this weather?"

"Sorry, none of us were polled about when to hold the massacre," I retorted sharply.

Steve winced. "Sorry. That was thoughtless. Are you sticking around all night?"

"No, I'm not up to the cold." I allowed myself a smile of forgiveness. "I'm just here for the ceremony, and then I don't know. I haven't spotted Leo or Arno anywhere, and they were on the committee. Julian is over there behind the stairs, helping steady the sound booth's baffles or some such." I shrugged. "I really don't know if anything is on for later, besides the vigil. I guess it depends on what Grace and Denise are up to. I hadn't really thought much past seven-thirty, to tell you the truth."

Heather, one of the most marvelous voices to ever come out of the music department, was stepping up to the microphone. She didn't stand too close. I'd heard her sing in Convocation Hall once and figured she didn't even need the mike. She had the look of a tragic heroine from some opera as she began a spiritual, "All My Troubles, Lord, Soon Be Over." The gong miraculously slid right into the music. Someone in the front of the crowd began to weep openly.

Steve stiffened. I looked up at him questioningly.

"Randy, meet me on the steps of St. Joe's. Go now, please!"

I couldn't figure out what he was talking about, but he moved off before I could speak. I started to move back across the bus route to the Catholic College. I wasn't sure why I was letting a man dictate my movements on tonight of all nights, but there had been something in Steve's voice that made me listen.

It made no difference in the long run.

While we had all been focusing on Heather, several figures in red jackets and full head masks had circled the crowd. The ones between me and St. Joe's had on a gorilla mask and a Nixon mask, respectively. They were shouting, "Chill out, bitches," so loudly that they were able to drown out Heather's voice. Or maybe she had stopped singing anyway. The crowd turned toward their voices, and everyone began to scream at once. The masked offenders were letting loose cold water from huge, luridly-colored water rifles.

Any other time it would have been offensive. On a chilly December night it was dangerous. People were getting drenched. The ground was quickly becoming treacherous. I wasn't sure where Steve was, but his so-called crowd control folks weren't all that obvious to me. I got off lightly with a quick spraying, since I'd already been moving out of range. The folks near the front weren't as lucky. Denise tried to get to the mike to stop the panic, but the technician warned her away, since the equipment had already had a dousing.

I saw one cop chasing one of the guys in red, who flung his water gun away and loped off toward the Education Building. Another couple headed for the entrances to the Light Rail Transit subway. They wouldn't get away, unless there happened to be a convenient train waiting.

People were milling toward the entrances to the Student Union Building, shivering and baffled by their brush with hatred. I stamped my feet to keep myself warm, waiting for Steve.

I whirled around when I heard someone behind me, but it was just a small priest in a raggedy black sweater opening the door for me.

"Wouldn't you rather step inside, dear?"

"Thanks. I'm supposed to meet someone here."

"You can watch through the door. Just what on earth is happening?"

I explained as best I could to Father Masson, who had asked a passing student to fetch me a cup of coffee. He tutted and shook his head. Coffee arrived at the same time as Steve.

Father Masson brightened at the sight of him.

"Steve Browning! How are you?"

"Hello, Father. I see you've met Randy. Thank you for the sanctuary, as it were."

Steve turned to me.

"I took a course on Christian Platonics from Father Masson. That must have been fifteen years ago. I can't believe you remember the names of all your students."

"Only the argumentative ones," said the old priest fondly. "So you are now a policeman?"

"For my sins." Steve grinned back.

I was starting to feel left out. "What's happening out there?" I asked Steve.

"We managed to catch one of the pranksters, and he's being hauled downtown now. Most of the vigil attendees are shivering in SUB, and some officers are in there taking statements. Your friend Grace has made a call for pizza, and said something about "blowing the hysterical budget," but I'm not sure what she was on about."

"*HYSTERICAL*, not hysterical," I explained, and then realized that they couldn't be expected to hear my distinction of all capitals. "I mean the periodical. Trust Grace to do something like that. Are they looking for me?"

"Right now they probably don't know you're missing, but we could head over there anyway."

He turned toward my diminutive host. "Thanks again, Father. It was good to run into you."

I shook hands with Father Masson, who told me to give my best to Dr. Tarrant before ushering us out. Seems he was a subscriber to HYSTERICAL and a friend of Grace's. I swear someday I'll learn never to second-guess people. He waved from the doorway as we made our way across the impromptu ice rink in front of the Administration Building.

"Christian Platonics?" I asked Steve as soon as we were out of earshot of Father Masson.

"I had a hankering to have a course in a real old college. Probably came from reading too many Oxbridge novels. St. Joe's was the only one available, and C.P. was the only course I could justify. It wasn't bad, all in all."

"So, you're Catholic?" I couldn't believe it. Here in the middle of a crisis I was probing the background of my boyfriend. If he *was* still my boyfriend.

"Only in my tastes," Steve laughed and hugged me around the shoulders.

I hugged him back.

"Randy, I've got to apologize for this last week. I was wrong to shut you out like that. I know you didn't deliberately scupper anything, and if you say there was nothing of note in the journal, then I believe you."

We had stopped just outside the stage doors to the Horowitz Theatre. I reached up a mittened hand to touch his cheek.

"I'm sorry, too. I've missed you."

"So, no more than one slice of pizza and I'll see you home, okay?"

"You don't have to stay and work?"

"I'm thinking of going deep undercover tonight." He laughed.

Thank goodness it was dark. The blush had me almost warm by the time we got into the SUB lobby.

T HE PLACE WAS BUZZING. I'VE NOT FOUND MUCH reason to go into SUB since my early days on campus, especially since they tarted it up. Once it had looked like a students' union, with the focus on the bookstore, a good inexpensive cafeteria, a common area complete with fire pit, and a large seating area that was by day eating space and by weekend a cabaret. RATT, the Room at the Top, was the rowdier of the three campus bars. Now, although RATT still maintained its reputation, the whole place looked as antiseptic as a shopping mall, with nailed-down seating arrangements surrounded by fast-food kiosks.

Two camps had congregated. One had formed around Denise, spouting indignation and a little bit of excitement to be caught up in a real live adventure. Police officers were pulling them off two at a time to take statements at one of the food court tables.

The other group just looked wet and cold and bewildered. Grace seemed to be in charge of them, hustling around the perimeter, organizing them to remove wet outerwear and line up for the telephones.

I wasn't sure where I might be needed and was selfishly trying to make sure I wouldn't be indispensable anywhere. Denise caught sight of Steve and me, and waved us toward her melee.

"Randy! Are you all right? I wasn't sure where you were standing when the chaos began." She broke off to address Steve. "Are you in charge of the officers this evening? Because if you are, I have to express my disappointment in their ability to maintain what had been an orderly demonstration."

"Sorry, no." Steve broke in before she could really get rolling. "I was here on my own time, although I have a feeling this investigation will probably lead back to mine."

Denise's eyebrow shot up in a question, but she refrained from quizzing him.

"Grace has ordered pizzas," she said. "Lord knows what her credit card is going to look like after tonight, but we can't just let these kids go home covered in icicles. Some of them are calling friends to bring dry clothes. Others who live on campus will just hurry home after the officers have finished their questions."

"Did you see anything from where you were standing?" Steve asked Denise.

"I've been wondering." She pursed out her bottom lip, thoughtfully. "I was toward the back on the top steps of the Admin Building. We had one arc light focused on the stairs for the speakers, so maybe my eyes weren't working on full night vision. All I really know is that just as Heather got into the chorus of the spiritual, she got drowned out by shouting. It was so sudden, and from so many directions, I'm not sure exactly what they were shouting."

"The ones behind me were chanting 'Chill out, bitches,' but I'm pretty sure that's not all that was being said," I offered.

Steve looked tired and more than a little bit frustrated. He put out his hand to Denise, who shook it.

"On behalf of sane men everywhere, I apologize for the disruption of your ceremony. The only statement I can make officially is that we have apprehended one perpetrator, and we hope to run all the hooligans to ground soon."

Denise looked impressed, and nudged me when Steve left

for a moment to talk to the officers in charge. "I have to say, Randy, there goes a good man."

"I'll say."

"We should have him stuffed and mounted."

"Denise!"

"Just kidding. I take it you're not going to stick around for pizza?"

"Uh, I figured, as long as I'm not really needed . . ."

"Go on, Craig, you are so transparent. If it makes you feel any better, think of yourself as a mole for the sisterhood."

"Yeah, right, that makes me feel a whole lot better."

Steve returned before I could say anything more damaging and we left through the west doors toward the car park and Steve's car.

"Do you really think you'll get anything out of the guy you caught?"

"Well, I'm banking on him being a frightened freshman unaware of his rights, but it would have been a lot easier if we'd caught two of them. Then we could play one off against the other."

Steve opened the car door for me, a gesture I hadn't seen in a while. I guess too many guys are afraid of being rebuffed for the manners that their mamas instilled.

"What I hope to find out is if there's a ring of assholes out there, or if there's just a whole lot of nasty people working individually."

"You mean the letter-writers and the door scribbler and these hooligans tonight might all be the same guys?"

"Could be. We managed to get only three guys to admit to the letter-writing, and though all of them said there were more than three people in the room, none of them would name any other names."

"Could one of them have actually murdered Gwen?"

"Jeez, Randy, I hope not." Steve pulled up in front of my place and stopped the car. He held on to the steering wheel and stared through the windscreen at the frigid night. "Not trying to downplay what happened tonight as less than it is, but I have a personal hierarchy of malfeasance. This was pranksterism, and one could argue the same for the letters, although they were really ugly and ill conceived. The doors are one step further down the ladder, but murder is at the very bottom, and I hate to think that kids who are supposed to be worried about their mid-terms are capable of it."

"I know what you mean," I said, "but that's something you have to get beyond."

"What?" He turned to face me.

"That someone in a university is somehow beyond basic ugliness. I was shocked when I attended my first faculty meeting, because I always figured that folks who had spent their lives studying greatness wouldn't themselves be petty. But to be human is to be petty, I think. It just hurts more to see it in the ivory tower than to see it in the boardroom or the staff canteen."

" 'We are all of us lying in the gutter, but some of us are looking at the stars'," Steve intoned.

"Are you quoting the original Oscar Wilde or Tennessee Williams?" I laughed.

"Tell me the Tennessee Williams."

"It comes from *Summer and Smoke* where Alma the goody-goody is in love with the ne'er-do-well doctor's son. She says 'Who said, 'We are all of us lying in the gutter but some of us are looking at the stars', and John says, 'I think it was Oscar Wilde,' and she gets huffy and says 'Well, it doesn't matter who said it, it's still a lovely sentiment!' "

Steve laughed. "How about, we are all of us freezing in December, but some of us are sitting in our cars?"

"Now that's an original. C'mon, I'll make you some cocoa."

"Are you trying to bribe an officer of the law, ma'am?"

"Would it work?"

"There's just one way to find out."

THE NEXT MORNING, AFTER AN AMAZINGLY restrained shower, I found Steve sorting through the wilted vegetables in my crisper when I swanned into the kitchen.

"If this is a search, you'd better have a warrant."

He smiled. "I thought I'd surprise you with a Browning original. Slumgullion omelet coming right up."

"And he cooks too. Just wait till my mother phones next."

The coffee was already dripped through, so I reached across the action on the cutting board for a mug that hung off a hook under the cupboard and helped myself. I could get used to this.

Steve looked up at me and smiled, making me wonder if I'd said the words out loud.

"You don't have to rush off?"

"It's my day off. Mayhem will have to wait. Actually, that's some of the best advice I ever learned, and they don't mention it in the academy. It was my first sergeant who took me aside and said, 'Shit just keeps on happening, whether you're there or not, and you have to rest sometime.'"

"Quite the philosopher."

"Wasn't he just? One of the few cops I ever met who had a fifty-year marriage and a happy retirement, so I figure he was worth listening to."

"But what happened to the thing you read in mystery

novels, where you have to work like the devil so the trail isn't forty-eight hours cold?"

"Oh, there's overtime for that sort of thing, and it happens more than I like, but you get resigned to wearing a beeper, and you gather your rosebuds where you may. That's your actual poetry, just for you."

"Charmed, I'm sure."

Steve dumped a mass of chopped tomato, green pepper, onion and potato into the egg mixture bubbling on the stove and stooped to kiss me on the nose.

"I think I'm in heaven."

"Set the table, and you'll find out for sure."

In a few minutes I was digging into a wonderful breakfast, vowing in the back of my mind to get back to Muffets the next morning. It was astonishingly good to sit across from someone in the early morning and share a meal. I wondered if long-married couples realized their blessings, or buried themselves in newspapers and missed the glow.

"Well, I'm off today, too. In fact, I'm done till a week Monday, when I sit exams."

"Really? What are you doing with your week?"

"Well, I was planning to reread *Love Medicine*, and I should do a deep-clean on this place, especially since even my rotting vegetables are no longer safe from prying eyes. Then there is Christmas shopping to think about, and card-writing . . ."

Steve looked up and gave me a questioning glance as I stopped speaking mid-sentence.

"You know, it feels strange to think about ordinary things when so much has been happening that's out of my normal existence."

"Meaning the murder investigation or the pranksters?"

"Both, I guess. And this too, this—what should we call it?—relationship." My laugh sounded surprisingly brittle. "Isn't that a stupid word?"

"It'll have to do, though. After all, 'affair' has taken on such tawdry overtones, and seems to indicate a presumed ending. You're the word person. You should come up with a new word."

"Words are hard, though, when you're uncertain."

"Are you uncertain?"

"I guess I'm worried about opening up emotionally and ..."

"Allowing your vulnerability to show?"

"More like scaring you away. Wasn't it Rita Rudner that once said she always got rid of unwanted men by saying, 'I love you'? I know I'm generalizing wildly here, but stereotypically, your gender is not known for clinging to commitment."

"Ah, I get you."

"Most of the women I know go by the tenet that it's best to hold back and wait until the guy expresses himself first. It's today's version of the junior high school dance ritual; girls on one side of the gym, guys huddled at the other side. All the girls trying desperately not to show how much they want someone to cross the gym and ask them to dance."

"And it would make you feel better if I told you that I showed up at the vigil last night hoping to find you because I've been realizing this last week that thoughts of you keep creeping into my mind?"

My face was getting tingly with heat. "It would."

Steve smiled, and stuck his hands in his pockets. He shuffled across the three feet separating us in my miniscule kitchen, until he stood barely an inch away.

"Well, a sunny kitchen wasn't exactly the atmosphere I had in mind for saying this, but, Randy Craig, would you like to dance?"

I T WAS MID-AFTERNOON AND ANOTHER COBBLED together meal before Steve left. I filled the sudden emptiness with laundry and other mindless chores, trying to regain a bit of equilibrium. Everything in my world was changing, some of it for the better, but all of it a bit too fast for my liking. Mind you, continental drift is a bit too sudden for me at times, too, so I was trying not to get too stressed out.

When the place looked presentable again, I sank onto the sofa with a cup of coffee, and reached for a pad of paper and pencil. A list would help. I would probably take a pad of paper to a deserted island instead of the works of Shakespeare. My days would feel so much more structured: "Tuesday: make coconut soup, work on raft, get off island."

Steve's question of what I'd be doing with my week had made me panic a little. So much had been happening that I hadn't really thought ahead to this glorious week off. I liked this week better than the Christmas break, since during that time I was usually marking essays. It was more fun to loll about when everyone else was panicking over exams.

I did have to reread Louise Erdrich's book, but I'd taught it before, and my notes were pretty thorough, so I didn't foresee too much prep work for the lectures. Having had to clean my office last week had been a blessing in disguise; it was ready for next term already.

If I went out Christmas shopping tomorrow, I could wrap and send my parents their present in time for the twenty-fifth. They were the hardest to shop for, since I usually like to buy everyone books, but my mother screams over the price of postage, so my choices for her were predicated on their poundage. She wouldn't be needing another silk scarf. Maybe I'd find her some nice moccasins. I'd seen some hokey golf club covers for my father, with all the Sesame Street Muppet heads on them. I doubted if he'd use them, but they would make him laugh.

I would hit a bookstore for Fiona, Denise and Leo, and maybe get some Body Shop soaps for Grace. I felt a bit out of my element buying books for a full professor.

Steve would definitely be interesting to shop for. I wrote his name down and then had to shake myself out of a reverie to get back to my to-do list. One of the important chores would be to work on my Christmas letter this evening, and get it mailed off by the end of the week. Some of the people on my list only heard from me once a year. I wasn't sure how much of this autumn I wanted to commit to paper. I usually flipped through my wall calendar to remember what I'd done for the past twelve months. I hadn't kept a journal since undergraduate days. It seemed slightly hypocritical to demand regular journal-keeping from my freshmen when I myself was so lax about recording things for posterity, but hey, I was the boss.

Damn journals anyway. Thank goodness Steve had been big enough to forgive me my stupidity about Gwen's journal. He was right; there probably hadn't been anything of interest to the police in there, and I'd already told him about the therapist business.

Someone had thought it important, though—important enough to ransack my office. Unless they really had been after the exams and had just taken it for some unknown reason. Like a macabre souvenir.

The thought of some hooligan reading Gwen's diary made

me shudder. She'd been through enough without her inner-most thoughts being ravaged as well. I shook myself, literally as well as mentally. Talk about pathetic fallacy; here I was despairing over the violation of words, as if what had actually been done to Gwen was in some way less than the worst possible. I guess my mind still couldn't absorb what had happened as real. Maybe it was my sheltered background or the daily life on a university campus, but I didn't really have any identifying feelings for connecting to Gwen's annihilation. Words were my succor; they might well be my prison too.

Nothing like self-flagellation to work up an appetite. I made myself a pita stuffed with things Steve had overlooked or discarded as less than edible and went back to my list.

I folded the page lengthways, to begin again. There were a few things I had been wanting to ask Steve, but somehow didn't get around to in his presence. Even thinking that started the heat of a blush up my neck.

Was it the exam or the journal? I wrote at the top of the list, and then chewed a bit on the end of the pencil, stopping only when the tired eraser hit the roof of my mouth by accident. Yuck.

Did you find Jane the therapist?

What did she tell you? I figured I'd give it a try, although I had some preconceptions about therapist disclosures that made me think I wouldn't get much out of Steve, if indeed he'd got anything out of the therapist.

Are you going to tell Jane that the journal's missing?

I stared at the silk-screen print on the wall across from me. A friend of mine had done it when he was taking a Fine Arts degree, and titled it *Autumn Beach*. Sometimes I could almost see it, but tonight it was just some streaks of pleasant color with a few rock-shaped circles to one side.

What if whoever took the journal could find Jane too? She should be warned, even if whoever had the journal wasn't the sadist who had murdered Gwen.

The little editor on my shoulder tsked at me as I went rummaging for my Yellow Pages, but I wasn't in the mood to agree that this was precisely the sort of thing Steve would frown at. I shook off the feeling. It wasn't as if I was actually thinking of tracking Jane the therapist down myself. I was just going to find out how easy it might be to do so.

I flipped through to Physicians and Surgeons. Under Psychiatrists there was two-thirds of a column, none of them a Dr. Jane Anybody. I tried Psychologists, but they weren't listed. Nothing under Therapy either. I started flipping randomly, trying to think of another grouping. Under Marriage Counseling, I found two pages of listings, along with little advertisements. I liked the one that read *Relationship Therapy: Before, During & After Marriage*. I scanned all the names, finding only two Janes but several ads that read So and So and Associates, which didn't bode well. I made a note of the two Janes.

I was on a roll of sorts so I tried Counseling and again struck a windfall. Some of the marriage counselors were listed here again, as well as a few of the more marginal churches. There were several associations and networks listed too, making me think that perhaps Jane might be too layered in a bureaucracy to be discovered by some lunatic. Or me, for that matter.

One of the Janes was listed in both places, but her address placed her somewhere on the north side of town. I had a vague recollection of Gwen mentioning not having a car after years of relying on one, so it occurred to me she'd be looking closer to campus for an appointment.

I thumped the Yellow Pages closed and hit my head in the standard "I could have had a V-8" pose. Of course she'd look closer to campus. She'd be looking on the campus itself. I reached for last year's Campus Directory (I keep the current one in the office). Under Student Services I found the Campus Helpline.

On impulse, I picked up the phone and dialed the number. Several rings went by before someone answered. It didn't surprise me. The week before exams was bound to be a busy one for these guys.

"Campus Help," answered a friendly male voice.

I hadn't planned this call and wasn't really sure what I wanted to say. I was so busy thinking, my tongue took over for me, and I listened to myself say, "Is Jane there?"

"I'm afraid Jane's not in for a couple of days." The voice took on a saddened, friendly tone. "Can someone else help?"

"Uh, no thanks. I'll call back later. Oh, what are your hours?"

"The phone line is twenty-four hours. If you want to come in and see a counselor, they make bookings from eight-thirty till four-thirty, and till eight p.m. on Thursdays. I can make a booking for you now. Have you seen Jane before?"

"No, but I'd really like to talk to her."

"Could you make it in on Monday at ten-thirty?"

What the heck was I doing?

"Sure."

"And your name?"

"My name?"

"A first name will be fine. Everything here is confidential, don't worry."

"Randy."

"Okay, Randy. Monday at ten-thirty. Until then, stay loose, you hear?"

I put down the phone. Contrary to Steve's wishes, I was sleuthing on his territory. I had no idea if this Jane was Gwen's Jane, but I had a ten-thirty appointment with her on Monday.

Well, there was something else to put on my to-do list.

S TEVE CALLED THE NEXT MORNING TO SET A TIME for a late dinner, but he sounded rushed so I didn't mention his case. I'd bring up the list of questions later in the evening. I was dawdling about, half-heartedly getting ready to catch the bus for downtown shopping when the phone rang again.

It was Leo, wondering what I was up to. I admitted my Christmas shopping plans.

"Am I on your shopping list, or can I tag along?"

I laughed.

"Very clever ploy, Leo. Were you one of those kids who shook all the presents under the tree?"

"Of course not. I didn't need to. I used to find them hidden away before they were wrapped."

We agreed to meet up at Audrey's, one of my very favorite bookstores in town, at twelve-thirty and find a spot of lunch together. I figured that, if I timed things right, I could be down there early enough to pick up Leo's present and have it bagged before he made it downtown.

It was such a nice, bright day that I decided against waiting for a bus, and headed for the High Level Bridge. I have a distinct fear of bridges, and you'd think a structure a half-mile long would send me catatonic. Paradoxically, the High Level was the only one I wasn't too bad on. The High Level spanned the river valley from high bank to bank, whereas all the other bridges demanded that cars drive down one steep bank and up the other. It was huge and black, with railroad tracks on the upper level, and two lanes of traffic heading south underneath. The pedestrian/bike lane was on the outside of the driving level, overhanging the river. I refused to bike across it, feeling that the winds might knock me over the metal balustrade, but if I kept my eyes on the tips of my boots I could walk across in about fifteen minutes.

The slight sweat brought about by fear made me warmer still. I walked into Audrey's about half an hour after leaving my apartment. So much for getting the drop on Leo, though. He was already at there and gave me a huge hug as if we'd just met up by accident after seventeen years.

"*Cara mia,*" he gushed, and kissed me on both cheeks. I wonder if Shelley or Byron had ever really been this flamboyant.

"Am I late?" I asked. "Can we look around for a bit here before lunch?"

"But of course! I have a few things I want to pick up too. How about we meet in cookbooks in half an hour?"

"Why cookbooks?"

"To get an idea of what we want for lunch."

I smiled and sidled away from him through the crunch in the aisles. No matter what time of year, Audrey's always seemed to be packed. Maybe it is because it's on Jasper Avenue, the main drag of downtown, or maybe the big window displays that wrap around the corner just lure people in, but I couldn't recall ever being there without having to mutter "Excuse me" more than once while meandering through the aisles. Nice tall stacks make it possible to browse for hours, and no one comes up behind you with a frown. There is an air of sanctity for the printed page, the same feeling you'd get in some medieval ecclesiastical library. The sun coming through the windows and dappling the dark wood helps the image. Every so often along the stacks a Lucite notice board holding a recent review or announcement of a local reading would grab my attention. I stuck to the main floor, and edged around the banistered stairwell to get to the fiction. The children's section downstairs was wonderful, but I had grown-ups to buy for.

The new Ondaatje would suit Greg. I picked up a paperback copy of Paul Quarrington's *Whale Music* for Fiona, thinking I'd wrap it with a Pavarotti tape as a joke. Her and her tenors. Give me a baritone any day. I'd seen Carolyn Heilbrun's *Hamlet's Mother* on Denise's desk the other day, and it had given me the idea of getting her a couple of Amanda Cross mysteries, Heilbrun's other, distaff literary offerings. I picked *The Players Come Again* and *The James Joyce Murder*. While I was in the mysteries section, the title *Literary Murder* jumped out at me. I picked up the book. It was by an Israeli named Batya Gur, and apparently about a sensitive policeman solving a murder at a university. How could I resist?

There was no point in searching for something for Leo, with him leering over shelves at me. I checked my watch and dutifully headed for the cookbook section. Leo was already there with a Vietnamese cookbook in his hands.

"Are you feeling like noodles? There's a wonderful place just a block from here."

"Lead on, Macduff. Just let me pay for these first."

We chatted as I waited to get near the till. Leo was thinking of taking a week off in Puerto Vallarta during exams.

"A fellow I know says there's a charter heading down that needs a few more people. I have to get some reading done before I tackle the next chapter of the thesis. Why not read on the beach?"

"It all depends on how much you can absorb mentally while absorbing margaritas and cervezas." I sounded like my grandmother, who had, I was certain, personally coined the phrase "No play before work." There's nothing like someone else's talk of escape to make me curmudgeonly.

"Well, there is that." Leo looked as pensive as Leo could, a pathetic attempt on his part. "And, one has to wonder how one's supervisor will feel when one turns up looking like a bronzed god among the pasty-faced intellectuals."

"What with melanoma scares, pasty-faced is high fashion now," I reminded him.

"Right, just like skinny is out for gay men. Now we've all got to have washboard abs and rippling pectorals. Nothing like a disease or two to set the fashion wheels making U-turns."

I constantly marvel at Leo's ability to hold nothing sacred. Just then my turn came at the counter, and I burrowed for my MasterCard, thankful that I now didn't have to come up with a rejoinder.

The cashier slid a slip toward me and I blithely signed without checking the total. It comes, I swear, from being an English major as an undergrad. After being sent to the bookstore with mile-long required text lists, I have no qualms about dropping sixty or seventy bucks at a time in bookstores. On the other hand, I will agonize over cheap cuts of meat and small trays of chicken breasts, buy generic toilet paper and keep all business-sized envelopes for making lists on the backs. Go figure.

Leo bustled me out of the warm and cozy store and onto Jasper Avenue, heading east.

I was glad Leo knew where he was going, because I'd have missed it. Behind an unassuming glass door was a long narrow restaurant with the trademark look the best oriental restaurants have: they all look as if the owners had asked someone's Aunt Vera to replicate the look of her fabulous fifties kitchen, only with thirty-five chrome tables instead of one. The menus had clear plastic covers over mimeographed sheets (well, it was probably laser printer made to resemble mimeograph), and the waitress smiled and nodded as we covered the extra two chairs in various layers of outerwear.

Leo ordered a pot of tea and two big bowls of vermicelli

noodles, assuring me I'd love it. The waitress smiled and nodded and took off for the nether regions of the restaurant.

"So," said Leo, as he poured the tea that arrived with another waiter. "I want to hear your thoughts on the vigil, and Denise's reporter, and your policeman. In any order which you might care to proceed." He sipped his tea, and offered up one of his infuriating smug grins.

"What don't you know?" It was impossible to keep anything from Leo, but there was no need to go over stale ground. Besides, I wouldn't mind knowing about "Denise's reporter" too.

"Well, Denise was in the department yesterday, moaning about the destruction of the spirituality of the convening moment . . ."

"She was not."

"Oh all right. She was bitching about getting wet in subarctic weather. But she did say something about you disappearing with the boy in blue."

I might have known that Leo would get hold of that tidbit of information. Luckily our lunch arrived just then, and Leo proceeded to explain how to pour the small bowl of fish sauce over the noodles and salad greens and spring rolls piled into the medium-sized serving bowl set in front of me. It was fabulous, and for a few minutes neither of us spoke. Finally, pouring us each another small cup of tea, I got back to the topic at hand.

"So what about the reporter?"

"Oh. Well, Denise was giving us a blow by blow . . ."

"Us?"

"Me, Greg, some MAs I don't really know: the girl with the frizzy boot-black hair and the guy with the lace-up boots, and Julian, who had been at the ceremony. I think Arno was in the background mooching a cup of coffee, but I don't recall him having anything to add. I take it he wasn't there on the evening?"

"No, he wasn't. And that begs the question of where you were. Why weren't you out freezing along with us, bucky?"

"Did you really expect me to be shivering in the frigid evening air, Miranda darling?" Leo looked down his not inconsiderable nose, and sniffed. "I'm perfectly willing to fold the odd leaflet, but I draw the line at shivering in the cold. As it happens, I was at the club, and I think it was Emma Goldman who suggested that 'if I can't dance, I don't want to be part of the revolution,' wasn't it?"

"That is not at all what she meant, you nitwit."

"May I continue?"

I nodded.

"So as Denise was telling us about these masked offenders spraying you all with water and chanting obscenities, in walks this guy from the *Edmonton Journal*. Our Lady of Perpetual Vigils stops in mid-sentence and, I do not tell a lie, begins to flirt with him."

"Denise? Our Denise, flirting?"

"Well, it sure looked like it from where I was. She looked at him through her eyebrows, you know the way Lauren Bacall used on killers, and then she slid off the edge of the table and went off to lunch with him."

I took a gulp of tea and proceeded to burn my tongue. I couldn't imagine what Denise might see in Mark Paulson, but then who could tell which pheromones might call out to whom? I'd often wondered what sort of a guy might catch Denise's fancy—she whom I figured could just crook a finger at almost anyone. If Leo was right, Denise was playing a dangerous game. I remembered what McNeely had said to me about consorting with the police. Just imagine what he'd say about Denise and the fourth estate.

"Okay, so that takes care of La Wolff." Leo grinned. "What about you and the thin blue line?"

I proceeded to tell Leo a slightly more risqué version than I'd tell my mother, but highly censored from what I'd write in a diary. I could trust Leo not to blab my private life if he thought he was getting an exclusive. He's very proprietorial about his gossip, figuring his right to know is obvious and everyone else's prurient.

"This is wonderful, and just in time for expensive presents! What are you getting him?"

I showed him the book, and he questioned me about Steve's off-duty taste in clothes. We decided to take a look through Holt Renfrew for ties on our way to the Edmonton Centre mall. The noodle dish had been extremely filling, but Leo was already talking afternoon tea at the restaurant in Holt's. I looked at my ensemble and decided I could look inconspicuous enough among the beautiful people to risk it. A leather bomber jacket is so ambiguous, and for once my hat, mitts and scarf all matched.

Leo passed on the power ties and began flipping through some novelty ties with Tin Tin and Asterix the Gaul on them. That's what happens when the head office of your retail chain is in Montreal. I heard him giggle and turned from my examination of silk boxer shorts.

He was holding out a navy silk tie with what looked like a running pattern of little circles. I came closer and realized they were tiny sets of scarlet handcuffs dotted across the blue.

"It's perfect," Leo gushed.

"Are you sure? What if it's supposed to be a signal that you're into bondage or something?"

"Trust me, those signals are a wee bit more obvious that this. With this and the book and a tape of the first record you listened to together, you're set for a perfect evening beneath the winking lights of the tree."

I bought it and agreed to have it gift-boxed. I had over half my list filled, and I paid for the tea to thank Leo for his help. We moved onto Sam the Record Man for Fiona's tape and a copy of Joni Mitchell's *Blue* (who am I to argue with Leo when it comes to romance?), the Den for Men for my dad's golf warmers, and I snapped up a snazzy cotton sweater shot with metallic thread that Mom could couple with her chiffon evening trousers for a simple evening ensemble on their next cruise.

Leo took his leave around four to meet some friends at the Bistro Praha. We made plans to see each other at Grace's Christmas party and have a dinner together if he didn't jet off to the Mexican Riviera.

"It's still nebulous, but I'm one level of frostbite away from signing onto the charter."

"If you do go, I hope the mariachi band plays 'Guadalajara' under your window all night, every night."

"You're so supportive, *cherie.*"

After another European kiss, he was off in a flurry of scarves and coattails. I watched him cross the street then turned back into the mall to head to the SmithBooks on the main level. I wanted to check if there was a published filmscript of Ken Russell's *Gothic*, the movie he'd made about Shelley and Mary and Polidori all daring each other to write horror novels. That, or the actual video, would be a coup for Leo.

They didn't have anything of the sort, but the salesclerk suggested I try one of the record stores in the mall. I wandered about from floor to floor, watching the people move about like ants up and down the escalators. I decided to give up when the old Christmas angst started wafting around me. A little carolling might be nice, but the thousand strings doing *Jingle Bells* can drive me into a slump like nobody's business. I headed for the exit doors that would bring me out closest to my bus stop.

Luck was with me and a bus was waiting. I pushed on, holding my shopping in front of me. After dropping coins in the box, I lumbered toward the back door, looking for a double seat that could hold both me and my bags. The bus started rolling as I found a seat, and I just avoided crushing an older woman by turning as I fell onto the bench.

It took me twenty minutes to get home. I dropped the bags on the chair by the door, shucked off my boots and started pulling off my scarf as I made my way to the blinking red light of my answering machine. I paused to count the blinks before pushing the pulsing red button. Four calls.

The first was from Denise, with a terse message to call her. The second and third were both from Steve, to tell me that he loved me and that he'd be picking me up around seven. The fourth voice I didn't recognize.

"Keep your nose clean and stick with dead writers, Professor Craig, unless you want to have something in common with them."

I stood frozen in my little apartment, staring at the machine as the red light began to pulse once more. Then, in a frenzy, I ran to the windows and pulled closed all the blinds.

STEVE ARRIVED ABOUT WHEN HE'D SAID HE WOULD, and found me hunched up in the corner of my sofa trying to read. The fact that I'd spent the last hour on the same page hadn't registered. I had been straining at every sound in the hallway and startling at every set of headlights shining through the kitchen blind.

I played him the tape, which he removed from my machine wordlessly. Suddenly I found myself unable to stop talking. I blathered on about shopping, and Leo's gossip and Denise's call, which I still hadn't returned, and my appointment with the possible Jane.

Steve called in a report of the tape message, and after a short delay the word came back to him that the call had come from a pay phone on campus. He shrugged, replaced the receiver, then turned to me.

"Get your coat on."

"Where are we going?"

"Once I've dropped this off at the station, we have reservations for Jack's Grill."

I was going to demur and admit I had no stomach for supper, but the thought of remaining home alone, coupled with the offer to eat at one of the best restaurants in town, was too much to deal with. Steve helped me on with my coat, which lay abandoned on a chair by the door, and after making sure the door was securely locked, we headed for his car.

I went into the station with Steve. He typed up the gist of what I'd told him, and I signed. After chatting with a couple of people whom I presumed were detectives since they were wearing jeans and sweaters, we drove off to a little strip mall in the southwestern corner of the city.

Jack's Grill is one of those places where you never have to worry about whether or not you'll like what you order. It's all fabulous. For such an out of the way place, the reservation list is months long. I wondered how Steve had managed to score us a sitting.

The tablecloths are paper, and there's a glass of crayons on the table for doodling while you wait for your meal. I chose a green crayon and did my usual doodle, lots of grass with a couple of dandelions sprouting. I looked over at Steve, who had taken a red crayon and was embellishing a huge Valentine with S and R in the middle. How could I not love this guy?

"I'm going with you to see Jane tomorrow, " Steve said over a very nice glass of wine.

"I was meaning to ask if you'd talked with her already," I said after I'd swallowed the last crab-stuffed mushroom.

"I asked, and no one had followed up on it, although I'd put it in my initial report. What made you think of it, especially after I thought we'd agreed you wouldn't be featuring any more than necessary in this investigation?"

Steve was smiling, but I felt reprimanded.

"Well, it's not as if I'm completely out of it after tonight, am I? I'm not getting death threats for my fashion sense, after all." It wasn't until I'd actually verbalized the term that the reality hit me. I'd received a death threat. I took a quick swallow of wine to stop the sudden shakes.

"Actually, tonight's business is keeping me from really yelling at you. Randy, I know you're going through some awful times right now, and if I could change it I would, but you've got to stay clear of this stuff. If not for your own safety, think of my job. I'm not supposed to bandy around what I do as pillow talk."

"Pillow talk?" I spluttered.

"That's what it will be seen as if it gets out, and it will."

"How do you know?"

"Because the death threat is the fourth on your tape. My supervisors will be listening to me swear undying affection for you. Most of them have been detectives long enough to make the connection."

"Oh." That hadn't occurred to me. This could be dicey for Steve.

"Okay, so you'll come along to the interview with Jane." I was into placatory mode, since I certainly didn't want to ruin the meal I saw the waiter bringing our way. "If she's the right Jane, anyway," I continued, after the waiter had advised us on the heat of our plates, ground pepper at us, and wished us an enjoyable feast, "I'm just riding a hunch, after all."

Steve dug into his entree with gusto. I suppose death threats are nothing to a man in uniform.

"What made you go looking for her in the first place?"

"I thought she should know about the journal going missing. If she is the right Jane, that makes her pretty easy to find. I mean, even I found her, and if the murderer took the journal, he could find her too."

"Don't sell yourself short. You made some pretty astute leaps of logic. In fact, unless the perpetrator is campus savvy, I think Jane might stay safely incommunicado."

"Does that mean you think it was Gwen's husband who did it? Stole the journal, I mean?"

"I'm not going to continue this discussion. How's your chicken?"

I pretended to sulk, but allowed myself to be guided to other topics pretty easily. Murder wasn't something I really wanted to dwell on. Not here, not with this wonderful man.

Not with someone out there hating me.

S TEVE HADN'T BEEN ABLE TO STAY THE NIGHT, and my sleep had been restless even with the kitchen chair shoved under the doorknob of the apartment door. I woke grumbling, with my hair squashed onto my face leaving red fossil traces on my cheek. I was still feeling hard done by, but very clean, after a hot shower.

Steve arrived in time for a coffee before we headed off to our meeting with the possible Jane.

Student Help was located in the basement of Athabasca Hall, one of the oldest buildings at the university. It was an older, burgundy brick building, structured like a U created by a north and south wing jutting outward on either end of the building. The result was a nice small quad in front of the main entrance. One entered Student Help through a door at the end of the south wing.

Steve had dressed in detective clothes, which meant he looked like a cop on holiday. When we approached the woman at the reception desk, he let me do the talking.

"My name is Randy. I've got an appointment to see Jane at ten-thirty."

She smiled and checked the register. "That's right. Jane will be with you shortly. She's just finishing with someone else. Would you like to have a seat?" She then looked quizzically at Steve.

"I'm with Randy," Steve said curtly.

We sat on institution chairs placed around the perimeter of the area. Several *People* magazines and a couple of *New Trails* littered the top of the central round coffee table. Steve picked up one of the alumni magazines. I looked around, trying to imagine what the receptionist was making of the two of us. Maybe she thought I was pregnant and in distress, and Steve was the father. Or maybe he was my older brother, and I was having some sort of repressed memory of our father abusing me. Or maybe she figured I was in trouble with the law, and Steve was my minder. Perhaps she had no theories whatso-ever, though that to me seemed the most fantastical possibility. I never believe people when they say they have no imagination.

Before I could decide what she might or might not be thinking, she answered a softly beeping phone, and motioned us to go with her. She led us down a small hallway and opened a plain door.

"Jane? This is Randy and friend to see you." She motioned gracefully for us to enter and closed the door quietly behind us.

Jane's office was pleasant and non-threatening. There was a desk in the corner under the one window and another of those circular coffee tables sat in front of two chairs and a small sofa in the other corner. I took in a couple of bookcases, some plants, and an inordinate number of Kleenex boxes placed practically everywhere. Tool of choice for therapists, I guessed.

Steve and I sat on the sofa. Jane took one of the matching chairs.

She was an interesting-looking woman, not beautiful but not plain. Her eyebrows were not quite as thick as Brooke Shields' but they managed to make a statement. Her eyes were large and discreetly made up. She wore her black hair in a Louise Brooks chop, but it suited her. She smiled with her entire face, which is not something you see every day.

"Which one of you is Randy?"

"That's me. This is Steve Browning, who asked to come with me today. I'm afraid we might be wasting your time, but we felt it was important to see you."

"Go on."

"I'm a sessional lecturer in the English department here, and Steve is a police officer. We're, well, I mean, he is investigating the murder of Gwen Devlin. The reason we're here seeing you is that Gwen wrote of her therapist named Jane in a journal she was keeping for my class, and we thought it might be you to whom she was referring.

"I'm not sure what I'd be allowed to tell you," Jane said.

Steve broke in. "Then you are the Jane that Gwen referred to?"

Jane smiled. "I suppose I can tell you that much. Yes, I am. She contacted me shortly after term began, and we met regularly. I was very saddened to read of her death."

It was my turn to break in on Steve. "The reason we wanted to come see you is that the journal you're mentioned in was taken from my office last week, and we thought you should be aware of that."

Jane looked puzzled but not frightened. I guess knowing other people's nightmares keeps you from jumping into your own.

Steve took over again. "I would appreciate it if you could tell me the gist of what you and Ms Devlin spoke of in her sessions. If you need to consult with your superiors for approval, I'll understand, but this is a police investigation, and we are pursuing several leads. If she mentioned that she was afraid of someone, or had dealings with someone unsavory, or hurt someone's feelings, it might shine a light on why she was murdered."

Jane now looked a little unhappy.

"If you want me to, I'll wait outside," I offered, praying they wouldn't take me up on it.

Steve nodded to me. "If you wouldn't mind, I think that would be best, Randy." Damn him anyway. I left and sat flipping through magazines, wondering what the kindly receptionist made of my exclusion. She asked if I'd like a cup of coffee. Perhaps she really didn't have any imagination.

Steve came out in another twenty minutes. I got up and we stepped out into the bright December morning. I had to hurry to keep up with Steve. We were heading for the back entrance to the Student Union Building.

As Steve held the door open for me, I stopped.

"Well?"

He grinned. "It may take more than a large café latte and cherry Bismarck to get it out of me, and it may not."

"You're on." I laughed.

IT TOOK TWO CHERRY BISMARCKS AND A LONG JOHN to get Steve to tell me that Jane Campbell had been less than forthcoming. Instead of expounding on her meetings with Gwen, she had agreed to answer questions Steve posed her.

"The trouble was knowing what questions to ask," he mumbled through icing sugar-coated lips. "I asked about her marriage, and whether she was afraid of her husband, and her adjustment to living in residence and whether anyone there had harassed her, and her classes, but what I'd really like to know is what took her to see a therapist in the first place, and that was strictly off limits."

"Is there anyway you can subpoena her files on Gwen?"

"It's not an issue anyone likes to force without obvious cause. We've had reports back from the staff in Fort McMurray who interviewed Gwen's friends and neighbors there, but getting access to medical files is tricky. You can't get anything without probable cause, and if you have enough evidence to get into the restricted files, you usually don't need to see what is there. Chicken and egg."

"Guilt might have been her reason for therapy."

"Guilt?"

"For leaving her children. Or if not guilt, then trying to deal with the lack of it. No matter how you play it, it's not the accepted thing for a mother to leave her children. Maybe Gwen was finding that difficult."

Steve nodded as he bit into the long john. Watching all that sugar consumption was making me fairly weak. I broke off a bit of my low-fat cranberry muffin.

"Did you get a sense of what kind of mother she was from the McMurray reports?" I asked.

"They talked to the kids' day care teachers and the next-door neighbors. All of them seemed surprised by her abandoning them. Seems she was a devoted mother."

"See? Even you think she abandoned them. Maybe someone's sitting in judgment on her for leaving. I wonder who's taking care of them while her husband's down here." I found myself scanning the tables for Rod Devlin's face. "He is still down here?"

"As far as we know. He was asked to keep us posted of his movements. The last address posted is a hotel down in Old Strathcona. He comes in every couple of days to see what's happening. He seems pretty lost. As for the kids, I think they're with his mom up there." Steve was finished his doughnuts, but still looking interested in the display. There must be a doughnut gene in cops, there really must be. I broke off the lower part of my muffin and slid it across the table to him. He smiled and began happily to eat again. Between bites, he continued filling me in on the Fort McMurray aspects of Gwen's life. Some of it I recognized from the journal, but not all. I wonder if there is a quantifiable number of sides to any given story. Here was a whole new view of Gwen's world.

"Gwen and Rod were high school sweethearts and from the sounds of it the beautiful couple of grade twelve. She was the editor of the yearbook and the captain of the girls' basketball team. He was, of course, on the football team. They connected through some peer tutorial system and started going together in the middle of grade ten. They got married a year after grade twelve."

I was shaking my head in disbelief.

"This sounds like a Ronald Reagan movie. Let me guess, she tutored him through poetry so he could play in the big game?"

Steve laughed.

"Actually, Spielberg, he tutored her through chemistry, physics and calculus. Seems Rod Devlin is really left-brained and Gwen was completely right-brained. She won all the essay contests, and he kept her from inadvertently blowing up the chem lab." Steve's face took on a more serious look. "You know, I have to give the guy credit. He didn't want to lose her but he has been taking care of the kids and kept things going up there all this term. Even though he was probably figuring she'd fall on her face and come back home to him, he was graceful enough to let her try. It couldn't have been easy on him."

I nodded sadly. Taking care of kids looked to me like the one of those labors that the gods tested folks with. Even Hercules wouldn't touch that one on his own. I had lots of respect for single parents, but I found myself not being able to pity Rod Devlin. Even though I had initially felt warmth toward him, he was tarred by being discarded by someone I had really liked, and there was something else, besides. Since he was one of the few people, other than students, who had been to the House this term since all the hoopla had begun, I found that I was subconsciously associating him with the night my office had been raided.

"Do you think he's the one who stole the journal?"

"It's a possibility." Steve was noncommittal.

"What about Mark Paulson, though?"

"You really don't much care for that reporter, do you, Randy?"

"But if he overheard us at the Diner, then he knew where it was."

"As did sixty of your students, some of your colleagues, not to mention the possibility that someone looking for your exam to sell or use just happened upon it. You can't just manufacture a case to suit yourself, you have to build it with blocks of provable evidence. And speaking of the case, I shouldn't be."

"Do you really think you'll get any flak from my answering machine tape?"

"Too soon to tell. I have to report in to my boss tomorrow morning to brief him on the case, so I expect I may hear something then."

Steve shuffled a bit in his chair, and squared his shoulders. His body language said as much as his next words.

"So, other than all this, how are things with you? Have you got your shopping done?"

I am not completely adverse to subtlety. I changed the topic with a rueful smirk.

"I have to find something drop-dead"—I winced—"I mean suitably glamorous for Grace's party Friday night, but aside from that I'm pretty well on target."

"Does one go glamorous to a feminist's party? I would have thought it was somehow inappropriate."

"Feminism attempts to foster sincerity, honesty and equality. There is nothing in any handbook anywhere that says beauty and joy are incompatible. We want to be admired thoroughly, not objectified, that's all."

"Sorry, just a poor attempt at a joke. Actually, Grace struck me as a very nice person."

"She is really lovely, and her parties are wonderful. Would you like to come with me on Friday? You won't be the only non-English type there. You might have fun."

"And you wouldn't mind being seen to consort with a member of a bastion of male hierarchy?"

"Well, unless you intend to bring along some phallic-looking night stick, I don't suppose many of them would guess your real identity."

"In that case, you're on. Do we bring wine to this thing?"

"Yep, and I'm supposed to make something, so if you get the wine I'll rustle up a Mexican layered dip and we'll be set."

"When should I pick you up?"

We agreed to set off for the party about seven-thirty, and then Steve told me he had to dash. He offered me a ride back to my place, but I decided to check in at the department to see if any students had come groveling for exemptions to the exam. I waved as he headed back toward the Stadium Carpark, and then aimed my way eastward back to the libraries, HUB and the Humanities Building. HUB was a zoo. I grabbed a Java Jive and an almond cookie to take with me to the department, and beat my way through the mass of undergraduate humanity. I didn't see a soul I knew, which brought back my feelings of paranoia I'd submerged during the morning. Somewhere out there was someone who hated me enough to voice it. Maybe I knew him; maybe I'd never laid eyes on him. Whoever it was had the edge on me, and that was not the way I liked it.

The crowds thinned out the further north you went in HUB, and there were very few people camped on the chairs in the walkway to the Humanities Building. I spotted Denise in the grad lounge as I came through the stairwell door on the third floor. She had her back to me, reading something she'd pulled from on top of the mail slots.

"Boo," I said, unimaginatively.

Denise jumped and turned in one movement. She looked wary—no, more than wary, guilty—before she recognized me and relaxed.

"Randy! I didn't expect to see you in this week."

"You looked as though you were expecting a lot worse than me, that's for sure. What's up?"

Denise glanced around, as if the walls would suddenly glow neon where she suspected listening devices had been secreted. I decided that I was in no mood for deep conversation anyhow, so I tried a lighter gambit.

"Leo tells me you have a boyfriend."

This obviously wasn't the icebreaker I'd thought it might be. Denise's defenses seemed to get even more rigid.

"What's he been spreading about?"

"Not much, really." I back-pedalled quickly. "You know Leo. He just saw you heading off for coffee with that reporter..."

"Shhh." Denise's actions were a parody of spy thrillers. She craned her neck about madly and leaned toward me, conspiratorially.

"Let's go for coffee. We can talk there."

I looked down at the sweating styrofoam cup of Java Jive still in my hand, but innate nosiness won out.

"Sure," I said.

D ENISE AND I FOUND A TABLE IN THE UKRAINIAN restaurant at the south end of HUB mall. Neither of us were what I would call perogy fanatics, but it was one of the only places you could actually sit down to eat within the restaurant itself, so we chose muffins and coffee (the woman looked askance at my Java Jive container and bullied me into buying a carton of skim milk) and found a table in the back corner.

Only a couple of other tables were occupied, but Denise kept her tones low anyway.

"I'm sorry to drag you into this, but I've got to talk to someone, and I don't know who else to trust."

This was sounding like more secret than I wanted to know, but Denise looked ready to explode, so I just nodded my encouragement.

"I don't know what I'll do if McNeely finds out, and knowing him, he probably will."

"Finds out what? That you're dating a reporter?"

"I know I'm sounding paranoid, but after what he said to you, I have a feeling he'll see me as a traitor to the university."

"Well, how's he going to find out, and what's to find out? It's not as if you're feeding the guy information, after all."

Denise was silent.

"You're not feeding him information, are you?" I tried

again, beginning to detect the chasm opening up in front of our collective feet.

Denise blushed and reached down beside her chair into her briefcase. She pulled out today's paper which she'd folded the way people on commuter trains do. I realized with a start that I hadn't seen the morning's paper. I'd been too caught up in last night's phone message and this morning's meeting with the psychologist. Denise handed me the paper and I could see it wasn't the crossword she had folded upwards. It was Mark Paulson's by-line, and the headline read "Sexist Pranks Aimed at U of A Feminists."

"Shit," I breathed.

I scanned the article as if I could vacuum up all the damage with my eyes. He had linked the disruption of the vigil with the department graffiti. He went on to question the university's stance on harassment and to ponder the trail leading from the letters preceding Gwen's murder through to the December 6th fiasco. It was with no great pleasure that I noted he'd spelled my name correctly.

After I'd read it through a second time, I looked up to find Denise reading it upside down, shaking her head woefully.

"You know McNeely's going to have a bird," I said.

"It's not as if we signed some official Secrets Act or anything." Denise looked at me with three parts fear mixed with one dash of defiance.

I looked at her.

"It just came out." Her face crumpled a bit. "We have been seeing each other, and I felt as though I was talking with a friend, not being interviewed by a reporter."

I understood the feeling. Sometimes I forgot that Steve might just as well be taking down a statement.

"Didn't he tell you he was going to use it?" I asked.

"He told me he was going to look into it and question some other sources about it, so it wouldn't be traced right back to me. And I think he tried. We really are more than just reporter and source, I think. But McNeely's going to know, isn't he?"

"I know it really isn't any of my business, but aren't you forgetting that it was Paulson who printed Gwen's letter in the first place?"

"So?" Denise's tone told me that it hadn't escaped her.

"So, it occurs to me that he might just share a little culpability here."

"Randy, Mark didn't kill Gwen. In fact, he has been the only one actually doing his appointed job in this whole thing. He's supposed to inform the public of what's going on. The university is supposed to act on complaints, which they didn't do. Students are supposed to spend their evenings studying, not harassing other people. The police are supposed to find the bad guys."

Denise looked as though she was about to crack, so I refrained from an argument on prurience versus the public's right to information. If I kept this up, I would be the next ambassador to the UN.

I spent the better part of an hour comforting Denise. By the time we were through, I had her halfway believing that McNeely wasn't adept enough to trace the leak to her. We agreed to meet up at Grace's party (which Paulson would not be going to), and I headed once again back to the department.

I felt just as burdened as before, since I'd been unable to talk to her about any of my troubles. It didn't take a rocket scientist to see she was smitten with someone who was after a Michener award more than a lifemate; and there was no way I was going to jeopardize Steve's case any more than I already had. I just couldn't trust Denise to keep anything I might say to herself.

I went past the Reading Room to Mail Room B, hoping that something nice had arrived for me in the afternoon mail. A couple of friends use my university address for personal mail, so I was perpetually hoping for more than departmental flyers.

The only thing in my box was a pink message slip asking me to report as soon as possible to the chairman's office.

For once I'd been right. McNeely hadn't traced the news story back to Denise. He had me fingered for the job.

NOW THERE ARE GOING TO BE SOME PEOPLE who will figure I should have kept completely silent as the chairman's enraged rhetoric spewed over me. Others will probably call me on not ratting on Denise as soon as possible. In order to disappoint the maximum number of people, I opted for the middle ground.

Once McNeely finished, I began haltingly to admit I'd seen the newspaper article, and that while I had talked to the reporter in question at the vigil (McNeely looked a bit purple at this admission), I quickly underlined the fact that I hadn't been discussing the case at all, and that Paulson had gone off to talk to others.

McNeely did his best to mop up his vitriol, but I could tell he wasn't absolutely convinced I was being honest with him. I tried to assure him that I, of all people, wouldn't talk to reporters since I was dating one of the police officers handling the case, and it wouldn't be proper to speak of anything that might become part of a police inquiry.

I wasn't sure whether this piece of information calmed McNeely down the way I'd thought it might. Instead of Deep Throat, he'd found a police snitch. He tried to intimate that allowing the police to bumble through without overtly aiding them would be in everyone's best interests. I remarked that I wasn't directly involved with the case and that my friend certainly didn't discuss things with me after hours, and that seemed to mollify him somewhat.

I left the office figuring it was just a matter of time before Denise was hauled into the inner sanctum. As a full-time sessional, she would be suspected before a tenured professor like Grace. I, of course, being the lowliest of the low, would have been the odds-on favorite, but even department chairs can't have it all their own way.

There was no way I was going to get anything productive done so I headed home. My plan was to phone Denise and warn her about McNeely, but the phone machine was blinking as I walked into my apartment, bringing back the horror of the night before.

Gingerly, I pressed the blinking red button, expecting anything, or so I thought.

Mark Paulson's voice was the last thing I expected.

"Randy? This is Mark Paulson. We spoke at the vigil on the sixth. Could you return my call as soon as possible, please?" He rattled off the number, and I automatically scribbled it onto a scrap of paper.

The next call was from Leo, who sadly informed me that he wouldn't be winging it southward and would see me at Grace's party.

Steve's voice sounded strained in the following message. I suppose he was calling from work, judging by the ambient noise in the background.

"Hi Randy. The manure has hit the proverbial cooling element here. Would it be possible for you to meet me here at the station around six? My boss would like to talk with you. Call me."

I dialed his beeper number and left my name and number, hoping he'd call back soon. He did, almost immediately.

"Can you make it over, or would you like me to come get you?"

"What's this all about?"

"I really can't say at the moment. My supervisor, Staff Superintendent Keller, would like to discuss your apparent involvement with my case."

"As in my being threatened, locked up, and harassed, or as in my sleeping with the officer in charge?" I asked, wondering how much Steve could reply, and whether they tapped police lines. After my run in with McNeely, I didn't really care. After all, Staff Superintendent Keller didn't have the authority to fire me.

"A bit of both, I'd say."

Well, it seemed like it was going to be my day for being raked over the coals. I told Steve I'd grab a bus and be there in about forty-five minutes. In reality, it took an hour, since the 69 heading down 51st Street didn't show up until twenty minutes after the schedule had it pegged.

Steve came to meet me at the front desk after the officer there had made a quick call announcing my presence. We walked through the half-gate and down the hall I'd been in just the night before to deliver my answering machine tape.

We passed through the open area and knocked on a door in the corner. Steve gave my arm a quick squeeze, and I think I saw him wink as he opened the door for me.

Staff Superintendent Keller was everything you'd expect him to be. He was about fifty-five and probably had joined when there were still height restrictions for the police force. He rose to greet me and stuck out an enormous hand for me to shake. His hair, sort of sandy-gray, had probably been a honey brown in his youth, and was cut regulation short.

Keller waited until I was seated in one of the two chairs in front of his desk. Steve took the other. He looked us over, the way a liberal father would after catching his teenaged daughter out with her boyfriend.

"It seems to me that we have to deal with things before we get carried away here," he began, and I felt myself starting to blush. He noticed, which made me feel even hotter. McNeely should have taken lessons from this guy.

"I realize, Ms Craig, that we approached you to help us in our investigation, so I am not about to chastise you for interference in a police effort. I realize as well that you have become involved through no fault of your own. I am referring to the telephone threat."

He looked down at some notes on his desk, and I took the moment to steal a glance at Steve. He was staring straight ahead, impassive. I looked down at my hands. Keller cleared his throat. I looked back up.

"However, it has come to light that this investigation might be seen to be compromised by your involvement with Officer Browning. While I am not so antediluvian as to restrict the social lives of my staff, I cannot have their professional conduct questioned. Do you understand?"

"Yes, sir."

"There are a couple of solutions to this problem as I see it. The first would be to remove Officer Browning from the case. I hesitate to do this, in that he has an admirable handle on it. But he could remain in contact with the new officer in charge. The second solution would be to ask you to forego any further involvement with either the investigation or Officer Browning."

Steve spoke up. "It's going to be hard for Randy to extricate herself from some wacko's threats, and with respect, sir, I think it would be safer if she felt she could contact us should anything more transpire."

"Point taken. So, are you willing to remove yourself from the case?"

"I am. I can hand over the files and brief whomever you choose to replace me. I will, of course, be available to the officers in charge for background."

I couldn't keep all the permutations and combinations straight in my mind.

"Excuse me, could you spell it out a little more clearly for me?"

"Certainly, Ms Craig." Superintendent Keller smiled. "From this moment on, you are no longer an advisor on this case. You are a possible target and will be guarded accordingly. Officer Browning, who no longer will be assigned to the case, will likely be more circumspect when speaking into your answering machine."

"So I can talk to Steve about things?"

"Yes, but should the need arise, you will report to Detectives Simon and Anderson. Is that clear?"

"Yes, sir. And I'd just like to say I'm sorry to have caused any difficulties, but that Officer Browning was never unprofessional when dealing with the problems at the university."

"I'm sure you are right, and I will make note of that in my report. I hope you understand the need for this meeting, though. I would hate for something innocent to blacken the record of one of my officers."

Keller rose again from his desk, like a whale cresting. I stood, to avoid being bested by the shadow of his presence, and the next thing I knew Steve was ushering me out the door. He took me down the hall to an office where a man and a woman sat at neighboring desks.

"Karen Simon, Kevin Anderson, this is Randy Craig. She received a threatening message on her phone last night, and we think it might tie in to the murder of Gwen Devlin. Ms Craig was Gwen's English prof."

I nodded to the two detectives. Karen Simon asked for my address and phone number, which I gave her. We agreed on a time for them to come and interview me, then Steve led me out of the station.

I was the first one to break the silence as he drove me home. Makes sense, I'm the wordy one.

"So," I said.

Steve grinned a flat smile, keeping his eyes on the road.

"So," he replied.

"What could I have done differently back there?"

"What do you mean?"

"Well, I feel as though it's my fault you've been thrown off the team, or whatever that was back there, but I can't figure out what I did in the first place, or just now, that could have changed how it came down."

We were pulling up in front of my building. Steve parked, and turned to look at me.

"Look Randy. I wasn't thrown off of any team. The case has just been reassigned. Tomorrow I'll go to work on other cases, and Karen and Kevin will take up the slack on this case, and things will go on. You didn't cause that to happen. The we/us thing sort of complicated matters, but that's not something I want to give up on for the sake of a case. Do you?"

I hadn't realized until he said it that that was exactly what I'd been worried about. I felt one of those Monty Python sixteen-ton weights come off my shoulders.

He agreed to pick me up for Grace's party at seven-thirty Friday, and kissed me quick before I hopped out of the car. I waved as he drove off, then hummed my way into the building, stopping briefly to peer into my mailbox and see if it was worth unlocking. I grabbed the three flyers and a please letter from the David Suzuki Foundation, and headed down the once-again serene hallway.

All was okay in my world. I could put the case behind me just as easily as Steve could. That is, unless I became the next victim.

GRACE'S PARTY WAS PROBABLY NOT THE EVENT of the season by everybody's standards, but I'd come to mark my Christmas revelry by it. I would pull out my red and green chenille sweater, braid the annual stalk of mistletoe into my hair, and fiddle with layers of refried beans, cheese, salsa, and sour cream. This year I'd begged a few holly leaves from the florist down the street, and placed them in each corner of the pan. I just hoped no one would think they were a new type of nacho chip.

Tomorrow afternoon I was planning to head down to the tree lot, which was set up annually in the Garneau tennis court, and drag home a Charlie Brownish tree for the apartment. Maybe I could persuade Steve to string some popcorn with me while watching *Miracle on 34th Street*, which I'd noted in the TV listings.

I was trying to banish all thoughts of murder, threatening phone calls, and anti-feminist attacks. Whenever something popped into my mind, I started humming "I Saw Three Ships," which I'm sure was the medieval equivalent of "Rudolph the Red Nosed Reindeer."

Leo had called to ask if he could bum a ride to Grace's with us, and I'd agreed without checking with Steve, mainly because I was chary of calling him at work. Leo was situated about halfway between my apartment and Grace's house in

Pleasantview, so I didn't think that Steve would mind.

I thought about calling Denise, but that made me think about Mark Paulson's phone message, to which I hadn't replied. I figured I could get Denise aside at the party sometime tonight and let her know about McNeely and Paulson's call. Maybe she could call off Paulson. I didn't want to have to deal with him, especially after placing Steve in the situation he was in at work. If it looked as though his girlfriend was blabbing things to the press, I had a feeling Keller wouldn't be quite so understanding with him. It was all getting so complicated. "And who was on those ships all three? On Christmas Day, on Christmas Day . . ."

At seven-fifteen, just as I was wiping off the blotchy mascara I'd inexpertly tried to apply and was starting again, there was a knock at the door. I blinked through the cream, and stumbled into the living room to open the door. Steve stood there, looking blurry, gorgeous and irritated.

"Jesus, Randy, don't you even ask who it is? What about the door chain?"

"I knew it was you."

"I'm going to put a peephole in your door on the weekend."

"Just as long as you don't think it'll count as my Christmas present."

He laughed, kissed me, and told me how wonderful I looked. I was torn between wanting to continue, and wanting to see for the rest of my life. Eyesight won out, and I shuffled off to wipe the eye gunk off. Five minutes later, sporting eyelashes like little spiders, I returned.

Steve was reading the Christmas cards on my mantel. He turned, and his admiring look was enough to make me feel beautiful for the whole evening.

We were heading down the hall to the front door, when I remembered to tell him we were picking up Leo.

"Leo is the fellow who found you locked in the bathroom?"

"That's right. I'd forgotten you'd met. Maybe I was just

trying to block that whole episode. You know, I can understand the whole repressed memory stuff now. Some things
are just too nasty to keep in your head."

"The point is you do keep them. Have you considered seeing someone about that episode?"

"Not really. Do you think I should?"

"Trauma is trauma. It might not hurt. What about Jane
Campbell?"

I looked at him, trying to figure out what he was saying.
Was he really just thinking of my mental health (and if so,
was that necessarily a good thing?) or was he trying to tell me
subtly to keep asking questions? He looked at me and raised
his eyebrows.

"That's not a bad idea, I guess. Maybe I should talk to
someone about it. I was pretty scared, and maybe that's what
is making the phone messages so frightening."

"Messages? Have you had another?"

"No, it's just that it feels as though the second shoe hasn't
dropped yet. Turn here. It doesn't matter that I've promised
your boss to stay out of things; somehow I'm in the middle of
it, and I don't see an end so far."

It might have been a productive conversation, and it might
have kept me out of future trouble, but I had to break off just
then to point out Leo's house. I hopped out of the car to
knock on the basement window, and Leo soon joined us,
exuding good cheer and small German cookies in wreath
shapes.

We weren't the first to arrive at Grace's, and more soon
arrived. At one point, just before nine o'clock, I passed the
bedroom where Grace had motioned us to throw our coats. A
mound the size of Mount Robson hid any sign of my leather
jacket.

As at any party, there was a crowd in the kitchen. Denise
and Julian were leaning against the fridge, discussing post-
modernist renditions of the classics and trying to determine if

Stoppard's *Rosencrantz and Guildenstern are Dead* was a prime example or just darned good theater.

Leo was sitting cross-legged on top of the dishwasher, flipping back his silk scarf in order to eat a piece of sashimi with proper panache. Grace was flitting between the sink and the dining room door, ferrying more and more platters of goodies onto the already heaping table. Steve seemed happy in the dining room chatting with Arno, Karen Hanson, Marni Livingstone and two of the younger members of the department I didn't know all that well. Marni was talking about her adventures climbing in the Rockies the summer before.

"I can't even manage one of those climbing walls at the gym," Chris was complaining.

"Do you use the Van Vliet Centre?" Arno asked. "I've been thinking of starting some work-out programs. Several fellows in my classes swear by the facilities. I have to admit, teaching buff eighteen-year-olds is a humbling experience."

"You're not old enough to be feeling old, Arno." Marni was flirting mildly.

Arno shook his head, smiling. "I'm not ancient, but I'm certainly not as young as some of the newer folks being hired. It's a tad harder to be hired if you're not the flavor of the month. I'm not complaining, though. It did give me a chance to get my book written."

"You wrote a book while sessionaling? I'm impressed," Steve said. "From what I've seen, it's a grind of marking."

"Are you intimating that I am just grinding away, Steve?" I asked in mock horror. "I'll have you know that I can usually manage a few freelance gigs at the same time as teaching a full load."

Marni nodded her agreement with me. "It's tough, but it can be done. Especially after you've taught the course once. Then, at least, you don't need to be running about creating lecture notes or new handouts. The marking, though, ooh la la."

The last thing I wanted to think about in the middle of the party was marking, so I smiled at Steve, who had turned back to talk with Arno and Marni, and drifted down the hall to the living room.

Grace's living room was a study in polished surfaces. It reminded me of the set in Annouihl's *The Enchanted* where the girl tries to attract the ghost by putting shiny surfaces all about the room. The hardwood floor gleamed around several Persian rugs. Brass and copper bowls and, I think, spittoons held cut flowers on various wooden tables and sideboards. The sitting furniture was big and plush and comfy. I plunked myself down next to Chantal, one of my colleagues from the House, and Loretta Monterey, this year's writer-in-residence, a poet from one of those artsy islands off BC, and felt myself sinking for longer than I'd anticipated.

Chantal smiled and leaned back to make room for me in their conversation. I'd met Loretta briefly at her official opening reading in the fall, but hadn't really spoken to her since. She and Chantal had been discussing the latest Governor General awards. Loretta had been nominated for her new book of poetry, *Pebbles from the Sea of Japan*, but lost out to a fellow who hadn't received one before (Loretta already had two for poetry and one for a play she'd written in the eighties). Chantal was arguing that the award should go to the best work of the year, but Loretta seemed serene about the attitude that it was all right to share it around.

"How does it feel to be nominated?" I asked, figuring that her telling me was probably the only way in this lifetime I'd ever find out.

"That's the best part, really. They phone you about ten days before they release the shortlist, and that's the hardest thing, because they ask you to keep quiet about it until the list comes out. Those are the hardest ten days, though the two weeks that follow are pretty hectic once your publisher's rep gets hold of you. I must have done seventeen interviews in three days on *Pebbles*. It paid off though, I guess. My publisher is now calling it a bestseller."

"That's fantastic," I said, as Chantal excused herself and heaved herself out of the people-eating couch in search of another drink.

Loretta shrugged. "Maybe by poetry standards, but it still doesn't mean much. Most houses see publishing poetry as a charitable donation to Canadian culture. I've been lucky."

Being the member of the intelligentsia that I am, the conversation soon drifted to the weather conditions off the coast of Vancouver Island, and shoe stores in Edmonton where one could purchase size eleven. Loretta was a very nice person, and I made a mental note to buy one of her books.

After Loretta and I finished our conversation, I headed back toward the kitchen, with the intention of saving Steve should he require it. McNeely gave me a partially thawed nod as I passed. He probably would never quite forgive me for not being culpable, but I could live with that.

Leo, who had been hovering in the living room archway, cornered me to ask what I'd been talking about with Loretta. He grimaced theatrically when I told him.

"You have the ear of one of the foremost poets in the land and you talk shoe stores? What are we going to do with you, Miranda?"

I grinned, but he shook his head at me.

"I'm serious. You can't disregard one moment of networking any more. Have you seen what the job situation is out there for sessionals? You have to be constantly on the make. You're only as good as your last article in this game, and believe me, it's even tougher if you're male."

"Oh come on, Leo. You make it sound like a Rollerball tournament or something. I am not about to do a song and dance number to get a job. Besides, I have a job. I get just enough courses to teach each year. I don't intend to get a Ph.D., so I have no chance of being hired full time."

"There is such a thing as a full-time sessional position, you know."

"Yes, but that's more for folks with a Ph.D. from the looks of things. People like Denise, and you."

"What is the point of having a Ph.D. if you can't teach senior level courses? They might as well be hiring MAs for those positions," Leo grumbled.

"Don't get so grumpy, dearheart. Chances are you'll get a job as soon as your dissertation comes back from the bindery." I pinched his cheek like an old auntie might.

He winced. "Sure, if all minorities and women candidates decided suddenly that they'd rather apply for jobs with the Peace Corps."

"Cheer up, maybe they'll designate homosexuals as a discriminated-against minority, and you too can jump queue!" I dodged his whipping me with his silk scarf and scampered into the kitchen.

Grace was slicing wedges of pita bread and stacking them on a platter Steve was holding for her. Denise was gone from the kitchen, although Julian was still hanging around, filching olives out of a bowl on the counter. Half the department seemed to be magnetically pulled toward the dining room. Trust arts types to stay where the food is.

I craned my neck up to nibble on Steve's ear and took a pita from his platter.

Grace looked up and saw me. "Randy, there you are! I haven't had a moment to call my own, or I'd be a better host."

"You're a wonderful host. This is the best party ever." I leaned over and kissed Grace's cheek for good measure.

"Is it?" Grace looked around. "The trouble with hosting a party is you never really get a sense of it till the post-mortem. Not that I mind. It makes me clean the house for the holidays, and it always feels so much bigger after everyone's left."

"After this crowd, it's bound to feel palatial," Steve said.

"How many people are here, do you think?"

"I'd say at least seventy," he said, scanning the dining room.

"Really?"

"How do you do that?" asked Grace. "Can you really estimate on a visual survey, or do you count a certain amount and extrapolate from that?"

"Yeah, how do they manage to estimate crowds?" I wondered out loud.

Steve laughed. "It's a talent. Actually, I trained myself for the heck of it when I used to attend functions as a St. John's Ambulance volunteer."

"You were a St. John's volunteer? I suppose you're now going to tell me you lead a Scout pack in your spare time."

"No, and there was very little altruism involved in it. I figured it was the most economical way to attend rock concerts when I was a high school student and an impoverished university student."

Grace and I laughed.

"Since there was no mosh pit back then, we treated the occasional sunstroke and spent the rest of the time standing around. I started to guesstimate crowd size, and then we'd bet on it, and check the tally at the gate. I usually won."

"So, how many people were at the vigil?" I asked.

Steve squinted, picturing, no doubt, the crowd from that freezing, fateful night.

"I would say a good eight hundred or so."

"That many?" I asked.

Grace shook her head.

"It sure felt like it trying to feed the wet ones." Grace commented.

"That's right. Who picked up the tab for that?" I asked.

"I tried to see if the university would help out, but they refused on the grounds that it wasn't a university-organized function, so the pizza bill came out of the *HYSTERICAL* budget. It's put us behind on the mailout, but Vera and Suzanne . . ."

"The department secretaries," I filled in for Steve.

"... have volunteered their time to help with the mailout, and we got some emergency funds from the Women's Studies folks, so it should get out early next week."

"Can I help? Aside from proctoring my exams, I've got nothing pressing till marking."

"Sure, we can use all the help we can get."

Grace and I made arrangements for Monday, and then she disappeared into the crowded dining room with her full platter of pita dippers.

Steve led me out of the kitchen and into the back room. The area would probably be a family room in anyone else's house, but Grace had turned it into an arboretum, with ficus and hibiscus trees and several others I didn't recognize. Fuzzy purple ivy laced a path across the ceiling, and tiny grapes hung from a latticed wall on one end. Wicker settees and chairs were tucked in among the plants. The effect was immensely peaceful, especially since there were few lights and no partiers.

Steve and I cozied up on a wicker love seat. I leaned back into the crook of his arm and listened to the subdued roar of the party going on beyond the archway. I asked Steve if he was enjoying himself. He squeezed my shoulder and smiled.

"Do you mean, can I stand your friends?"

"Well, technically they're more colleagues than friends, although I guess I could claim about half a dozen or so."

"It's a good party. Grace is really something."

"I think so, too. I'm glad you're getting a chance to see her on her own turf."

"It's interesting to see them all in a different environment."

"You mean outside of academe? Or outside of being suspects?"

"It's not my case."

"Yeah, right."

"Seriously, I can't be seen to have anything to do with it. I'm here solely as your date." He kissed me to prove it.

"Do you really think someone in the department might be involved?"

He nuzzled my ear, and whispered, "Randy, repeat after me, it is not my case."

I struggled up, half-heartedly, out of his embrace. "But someone who hated women wouldn't be caught dead at one of Grace's parties."

"If they don't want people to know their true colors, here is exactly where they'd be."

"But it's not your case."

Steve laughed. "C'mon, they're dancing in the basement."

"He locks up bad guys, he cooks, he dances. You are the perfect man, Steve Browning."

"Hold onto that thought."

That wasn't all I was hoping to hold onto.

THE NEXT MORNING, WHILE STEVE WAS TAKING a shower, I curled up in bed, thinking about something he'd said the night before. Was there someone in the department who hid his true stripes? Had there been a real misogynist at the party?

It was so hard to picture someone harboring hatred for half of the human race that I couldn't conjure up any faces. Of course, there was always Professor Dalgren, but he hadn't been at the party. He probably hung upside down in a cupboard somewhere after the sun went down. Besides, he was an equal opportunities misanthrope; just pick a category and he could ooze contempt. Women, undergrads, graduate students, high school drop-outs, First Nations, the French, the government, theorists, members of the department, members of other departments; I'd heard him wax vitriolic on all of them at one time or another. He probably would have harsh words for Desmond Tutu if given half a chance.

There had been some mutterings when six new professors had been hired a couple of years ago. The hiring policy had specified an intent to favor the previously marginalized, and four of the six positions had ended up filled by women. Since then, with publications and glowing student evaluations, they'd proved themselves, but I wondered if somewhere there was some untenured white guy with an axe to grind at losing out to a skirt. I thought about comments Leo had been making the night before at the party. How many people really felt that way?

Maybe I was getting in a rut myself. Did the murderer have to be a man? Maybe there was a woman who hated Gwen and saw her chance? Or maybe a woman was targeting women to highlight the misogyny on campus? Maybe I was going insane.

The shower stopped, and Steve emerged through a cloud of steam, dripping and grinning at the end of the bed. There'd be no need to turn on the humidifier this morning.

"My back is now realigned. It's like sleeping at attention in that bed of yours."

I agreed, but pointed out that sleep was not something we'd done a lot of. Steve replied by shaking his wet head on me. I yelped, and informed him I'd set the coffeepot going. I slid past him to see if he'd left any hot water in the building.

By the time I got into the kitchen, Steve had rustled up pancakes and was squeezing oranges into juice. I must have looked as shocked as I felt, because he asked what was the matter.

"I just keep wondering when I'm going to wake up and find out you're just a product of too many bananas before bed."

"Do you want me to pinch you?"

"Nah, why the heck would I want to wake up?"

After breakfast, Steve got ready to leave and I then busied myself about, trying to shake the buzz of unreality his presence in the morning always seemed to instill. I had promised to call Grace later to see about helping with the HYSTERICAL mailout, and I had to check my list for last-minute things to get done before the onslaught of exams and marking.

Marks have to be posted five business days after the final exam has been written. Every student takes this as gospel, but tends to demand the same results of mid-term and mid-session exams. It was always better to have an exam slated for mid-week, because then you had the weekend to add to marking time. My exams were both on Monday, the first day of exam week. If I wanted any peace at all, I'd have to have the marks posted on the door of the House by Friday.

I wondered if there was someone in my class presuming they had the questions in their possession. I wasn't really sure what a preview of the questions would do to benefit some of them. Sure, they could decide what essay question to tackle, and reread the text in question, but they'd still have to sit down and write the essay during the time frame of the exam.

I tended to mark exams on a different scale than in-term essays. I gave marks for an original approach and some form of consistent argument, and excused spelling and grammar a little more than usual. That's where writing in a journal every class came in handy; by the Christmas mid-term, my students were usually getting pretty adept at thinking on their feet.

Thinking of journals made me wonder once again just what had been the quest in the ransacking of my office. Scenes of the wreckage came back like snapshots in my mind. Funny how I'd managed to block it in the last couple of weeks. Maybe Steve was right, I should talk it through with someone. Before I backed off, I picked up the phone and dialed Student Help.

Another perky voice, this time female, answered on the second ring. I made an appointment to see Jane on Tuesday morning. I felt lucky, since I was pretty sure this would be an active week for the counselors. I hoped Jane wouldn't mind seeing me, after Steve and my visit to her last week. Oh well, if she did, she'd probably tell me and I could find someone else.

I checked the rest of my list. I'd done the majority of my shopping, but still needed to wrap my parents' presents and mail them off. I had to call Denise, since I hadn't had a chance to talk to her privately at the party last night. I had to update some notes on *Love Medicine*, and think up a couple of new essay topics for the February essay. Students complained if they didn't get topics a month ahead of the due date, yet it occurred to me that precious few of them did a thing before the last minute.

I wrapped my folks' present, after scrambling to find a brown paper bag to cut and turn inside out. I'd decided to walk up to the Shoppers Drug Mart postal outlet, then head down to Orlando Books for one of Loretta Monterey's books of poetry. On the way back, I could perhaps find a small tree for the apartment. I shoved the parcel into my knapsack and headed out into one of those brilliantly cold Alberta winter days.

My eyes stung a bit in the cold, and I was thankful for the scarf over the lower half of my face. Everyone was bundled today. Car tires squeaked on the snow, and huge plumes of puffy white exhaust trailed each one for two car lengths. I was glad of my knapsack, which allowed me to shove my mittened hands deep in my pockets. I passed two balaclavaed men and one bare-headed teen, hunched into his jean jacket. A tall woman replete in Linda Lundstrom pink stepped out of a white Sable and headed for the Turtle Creek Café. I felt a wild jab of envy for the pink coat with its matching pink fur rimming the parka hood. One part of my brain argued that investment in a coat like that would be appropriate given the extreme temperatures in Edmonton. The more levelheaded part of my brain argued for saving my budget for frivolities like food and shelter. I thought mean thoughts of how impractical pink boots would be in March slush, and then, feeling highly virtuous and self-righteous, I trudged on.

As I stood in the lineup for the post office, I happened to glance out the window and saw a familiar shape walk past. Head down, toque and scarf obscuring his face, hands burrowed deep into jacket pockets, high black skidoo boots on. I couldn't be sure of recognizing my own mother bundled on a day like today, but I was almost certain it was Rod Devlin walking down 109th Street. I looked around. I was still four people from the front of the line and several more folks stood behind me. I couldn't leave. And just what would it prove if I did follow him?

Steve and his boss had warned me off doing anything rash, so I fumed in the line, wanting to act in some way that might resolve the unsettledness of the whole situation. We'd had a murder, vicious graffiti, vandalism and personal attack (I was starting to embroider my sojourn in the basement washroom) and the ruin of the vigil, and nothing had been done about any of it.

I wasn't blaming Steve or the police; I couldn't see any solution either, but surely a murder as gruesome as Gwen's should have been solved by now. It seemed to hang over my head and possibly the whole university like that cloud that used to crown Li'l Abner's neighbor.

When I finally paid an exorbitant amount for postage that would guarantee an arrival prior to the twenty-fifth, I raced out of Shoppers and around the corner to see if I could still see the bundled potential Rod Devlin. There were plenty of people on Whyte Avenue, but I couldn't spot him, so I shrugged my knapsack into place and decided to stick to my original game plan.

The wind was crisper walking east, and I kept my head tucked down, glancing through my eyebrows to see where I was going. This did not qualify as a Lauren Bacall impression; I probably looked more like a cartoon bear walking against the wind. I barely avoided bumping into a woman with a stroller trying to keep her snowsuited child from pulling down his scarf.

One of the things that most impresses me about living in Edmonton is how the weather never seems to stop anyone. It can be forty below, and there will still be people lined up outside to get into the Paramount cinema downtown. Blizzards slow people down, but there will be a line of cars behind every snow plow. Today might be considered balmy by January standards, but it was still pretty damn cold out, and Whyte Avenue looked just as crowded as it did during the Fringe Festival in August.

Nine long blocks later, I was peeling my scarf off in Orlando Books. Jackie Dumas, the owner, a feisty activist for local culture and a gifted novelist herself, smiled at me and pointed toward the coffee machine against the wall. It was the best idea I'd come across all day. I poured a cup and silently toasted her.

Perversely, I avoided the poetry section until it was the only aisle I hadn't scoured. By the time I found a copy of Loretta's *Pebbles*, I had to pile it on top of the new Alice Munro, a Dana Stabenow mystery I hadn't read, a Haruki Murakami I'd never gotten around to buying, and some new calendar pages for my DayRunner. As I waited, patiently this time, in the cash line, I browsed through the selection of tiny books judiciously placed on the counter for impulse buying, and impulsively added a gorgeous little copy of Omar Kayyam's *Rubaiyat* to my purchases.

Leo be damned, I could come up with good ideas too. This, with a nice bottle of wine and loaf of bread all wrapped up in red gingham would be a wonderful present for Steve. I could picture it now, the lights twinkling on the tree, and a midnight picnic spread out on the floor.

Tree. Jeez, it was a good thing I'd brought the knapsack. I bundled the books into its depths as Jackie's cashier rang them up, foregoing a bag. It took two tries for my Interac card to get through, but the woman told me the connections had been like that all day.

"Christmas shopping tying up the phone lines, I guess. At least this way, there won't be any credit card bills to deal with in the New Year!"

Yeah, and no messy money cluttering up my account

either, I thought, Grinchlike. I smiled back at her, though, and let the thought pass quickly. Thinking about money made me think about my job, which in turn made me think of McNeely. Or maybe it was the blast of cold air hitting me as I left Orlando's that made me think of the chairman. Whatever, he in turn made me think of Denise, whom I hadn't yet called. And that made me think of Grace, whom I'd forgotten to call as well. It was as if I'd left a bundle of worries at the door of the bookstore, only to have to shoulder them again the minute I hit the sidewalk.

To add to everything, who should walk right past as I stood there, but the same collection of winter clothing I'd thought was Rod Devlin. Close up, I was sure, but judging by his non-reaction to me I figured he couldn't pick me out from any other polar explorer. He was heading west, briskly.

What the heck, I thought, and followed after him. Well, technically followed after him. I'd have been going that way, anyway. I could almost hear the excuses I was piling up for Steve's boss, Staff Sergeant Keller, in case I got caught. There were enough people on the street to make my following him unobtrusive, but he headed for the lobby of the Varscona Hotel, where not quite as many folks were congregating. I popped in after him, ostensibly to find a pay phone, but really just because I didn't know what else to do. My experience of tailing suspects comes directly from mystery novels, where the detective usually is quickly spotted and immediately beaten up. This wasn't the outcome I was hoping for.

I spotted a bank of phones, deposited a quarter in one, and dialed Denise's number while watching the elevator door close on Devlin, who had by now shown his face by removing his scarf. The elevator number stopped at four, which I noted as Denise came on the line.

"Randy! I was hoping you'd call. Where are you?"

"I'm at a pay phone on Whyte Avenue as a matter of fact, but . . ."

"Great, why don't I meet you down there in about"—she paused, probably to check her clock—"half an hour? The Mexican place across from the Army & Navy?"

"Well, I still have to get a tree, but . . ."

"You're not thinking of bringing a tree into a restaurant, are you?"

"No, I'll leave it to last, but I don't want to be down here all day."

"Half an hour to get there, and an hour tops, that's all. I promise. I'll buy. Go in and order a big plate of nachos and two Dos Equis. I really have to talk to you."

"Yeah, okay. I'd like to talk to you, too."

"See you there. Bye."

Eating nachos is not a bad way of combating cold weather. Eating them in Puerto Vallarta would be better, but Julio's Barrio was a good second. I looked over to the bank of elevators, thought about calling Steve or the other detectives, but figured they would just say Devlin was allowed to be in his hotel room, so I left and headed a couple of blocks back up Whyte.

I stopped into When Pigs Fly to see if they had something small in brass for Grace. Seeing her living room had given me the idea. The place was mobbed, and I beat a quick retreat so that I wouldn't be pushed into a stand of something valuable and fragile. I wonder if all Tauruses suffer from this phobia?

Julio's was just down the block, and mariachi music came floating out the door as I opened it, mingled with the smell of refritos and chilis. The waitress ushered me to a table of barrel chairs near the back of the restaurant. It was warm, being closer to the kitchen and farther from the street door. The place was active without being completely full, and a smiling waitress who thankfully didn't introduce herself hustled over to me with menus.

I gave her Denise's order, explaining I had a friend coming so that she wouldn't think me a lonely Christmas toper. It's so important what complete strangers think of you, after all. Speaking of, I took a moment to look around the darkened restaurant, checking to see if I actually did know anyone. I get accused of ignoring people out in public. I think I just make the assumption that I don't know that many people and never really look at folks. After teaching for a few years, though, the more faces were getting familiar the more places I went. Anywhere you look, you're bound to spot a university face. For instance, over in the front of Julio's sat Arno with several young men, very probably students. Thinking about what Denise had said about his campaigning for tenure votes, I wondered if he mightn't be getting some of his students to nominate him for a Rutherford Fellowship in Teaching Excellence. That wouldn't look half-bad when the tenure decisions were being made. I wondered what sort of teacher Arno was; he must be pretty swell to have students wanting to hang with him during study week.

I didn't think he had seen me, so I didn't bother trying to catch his eye. Instead, I reached into my backpack for one of the un-gifts I'd managed to snare in the day's foraging. The beer came before the nachos, but both had arrived before Denise breezed in and caught me on chapter three of *The Wind-Up Bird Chronicle*.

"Isn't it wonderful to be able to read what you want?" She nodded to my book, as she divested herself of parka, scarf, mitts and hat, and plunked herself down in the chair opposite. "I used to go into a bookstore the day after exams every year, pick up every single bestseller, and glut for a week or two."

"It's the calm-before-the-storm syndrome with me. Just knowing I have to mark seventy-five exams next week has me grasping at anyone who can complete a sentence. Literary merit is a bonus."

Denise took a long swig of Mexican beer and sighed. " This tastes so good. I think I may just run away and become a drunk. This marks two days in a row with alcohol. Do you think I'm on my way?"

We talked about the party. She mentioned speaking to Steve and probed a bit until I admitted that he'd been taken off the case. This interested her.

"That's it. I didn't think I was being interviewed, but just put it down to social graces."

"He wouldn't have interviewed you at a party, anyhow," I found myself defending him.

"No? Well, he and Leo seemed to be having a pretty intense discussion at one point, but I guess I was mistaken."

"Leo and Steve? He didn't mention it? They were fighting?"

"Not fighting. They just looked very serious. If it had been anyone but Leo, I'd have thought they were discussing hockey."

I tried to get off the topic of Steve. I somehow felt as if I was revealing secrets rather than comparing boyfriend notes with a friend. Mind you, this girlfriend was dating a reporter.

"Has McNeely been on to you yet?" I asked.

"I've managed to avoid him, although apparently there was a message in my mailbox to see him. Julian told me. I told him to leave it there, then I spent the evening ducking our chairman at Grace's. Thank goodness she has a big house. It's a nice house, isn't it? I'm not sure why they call it Pleasantview, though. The only real vista is of the cemetery."

Denise was sounding forced, which was unusual since she was normally the most direct person I know. Leo had once said of Denise that she wouldn't use a door if there was a wall handy, and he wasn't far wrong. Something was bugging her, and I had a feeling I knew what, or rather who, it was.

"How are things with you and your intrepid journalist?"

"Mark? He didn't take kindly to being left off the party list last night, but can you imagine what McNeely would have done if he'd seen him there? We could have just left him in the cemetery and saved trouble."

"Does Mark know the trouble he's put you in?"

"Intellectually I think he understands, but emotionally 'the truth' is in big neon letters and he can't get beyond that."

"Even if it means your job?"

"Randy, this is all going to get dealt with long before the review for next year's sessionals comes up. It will be history, and that, as they say, is another department."

"Are you sure? I was just thinking about how it's hanging over us all. I can't figure out how to make the cloud lift."

"Simple. They find the murderer. Then they find the graffiti artist. They punish the idiots in the Nixon masks who wrecked the vigil."

"So you think they're all disparate events? Unconnected?" I still wasn't sure what to think, and of course Denise didn't know about my threatening phone call. I felt sort of miffed that she was forgetting my office ransacking. Then again she hadn't been the one locked in the basement bathroom.

"Of course, in a way they are connected. I think the letters catalyzed the murder. I am not sure it would have happened without the letters, but I doubt any of the letter-writers was the murderer. I think the graffiti came as a result of the murder, and the vigil was ruined as a result of the graffiti. There is a sense of things being out of control."

" 'The center cannot hold . . .' " I quoted softly.

"Exactly. We have to come to some form of closure. If they find the culprits, we can punish them appropriately, and then we can all go back to normal. You remember normal? Where we pretend that we're all colleagues in pursuit of higher knowledge and wisdom?"

I grimaced. Maybe Denise should be going to see Jane instead of me. She sounded ready to snap. She probably heard the manic edge to her own voice, because she immediately apologized.

"I'm sorry, Randy. You're right. There is a cloud over us. I'm trying to think of Mark as the silver lining, but keeping things to myself at the same time as I'm exploring intimacy has got me rattled."

"He's worth the trouble?" I asked, more to keep her talking than for prurient reasons.

"He's terrific. He's funny, he's bright, and he's interested in my world. He's neither defensive nor egotistical about his own. And one of the best things, which in this case is also one of the worst things, he is taking all these events seriously."

"We're all taking them seriously, Denise," and I thought again about my phone message.

"No, not all of us. Everything, barring your student's murder, has been brushed off as hijinks. That's what made me talk to Mark in the first place." She polished off the last nacho, and washed it down with a gulp of beer. "Let McNeely do what he wants. It's not as if I signed some secrecy oath to be a sessional lecturer. Anything Mark got from me, he could have got from any first-year student with her eyes open for the last few weeks."

"Well, he probably had more fun getting it from you." I gave an approximation of a leer.

Denise grinned. "I'm sure he did."

We made plans to connect to help Grace on her mailout, then bundled up to brave the elements. Denise was off to Greenwood's for some present shopping, and I walked with her across the street to get a couple of red checkered dish-cloths and some long underwear from the Army & Navy. They were selling my favorite flowered Stanfields long johns three for $20, so I bought lavender, pink and mint green. I won over a suspicious lingerie clerk, who allowed me to put on one of my new purchases. I chose the mint green and felt much better on the trek home.

Whistling "It's a Marshmallow World in the Winter," I made it to the Garneau tree lot without encountering a single suspect. Kinsey Millhone might have thought it a washout, but I was claiming it as a minor accomplishment.

As soon as I got home, I phoned Grace. Actually, I tell a lie. After I found my yellow wash bucket, filled it with water and upended five old empty wine bottles into it to support the sad excuse of a Christmas tree I'd dragged home down 109th Street, and then swept up the ensuing needles from the floor, I called Grace. She was at home, cleaning up after the party. She explained that the mess wasn't enough to have taken the whole day; she'd just decided to have a lie-in for the morning, and had spent three hours in bed with the biography of Vera Nabokov I'd been wanting to read.

Her plan was for us to meet at her office at noon on Sunday, and sort and bundle the magazines into their mailing envelopes. That done, she could organize the whole postal sorting for Monday after office hours.

"It's no wonder the post office gives us a deal; we end up doing their whole job barring delivering it into mailboxes."

I promised to arrive via the High Level Diner, with warm cinnamon buns for everyone.

Grace laughingly agreed to supply Wet Ones for our inevitably sticky fingers, and I rang off.

The phone rang while my hand was still on the receiver, startling me a bit. I held onto it while it rang one more time, and then picked it up, sounding a little more hesitant than usual.

"You get the message, cop cunt?" said a muffled voice.

"Who is this?" I snapped, wishing at that moment for one of those newfangled Call Display phones.

"Keep your nose and your pig boyfriend's nose out of things, or you'll be sorry."

There was a sharp click, then dead air. I found myself holding the receiver to my ear anyway, trying to hear something that would tell me who was targeting me for this crap.

Finally, I put down the receiver and picked it up again, dialing Steve's pager number automatically.

He rang back within five minutes.

"I just got another call."

"Is it on tape?"

"No, I was home for this one."

There was a pause, then Steve spoke gently.

"Randy, I'm not the one you should be calling officially on this. Hang up and call Karen and Kevin. Tell them what was said, what time it came in and all that. I've got another half-hour here, and then I'll come over."

"Unofficially?"

"Most definitely unofficially."

"Thanks, Steve."

I put the kettle on before calling Detectives Simon and Anderson. It was Karen Simon who answered, and it sounded as if Steve had mentioned I'd be calling. I reported what happened, and agreed to come in the next day to sign the report.

Karen got me thinking when she asked the obvious question. "Who knows you're seeing a policeman?"

I promised her I'd try to get together a list of who might have seen us together, then hung up to go and make the tea.

Steve arrived at five-fifteen, five minutes later than he'd predicted. After holding me without words for a minute, he caught sight of the tree.

"A Charles Schultz fan, I presume?"

I laughed. "It isn't that bad, is it?"

We decided to head out to the Upper Crust for soup and munchies, and have popcorn for dessert.

"You're only allowed to eat the same amount as you string," I warned, when we were back in the apartment.

"You could moonlight as a slave driver," Steve grumbled, jabbing himself in the thumb with a needle as he threaded another puffed kernel onto the line.

"You ain't seen nothing yet," I teased, as I put my Muppets Christmas record on the turntable. Steve's eyebrows shot up into his hairline as he heard Miss Piggy yodelling to the *Twelve Days of Christmas*.

"That's supposed to set the mood?"

"I never said what mood, did I?"

Steve laughed with me, but I could hear the strain of trying to pretend everything was hunky-dory in both our voices. I slumped down in front of him and leaned back, using his knees as a backrest. His hands moved onto my shoulders and began to knead them into pliability.

"We might as well talk about it," he said gently.

"It's not going away no matter how much we try to ignore it," I agreed sadly.

I told him of Karen's question to me and the list I'd promised to make.

"If you want, we can start on it now," he suggested.

"Might as well." I nodded, shook myself into action, and stood up to get my trusty list pad and a pencil.

I returned and sat cross-legged in front of the tree. Steve slid off the couch and sat across from me. I wrote: PEOPLE WHO KNOW ABOUT US across the top of the list, and to be bloody-minded I put *Staff Superintendent Keller* right on top.

Steve, who was probably an expert at reading upside-down, smirked.

"Well," I said, "starting with the night in the downstairs toilet, there's Denise and Leo and your crime scene guys."

"I don't think you have to add Trent and Michaels; it doesn't sound like their MO."

"Then there's Grace, I guess. And everyone at Grace's party. And then there's your Father Masson from St. Joe's."

Steve smiled again, but I put the priest's name on the list anyhow.

"I'll bet you anything Denise told her reporter about us."

"Denise has a reporter?"

"Yes, Mark Paulson. She's the mole McNeely's really after. I met her today for nachos, and she's worrying me." I told Steve about Denise's rather zealous desire to duke it out with McNeely about freedom of the press. I also assured him that I hadn't told her any "inside" information about the investigation, including the nasty phone calls I'd received.

"The last thing I want is to see it in the paper, and I just can't trust Denise not to spill it all to Mark. She is really hung up on him."

"You sound as if being hung up on someone is a bad thing." Steve smiled, stroking my knee. I blushed.

"You just don't know Denise. She's usually so contemptuous of guys who fall for her looks."

"Maybe it's her brains he's after."

"Hmm." I thought back to my one encounter with Paulson. He hadn't struck me as much of an intellectual, but that could be me projecting my image of journalists on him. And my image of journalists was taken from movies like *The Front Page*, rather than from much first-hand knowledge.

I had one friend who worked for a newspaper, and she was well nigh bristling with integrity, so maybe I should be giving Paulson another chance. I thought that maybe what really burned me about Mark Paulson was that because of him I'd lost an access to confiding my own woes to Denise. Or maybe I was just jealous he was taking all her time.

I looked at the list. "Jane Campbell and the woman at the Student Help office, I suppose."

"Put them down, but I'm not sure if they would clue into the fact we're seeing each other from that visit."

It was tough to try to visualize who might know about aspects of my personal life. When it came down to it, any one of my students might have seen us together. Or someone might have seen us at a restaurant or a movie and known Steve was a cop from his questioning around campus. It didn't have to be someone I actually knew, either. Although it made my skin crawl to think an anonymous jerk was watching my movements, in a way it felt better than thinking it was someone close enough to know about my private life.

"I told McNeely I was seeing a member of the police force," I suddenly remembered. It gave me satisfaction to write his name down on my suspect list, not that I really considered any of the names we'd culled satisfactory suspects.

Steve was curious, so I told him about McNeely's raking me over the coals for the leak to the press. Steve was incredulous that the man thought he could keep wraps on the events that had occurred. Telling him made me think of someone else that might just know more about me than I wanted him to.

"Rod Devlin might have seen us together. He came to the House that day you were there." I tapped my pen on the pad resting on my knee. I was seeing Devlin walking into the Varscona Hotel again in my mind, wondering why it was he was still down here when his boys were up in Fort McMurray mourning their mother's death. Of course, that was me extrapolating. They might have been angry with her leaving earlier, so angry that her death was just another departure, not something to mourn as much as rail against.

What was Devlin doing here anyhow? How closely were the police monitoring him? He had seemed a sad and lonely man to me, someone to feel sorry for, but I'd heard of sad and lonely men opening fire on entire fast-food restaurants before.

Steve brought me back to the matter at hand. He took the list from me, and turned it so that he could read it in the conventional way. After a minute, he reached out a hand for my pencil. I put it into his palm the way nurses hand scalpels to surgeons. He began to notate the list. Finally, he looked up.

"Aside from the useful inclusions of 'All U of A students' and 'All U of A faculty', there are a few people here that Karen and Kevin might want to look at."

"Let's see."

I took the list back from him. He had started by putting checks and exes by names, and then finished off by circling several names. A couple of them I could understand, but some of the others surprised me.

"Grace? Denise? Do you really think they'd pull anti-feminist stuff?"

"We can't assume that all the events are the acts of the same person, and you have to look beyond obvious motivations sometimes."

"Well, I can see Rod Devlin, but McNeely? Not that I wouldn't mind him getting a taste of his own medicine, but I really can't see him ransacking my office."

"Why not?"

I paused, unable for a moment to explain. "Because books got hurt."

Steve's amazing eyebrows shot up again, so I rushed to try to explain my seemingly stupid answer.

"Whatever he is, he's an English prof. You don't get into this business without a deep-seated respect for the written word. There is no way I could see him pouring coffee on Shakespeare, no matter how tired the volume looked." I giggled, at my own unintended joke. "That goes the same for Denise and Grace, and Leo, for god sakes. Anyway, they're my friends, they wouldn't do anything to harm me."

"Technically, those phone messages are warnings. Friends warn friends away from perceived danger."

"Are you sure old Father Masson there wasn't a Jesuit? You argue too well." I was getting a little steamed with Steve. "And why didn't you circle Mark Paulson? Or consider it could be some kid in one of my classes?"

"Have you ever noticed one of your students when we've been together?" Steve asked patiently, in that smarmy interview tone I'm sure he took with the recently traumatized.

"No, but that doesn't mean a thing. One of them could have seen us from a distance. Or whoever it is could be stalking me." I tossed the list down on the floor. "I don't think this is such a useful exercise. It excludes too many variables. If you set your detectives sniffing after my friends, they may blinker themselves to another possibility."

"Who worries you most on that list?"

"Rod Devlin, of course." I spoke without hesitation.

"Why?"

"Because he was in the House. Because he's the husband of the murder victim. Because I don't know what makes him tick. Because he's big and big guys frighten me."

"Because you don't know him."

"Well, of course! Who wants to think that someone they know and maybe like wants to harm them? Anyhow, what about Paulson? I'm sure he overheard us talking about the journal. He could have headed right over and broken into my office."

"But he didn't."

"How do you know?"

"He didn't head right over, even though he knew you weren't there."

Steve had a point, but I didn't want to let Paulson off the hook. "So he went home and planned first. So what?"

Steve took my hand, and forced me to look him eye to eye. "Whose name on that list bothers you the most? I mean which name do you most not want to see there?"

"I don't know what you mean."

"Yes, you do."

"You mean Leo, don't you?"

"What makes you say that?"

"Denise said you were interrogating him at the party."

"Did she?"

"Were you?"

Steve tilted his head, like a puppy or a kid who has broken a window with his baseball. "We were talking. I couldn't be interrogating him. It's not my case."

I looked at him and wondered how well I actually knew this man who could probably draw an accurate map of every freckle on my body. Although I usually considered myself a pretty good judge of character, I'd been known to make mistakes before, especially when the pheromones kicked in.

"Okay, tell me, why should Leo be considered a suspect?"

"Well, we're looking for someone who has an antipathy to women."

"And Leo fits the bill because he's gay? That's ridiculous! Just because he doesn't want to bed them doesn't make him a misogynist. Most of Leo's pals are female."

"I just think you should keep an open mind about this, Randy. Your life might depend on it."

He was serious. Thoughts of Gwen leapt into my mind and I shivered.

"Okay, if it makes you happy they can call on Leo and Denise. But let them know that these guys are my friends, will you?"

"Who knows, maybe they've let it slip to someone you don't know about," Steve didn't sound too convincing.

Changing the subject, I told him about my appointment to see Jane. He seemed pleased by the news, but a little distracted.

"Do you still have the instruction book for your answering machine?" he asked, which led me to believe it was not my subtle vanilla-laced scent that had set his mind wandering.

"Sure, I guess so. You want to see it now?" So much for perfume. I hoisted myself up and went to rummage in the bottom drawer of my desk. I returned triumphant and handed him the manual.

Steve flipped through, then clicked his tongue as he found what he'd apparently been looking for.

"Look, Randy. It's possible to tape all your calls, even those you answer, without your caller being aware of it. All you do is press this button after you've picked up the phone."

I acknowledged that pushing a button would probably be better than having the police tap my phone line, although Steve warned me not to rule out the possibility.

"It'll be up to Kevin and Karen how they want to play it, but this guy is probably calling from a public phone booth. That's the great benefit of detective shows on TV; everyone's now too educated to leave prints or talk from their own phones."

"Or lick envelopes, or leave fibers in their car trunks," I added. "How do you guys ever catch up with the bad guys anymore?"

Steve winced, and I was sorry I'd joked. After all, Gwen's murderer was still at large.

"Luckily," he said, "most of the bad guys are too stupid to read, and all the really good plots are in books."

We ended up reminiscing about truly great mystery and thriller plots. I was voting for *Three Days of the Condor*, but Steve made a good case for *Wait Until Dark*. Talking about movies made us both realize that it was almost time for the eleven o'clock showing at the Garneau Theatre around the corner, so we bundled up and headed out, joking about overdosing on popcorn.

When we got back from a thoroughly forgettable and highly enjoyable two hours, I'd almost forgotten the phone call. That is, until we both saw the red light winking at us on the answering machine.

MAYBE IT'S MY MOTHER," I SAID WEAKLY, knowing full well she wouldn't call after eleven at night. Not unless it was an emergency. My stomach knotted. Maybe it was an emergency. I rushed to the machine with a burst of adrenaline.

With Steve right behind me, I punched the red blinking button. The machine whirred, and Denise's voice came on. I was so relieved it wasn't a family crisis or the nasty caller that it took a minute for her message to sink in. Steve's grip on my shoulders brought me back in focus.

"Randy." Denise's voice sounded strained and rushed. "I've just heard from Grace. Campus Security called her. There's been a fire at her office, and they want her over there. I'm meeting her there. Meet us at the Humanities Building if you get home to hear this. It's twelve-forty-five. Where are you?" Her last words sounded angry, but I assumed that she was just venting frustration.

I turned to look at Steve.

"She's probably just there now," he said. "Let me call in to the detachment to report it, and we can head over if you want."

"Do I have any choice?" I sighed, but Steve was already dialing.

I shuffled off to get my knapsack and put my camera in it.

If Denise had wanted pictures of the graffiti, she'd probably want photos of a fire. I already assumed it had to be arson. I couldn't imagine what could spontaneously ignite in an office in the English department. Grace's copy of *The Satanic Verses*?

Steve was off the phone.

"Karen and Kevin were still at the station. They'll meet us. The arson squad at the fire department is all over the place, we hear. It's not going to be pretty, but Karen says it'll be okay if we meet them there. Are you up for this?"

"What do you mean? There's no one dead, is there?"

"Not as far as I've heard. I just mean that your going over might be exactly what the caller told you not to do. Stick your nose in things."

"So I'm supposed to ignore the plea of a good friend because I've been warned off by some cowardly creep?" I was getting mad.

"That's better." Steve smiled. "You're getting some color back in your face. Let's go."

I checked around to make sure that nothing was plugged in on the tree before I left. Thoughts of fire will do that to you.

I was willing to walk, it was such a clear crisp night, but Steve vetoed the idea.

"It'll be really late by the time we're ready to leave, and by then you'll be exhausted. Let's take my car."

So, in the end, we beat Denise to the parking lot. She pulled up right behind us and caught up with us after locking the door of her Tercel. We stopped there for a moment to absorb the scene.

Three huge yellow fire trucks were pulled up on the walkway to the Humanities Building, dwarfing the two-story circular wing that held the lecture halls I loved to teach in. On the third floor of the main part of the building, one of the windows along the east wing of the chevron shape was broken and black smoke poured out. A ladder and hose were set up near to it, although water was no longer being pumped through the hose. Icicles hung from the windowsill, and a humped ice dam sat on the sill itself. I realized that I was seeing all of this so clearly because a huge spotlight had been trained on the site, like an Artaudian stage light waiting for some twisted Juliet to make her cue.

We walked past firefighters in full regalia, some of them (who had probably already been inside) looking filthy and reeking of smoke. Steve approached one of them, showed his ID, and asked if we could be allowed inside. We were pointed to a man in a black raincoat near the door.

"That'll be the arson squad," Steve told us, as we neared the building.

The arson guy told us that Grace was already inside with his boss, and that he figured it was all right to go in. He warned us that the elevators had shut down. He didn't have to tell us not to touch anything, but he did anyway.

Grace was standing in the hallway with the arson guy's superior. She looked very small and older than I'd ever seen her look. Crying can do that. She turned to us with tears rolling off her cheeks, making me think of the icicles dripping off her office window.

"Denise, Randy, thank you for coming. I didn't know who else to call. It's as if I've been raped; you don't really want the world to know."

The head arson guy, who introduced himself as Inspector Gibson, looked rather uncomfortable at Grace's simile. Once he had assessed that Denise and I were there for Grace, he turned to Steve. I wasn't sure whether he was trying to close ranks on a professional basis or if it was some sort of guy thing, so I was amused by his reaction when Steve disengaged himself by admitting he wasn't officially on the case.

"I'm here as a friend, Inspector Gibson," Steve said, just as Detectives Simon and Anderson came down the hallway. Steve turned to include them.

"These are Detectives Simon and Anderson; they're assigned to a murder case we think might be linked to these malicious events."

Karen Simon took over, questioning Gibson as to how much the arson squad might have discovered. The four of us stood in a doorway alcove across from Grace's office and listened to Gibson's findings. No one seemed to mind us there, probably because Steve was with us.

"The fire was deliberately set, using an accelerant doused on materials set along the west wall of the office. Most of the office was flammable, and there are noxious fumes from the upholstery in the chair. We got the call from Campus Security at the same time as the alarms at the firehouse went off. We managed to cut the air circulation once the fire was under control, so most of the smoke will have dissipated by morning. The offices surrounding have probably sustained some smoke damage, but the main damage is here in Dr. Tarrant's office."

Grace whimpered. Denise put her arms around her and rubbed her back.

"What was the accelerant used?" asked Anderson, who seemed to be in charge of writing notes while Karen Simon poked her head into the blackened dripping grotto that was Grace's office.

"Looks like starter fluid, but we'll be certain once the lab work is done."

Karen checked the doorknob of the office door. "They weren't very careful about breaking in. Crowbar to the joist from the looks of it. Was the door closed?"

"Yes, but not locked. There are smoke detectors in all the offices, so the alarms went off likely about four minutes post-flashpoint."

"How long did it take for anyone to get here?" Steve asked from our corner. Karen looked up and nodded her approval of the question. Gibson tried to calculate, but decided the safest answer would be to talk to Campus Security.

"The trucks were outside when I got here and the fire was out. I met two firefighters on my way up the stairs and there was a Campus Security cop at the end of the hallway to direct me. I've been here"—he checked his watch—"thirty-five minutes."

I turned to Steve. "There wasn't a Rent-a-Cop in the hall when we got here."

"No, but maybe he was dispatched to crowd control. I think half of HUB mall is out in the parking lot by now watching the show."

Simon and Gibson agreed to connect with reports by mid-afternoon, then the arson guy went back to work. After taking a couple of pictures, Anderson phoned in for a crime scene unit, then he and Simon asked if there was someplace they could talk with us, especially Grace.

Grace looked bereft, since her usual sanctuary was out of the question. Both Denise and I had keys to the grad lounge at the other end of the third floor, so we all filed down the narrow halls, saying little. It was weird to be in the department with only security lights on in the hallways, and the booming disembodied voices of firefighters echoing from time to time. I stopped in the staff washroom on the way and fumbled in the dark to the cubicle. On the way back out, I took a look through the window down on the circus scene outside. Steve was right, there were crowds of people standing outside the ring of yellow trucks, staring at the building. Several Campus Security cops, in their brown suits, were moving the crowd back. Some police cars were pulled up at the nearest edge of the parking lot, and I thought I saw a line formed near one of the cars. Someone got out of the car, and another person got in. Taking statements, I figured, and hurried out of the darkened anteroom to join the others in the grad lounge.

I found them sitting around the central table. Anderson was using a flashlight to write his notes. Simon was questioning Grace about the contents of her office, her movements in the past few days, and if she had a list of possible enemies.

"Anyone you failed recently? Maybe someone who felt put down in a class?"

Grace had enough spirit to look indignant. "I don't put people down in my classes, Detective."

Simon didn't break stride. "We have to consider all possibilities. Think about it. The arson squad figure the fire started on the west wall. What did you have on the table set against the west wall of your office?"

Anderson, who had sketched a quick diagram of the layout of Grace's office, pushed his notebook toward her and pointed with his pen to the rectangle in question.

"That table was piled high with padded envelopes, a file box of mailing labels, and about two hundred copies of *HYSTERICAL*. There were another six boxes filled with two hundred books each stacked under the table." Her voice broke. "Oh God, they're all burned, aren't they?"

"Hysterical?" questioned Anderson.

Denise stepped in, giving Grace time to regain composure. "It's a quarterly magazine. We were coming in tomorrow to get it ready for mailout."

"How many people know about this magazine? Would it have been a target?"

"Well, it's a feminist quarterly, but it's devoted to literature rather than polemic," Denise saw the question in Simon's eyes and rephrased her answer seamlessly. "It's not really political except in the way that any women's writing might be seen as a political statement. As for who knew about it, that's not an easy question. Everyone in the department knows that Grace is the editor; I don't know how many of them were aware of its mailing dates. I doubt if any undergraduates would even have heard of it, although it is sold at the university bookstore."

"We were discussing the mailout at Grace's party on Friday," I contributed. "I suppose anyone there might have overheard that."

"And I was in the general office on Thursday arranging some help from the department secretaries. People might have heard me," added Grace.

Simon sat back and thanked us. Steve reassured them that we could get Grace home. Anderson explained to her that her office would be restricted to crime scene access for a few days, and Grace slumped even further in her chair. Just then the lights flicked on, startling all of us.

"I guess everything's under control." Anderson smiled. "We'll be in touch later today, Dr. Tarrant."

He and Karen Simon left the three of us in the Grad Lounge. Denise and I turned on Steve to explain what would be happening now.

"My take on it is that there'll be two prongs of investigation, maybe three. They'll want to determine whether someonoe has targeted Grace personally. If not, and I doubt it's the case, they'll look to see if anyone has an axe to grind against the magazine itself. Then, with all of that ruled out, they'll try to tie it into the previous events. Access, availability, that sort of thing. With this being the third event of a distinctly anti-feminist nature connected to this department, we're bound to shake out some connections." He assured Grace that Simon and Anderson were the best there were, and we finally got up and pulled on our outerwear.

The crowds had thinned but not completely by the time we got to Steve's car. We couldn't persuade Grace to leave her car and come with us, so Denise drove Grace's car and Grace home. She said she could pick hers up later, and left a note on the dash to explain its presence to the parking Nazis.

Steve and I drove home in silence. I would have liked him to stay over, but understood when he said he should head in and file a report.

"I thought this wasn't your case," I teased mildly.

"I might not want it, but it seems to want me. Are you going to be all right?"

"Sure, once I shower this smell out of my hair."

"Put your clothes in a garbage bag and tie it off right away, or you'll be deodorizing your entire apartment for a week. There's only one smell worse than a fire scene to get out of your clothes."

"Yeah?" I said sleepily. "What's that?"

"A fatal fire scene," he said grimly.

I didn't feel sleepy any more.

I COULDN'T HELP IT; ON MONDAY MORNING I found myself walking past Grace's office on the way from the House to my exam. Even though it was the way I normally walked through the department, it felt ghoulish, like crawling past a traffic accident. There was yellow crime scene tape across the entrance and a massive padlock keeping the damaged door closed. Black soot smudged the white, bumpy stucco of the adjoining wall in ominous shadows like I've always imagined the fallout from Hiroshima. I hurried past.

There was nothing special for me in my mailbox, so I went down to HUB after grabbing a stack of examination booklets. I bought a large Java Jive and a packet of Fisherman's Friends lozenges for anyone who might get a coughing attack during the exams. I had half an hour to kill, but I intended to be at the lecture room ahead of schedule to reassure the worried students who might think they should be haunting one of the gymnasia instead. I was glad we in the English Department could hold exams in regular lecture rooms since our classes were, for the most part, manageable in size. Those rows upon rows of exam desks set on the tarps to protect the gym floors were so antiseptic I couldn't imagine intellectual thought being allowed to surface in the air. I recalled a Woody Allen routine about cheating on a metaphysics exam by looking into the soul of the student next to him, and chuckled out loud. A girl on a bench looked up at me, startled. I guess the sound of laughter before an exam is not widely heard.

I made it to the lecture hall by nine-fifteen and smiled at the three students already lounging near the door. I let them in, turned on the lights, and checked the hall for stray papers. Pristine. I set up my stack of exam booklets, exam papers, class list, novel and coffee on the desk, and started to write the various things on the board that I always tried to impress on my students.

"Read through the exam paper completely before beginning."

"There are two sides to the exam paper."

"Please put your name on your exam booklet."

"Use as many exam booklets as you need, number them in order."

"Write in pen."

"DOUBLE SPACE."

Students began to file in. I called the roll. There was one student missing, but I'd known about the absence already; something to do with four wisdom teeth being yanked. Deferment allowed in spades.

I passed exam booklets from left to right and papers from right to left. I closed both doors and went back to my chair at the front of the room. Although novel reading in the a.m. is best done in bed with a large quilt, I was soon well engrossed in Barbara Gowdy's *Mr. Sandman*, a novel I had wanted to read as soon as it had come out but hadn't got around to till now.

After the one-hour mark, some of the students began to shuffle forward for more exam booklets. I am always torn between happiness that I've engendered such dedication and the sincere and fervent hope that they just write big. I gave up on my novel about twenty minutes to the hour, and began to sort through my papers. A few students were flipping through their booklets, looking for obvious clunkers and spelling errors. I stood up and wrote "Merry Christmas" on the board, and sat down again to time the final minutes of the exam. By the time the buzzer sounded at ten to the hour, only three people were still writing.

"Time's up," I announced, and they resentfully closed their booklets.

A few people wished me a Happy Christmas as they left, but most were too wrapped up in either what they should have written or what they now had to study for. They filed out to their next Herculean labor. I gathered up their offerings (my own personal Augean stable droppings) and headed upstairs to the office to see if the ten o'clock mail had brought anything interesting.

There was a Christmas card from Guy and a postcard from Candy, a former grad student in the department. Did I really want to know she was enjoying a trip up the Nile? If I knew her, she'd be surrounded by willing Nubian fill-ins, as well. A notice informed me that the next Popular Culture Association's Conference would be held in Las Vegas, which seemed fitting, somehow. Maybe Disneyland would be the following year's choice.

One of the secretaries spotted my load of exams and tried to place a bet on when the students would first come round to check their marks. She was feeling smug since she wouldn't have to deal with them till April. Final marks were posted on official pink slips on two ring binders at the department office, and we could slip away from the hurly-burly then. It was up to us to try to get through hordes of mark-checkers at our office doors for mid-terms and mid-sessions.

I wondered idly where Grace would be posting her mid-term marks.

I was stuffing exams into the side pocket of my briefcase and checking on my afternoon exam papers when Chantal, Greg, and Thora breezed through the office into the copy room. They were heading into HUB for lunch and asked me along. I counted out sixty exam booklets, shoved them into the center of my briefcase, and announced I was ready.

Our choices were limited to the Korean restaurant or A & W, since Chantal smoked. The Korean place won hands down. It was pleasant to tuck into a bowl of *bibimbap* and listen to normal conversation for a change. The fire in Grace's office was dealt with, and we moved quickly on to other subjects such as exams, Christmas plans, the weather and the theory that the Internet was simply a plot to keep us from getting valid research done. Thora admitted to having been sucked into it for seven hours while making a random search for literary tours of the Lake District.

SInce Chantal and I had exams to proctor at two, we left the other two to a third cup of coffee and made our way back down the mall to the Humanities Building.

My second exam was on the second floor in one of the long, wide classrooms. I went up and down the rows of tables, making sure only two chairs were placed at each table to allow for mid-exam spread.

Some students had filed in by ten to the hour, so I self-consciously wrote my pre-exam messages on the board, praying all the *kimchi* I'd eaten at lunch wouldn't act up on me.

I scanned the heads bowed over the new, improved exam paper, searching for someone who might give away by body language that this was not the exam he or she was expecting. Sherlock Holmes might have noticed something, but I didn't. I wasn't really expecting to, anyhow. I was pretty certain that a student wanting to get away with stealing an exam wouldn't leave my office looking like a bomb site.

I managed to finish *Mr. Sandman* half an hour before the exam ended. They packed up, I packed up, and we all left the room. No bang, no whimper. Just business as usual.

I dumped the exams in my office at the House, and put in a quick call to Steve from my office phone. I told his machine that I was on my way home to cook a tuna casserole and that if he felt like comfort food he should come over about six-thirty. I took a quick look around the office to see if I was forgetting anything, and then locked up. I'd be in tomorrow, as soon as I'd seen Jane, to chain myself to my desk for a few hours to mark the exams I'd been hauling around. First-year students might never see my role of marking exams as harder than theirs of writing them, but they only had to write it once, whereas I'd be reading and commenting for two or three days.

Steve arrived at twenty after six with a bottle of German white.

"I wasn't sure what went with tuna casserole, so I made a fish/white sort of guess," he said, simultaneously kissing me, handing me the bottle and shrugging off his overcoat.

I laughed.

"Draft beer is probably more in keeping, but this should raise the tone of the evening."

And so it did.

I MADE AN EFFORT THE NEXT MORNING TO CLEAN the apartment up a bit, since I figured I wouldn't be getting back till late. My plan was to head in to Student Help and then straight to my office and mark until my eyes crossed. If I could dodge Leo and other sundry distractions, I figured I could get at least half of the exams marked. Posting my marks by Thursday morning would not only make me a hero with my students; it would give me two free days tacked onto the Christmas break.

I wasn't sure what to expect from my scheduled meeting with Jane. Steve hadn't been overly interested in knowing about it, so I still wasn't sure why he had suggested it. I myself was a little apprehensive about talking to a stranger, but I was cheered somewhat by the thought that she wouldn't be telling anyone. Especially the press.

The same sympathetic-looking woman was behind the desk when I arrived ten minutes early for my appointment. She nodded and checked me off in the book, and I took a seat to wait my turn. I'm not sure if Jane had anyone in with her before me, because I didn't see anyone exit, but at ten o'clock she appeared in the waiting area to lead me into her office.

"Have a seat," she said, gesturing toward the sofa/armchair grouping. I sat in a corner of the sofa and tried to think of what to do with my hands.

Jane picked up a legal pad and pen and sat across from me in one of the matching chairs. She crossed her legs easily and smiled. Her smile must have been what brought her into the counseling profession, because I doubted if that open sunniness that shone right through her eyes could have been learned in school. This was someone who wanted to listen, who wanted to help. My hands folded naturally onto my lap.

"I take it this is your first time seeing a counselor?" Jane intuited. I nodded. "Well, there's nothing much to it, but it can feel awkward at first. I suggest I ask you a few questions first, just to get the ball rolling, and then you can tell me what has brought you here, okay?" I nodded again.

She noted down my name, my connection to the university, my family connections and birth order, and several other innocuous things; the sorts of things you tell any potential friend in initial conversational forays. Then she paused.

"You were here last week with the policeman investigating Gwen's death. Does this visit have anything to do with that?"

The phrasing of her question startled me, not because I thought she hadn't recognized me, but because linking Gwen's death with my trauma so causally was something I hadn't really done until that moment.

"In a way," I said slowly, and started jerkily to tell her why I was there. I started with the episode in the basement bathroom, but by the time I finished with the threatening phone calls I was speaking much faster than normal. It was such a relief to actually talk about it. It was as if letting the words escape and hang in the air released them from my nightmare holding tank. When I stopped, Jane's response again surprised me. I guess I'd been expecting the stereotypical "Hmmm, and what do you think that means?" sort of answer that I'd seen in Woody Allen movies.

"Goodness," she said instead, "no wonder you needed to see someone. You've been through the wringer!"

Jane laughed at my startled look, and that made me laugh, more from stress release than any real humor.

"I think there are two or three things we might want to explore today. The first one is the feeling you have of not being connected to your friends. It occurs to me that you haven't spoken to Denise of your concern that your discussions wouldn't be confidential. Maybe you could broach that with her and see where it takes you. You have an ally in Steve and also a listening ear. Use it. As for your other friend, whom you think Steve suspects, I don't think that is your problem, is it?"

When she put it that way, I had to agree. Let Steve worry about Leo. Leo could take care of himself. And maybe I wasn't being fair to Denise. Already I felt better. No wonder Woody swore by analysis.

Jane went on. "The other issue is a little more serious. Are you being stalked and harassed personally, or were you just in the wrong place at what is definitely the wrong time? Either way, you didn't deserve it, or bring it upon yourself, and you know that. I sense a great deal of strength in you."

I raised an eyebrow in a reasonable facsimile of Steve's skeptical look.

"You're not allowing this to turn you into a victim. You've been through a traumatic situation. You've handled it maturely. There's some residue, which makes you uncomfortable enough to come see me, but that too is part of the mature way to deal with things."

"I don't know if it's maturity or automatic pilot," I admitted.

"What bothers you the most about the phone calls?"

I hesitated. "I guess it's the not knowing if this is all connected. So much has gone horribly wrong in the last little while, and things seem as though they must be connected since they're all awful. And is it worse or better if they aren't connected? There's this real sense of backlash against feminism everywhere on campus, and it feels like tentacles reaching out from the walls. Gwen gets murdered, and I get assaulted and my office gets trashed. The office doors are graffitied, and the vigil wrecked, and Grace's office burned. Are all these things linked, or is the link more tenuous, like just because we're all women on campus? How much is pranksterism, and how much is truly dangerous?"

I leaned forward, into Jane's sympathetic force field. "Part of me wants to think it's all random, so that I don't have to worry about a killer being after me personally. The other part of me almost hopes it is linked to one person, even though I know that more than one person disrupted the vigil. I just don't want to think there is that much misogyny out there. Does that make sense?"

Jane nodded. "Perfect sense. And I think that dichotomy is really what's bothering you, more than the after effects of your assault."

"So what can I do about it?" I said, with a little self-pity creeping into my voice. So what, I thought, this was my fifty minutes.

"The only way you're going to find out whether your enemy has one head or many is if the crimes are solved," said Jane matter-of-factly.

"And I've been told to stay clear, so my mental health is in the hands of others." Bitterness creeping in there, edging over to sit with the self-pity.

"You've been told to stay out of the police investigation," Jane clarified.

"Right, that's what I said."

"That doesn't mean you shouldn't keep your eyes open and your mind alert."

"If the Edmonton Police Service can't catch a murderer, what hope do I have?"

"Why not look at things from another angle? Let the police deal with Gwen's death. Concentrate on the events that had an impact on you personally. Maybe there's something you haven't picked up on, something only you could pick up on."

If I hadn't taken to her before, her proper use of the noun "impact" endeared Jane to me for life. If I could round up all the people who turned it into a verb and pour honey on them in wasp season, I'd be a happy camper.

Jane discreetly checked her watch and suggested we meet again in a week. I agreed and stood. We shook hands, which, though oddly formal, felt right.

I left the building by the side exit and walked purposefully off to my office in the other corner of campus. Jane was right. If I could figure out who had it in for me, I could put a face onto the evil. The irony of feeling better by knowing you had an enemy didn't escape me, but it still felt right. Maybe a series of lists would trigger something.

All of this would have to wait a couple of days, of course. I had exams to mark.

I STOPPED BY IN HUB TO PICK UP A CAFÉ LATTE from Java Jive; I needed a little pick-me-up to push me onward to all those waiting exams. I was meandering down the mall, licking the chocolate-sprinkled foam off the top of the cup before I set the lid on, and not taking much notice of the faces attached to the general ebb and flow. I was trying to stay on the right side of the mall, although that didn't always work during term. There were times when walking through HUB made me realize what a spawning salmon must go through.

I was pretty sure I had some foam on my upper lip, which was the Murphy's Law cue for me to bump into someone I knew, but not well. Right on time, just as I had my tongue extended upward toward my nose, I heard someone call out, "Randy!" It could have been worse; it could have been a student. I knew without turning that it wasn't a student calling me. They'd have called me Professor Craig, especially in this "sucking-up week" prior to results posting.

I looked around, swiping the perfectly lovely foam away on my coat sleeve. Mark Paulson appeared at my left elbow, and just about got said elbow in the chest for his troubles. He didn't exactly qualify as the last person I wanted to see, but he came close.

"Randy, I've been looking for you."

"Oh really?"

"I left a message on your answering machine."

Just the mention of my message machine made me tense up, and I nearly spilled my latte, but then I remembered that I had heard his message.

"I'm sorry, things have been a bit rushed."

"So I hear." he smiled wryly. He had a nice smile, I'd give him that. What the heck, for Denise's sake, I'd also give him a couple of minutes of my time.

"But not now."

"What?"

"Sorry, just thinking out loud. Look, Mark, I'm not sure what you want to talk about but I am really pressed for time right now and it's not exactly healthy for me to be seen conversing with the fourth estate. My chairman would have my head, for one thing."

"Oh, I understand. But look, here's my card. Call me tonight, okay? I'd really appreciate it."

"I guess, but . . ."

He was gone before I could ask him what I could possibly tell him that Denise couldn't. I put his card in my pocket, and shoved the lid on my latte. Just seeing him had taken the edge off the chocolate. I was fighting with the plastic rim of the lid, when I heard my name again. I looked up to see a swarm of English types observing me from across the mall. Oh great, if any one of them mentioned seeing me with the press to McNeely, I'd be tap-dancing in the chairman's office again.

I nodded to Carol Stanton, a sessional lecturer married to Geoff Stanton, the Moderns prof. They were clustered at stools around a precariously high table at the Pasta Place with Arno Maltzan. Maltzan was certainly making the rounds of the old guard. I felt as though I was watching a political campaign in action; first the students, now the tenured profs. I was betting this too had something to do with Arno's upcoming tenure review; maybe that was why we'd even been seeing him with Dalgren recently. Leo would probably have the dirt.

I wasn't sure how I felt about tenure anymore, having heard cogent arguments for both sides. It seemed to me that some sort of guarantee needed to be in place to offset status quo thinking, but on the other hand, I could find examples of people coasting for years on easy street as well. Maybe a ten-year term, with review policies might be the answer to keeping professors vital. I felt a bit of pity for folks like Arno, who were running the gauntlet of sitting on committees and pushing to publish in order to jump through all the standard prior-to-tenure hoops.

Still, I felt sorrier for Carol. She was just as qualified as Arno, and yet she'd probably never get higher than sessional status, just because the department knew it had her. Unless she wanted to split a marriage and seek employment else-where, she was stuck with sessional status because they'd already hired her husband.

Mind you, it was all relative (as in who are your relatives). Carol was a rung above Denise, who couldn't depend on her contract being renewed, and with three qualified Shakespeare profs on faculty, the chances of her qualifying for an interview were incredibly slim. As well, Geoff probably had some pull in getting Carol's contract renewed endlessly. And then there was me, a lowly MA, destined never to teach more than fresh-man English, and wondering every eight months if I'd be able to pay next year's rent.

There was no mail in the department mailbox, so I had no other excuses. I trudged over to the House, let myself in with my key, and made my way slowly up the stairs.

I'd just got comfy at my desk when my phone rang. It was Steve, wondering how my morning had gone.

"Great. But right now I'm looking at a stack of essays."

We decided I'd be in need of a back rub around eight-thirty

at my place, and I set down the phone feeling markedly more cheerful. I wonder if studies had been done on rating productivity at the workplace with getting enough good sex. I was more than willing to sign up for the core group.

Whatever the factors involved, I managed to get through twenty-three papers before my bladder called for a truce. I was pleased to see the upstairs bathroom had been fixed. I didn't need to revisit the lower bathroom, especially after rekindling the memories so vividly during the morning's session with Jane. I washed my hands, and headed back for more torture.

Actually, they weren't too bad. The essay questions on *Twelfth Night* were bringing me back to thoughts of the murder and ensuing days. It was obvious from the tone of the essays that the similarities of the incidents hadn't escaped many of the students, either. There were references to anonymous letters, and masquerading as someone else to gain understanding of another. I wondered again who it was masquerading in Gwen's life. Was she Olivia, being wooed from afar and courted by a pretender? Or was she cast as Viola, dressed up and playing make-believe in a world that wasn't hers? One of the students even drew a parallel between Malvolio's incarceration and the fears of the students who had received poison pen letters. It seems several of them had dropped out of school since the whole incident had begun. This was the first I'd heard of it. What a dreadful pity. One horrid, stupid action, like a pebble into a murky still pond, brought ripple after ripple of effects and after-shocks. I knew I was mixing up my geomorphology. What the heck. I rolled my shoulders a few times, and went back to marking.

It was going pretty quickly, all in all. Aside from the Shakespeare fans, most of them were settling for safer topics on the essay component, but a few had attempted to analyze the poem I'd included, which made for some hilarious reading. It was Snodgrass's "Leaving the Motel," which depicts an adulterous liaison. Most of my babies read a family vacation into the words, rather than a bittersweet extra-marital affair. One of the girls analyzing it (wrongly) did come up with the most telling aspect of the poem: although it is written in rhyming couplets, to make sense of the words one must read beyond the set feet, and find that it doesn't rhyme at all. To me, this was Snodgrass' comment on illicit love. To her, it was a flaw. And to think I still had four months worth of pearls for them to stomp on.

I wondered, idly, what Gwen would have made of "Leaving the Motel," given her situation. I was sure Devlin must have been having an affair or something, to give her such a hard, cold take in the essay on Gatsby that she never was allowed to submit. I had recorded the 8.5 I'd have given it in my records, anyway. Even without the rest of the grades, she still would have fared better than some of the students still left in the class. In fact, I'd have given her a nine had she not mixed up Daisy and Myrtle in her synopsis of the Valley of Ashes. Having Tom punch out his wife would give an American classic a whole new twist.

I started. That was it. Rod Devlin wasn't a philanderer; he was a wife beater. No wonder she'd mixed up the names. No wonder she had left him. No wonder he had killed her. I reached for the telephone to call Steve, then thought better of it. I'd be seeing him this evening. I had essays to mark. And I wasn't Nancy Drew. I wasn't going to somehow solve all this mess by some inadvertent transposition in a student's essay. I would tell him, though. It might be enough reason for him to question Gwen's doctors back home, or something. Maybe I should just call him quickly. Anything to hear his voice, and avoid marking another essay just yet.

My willpower didn't have to be tested, since the phone rang just as my hand was reaching for the receiver.

It was Steve, which just goes to show that we were made for each other. Or something.

"Hey, I was going to call you. Do you remember asking me about the essay Gwen wrote? Well I think maybe there was something in there for you to check out."

"Randy, listen to me, I've got something important to tell you."

"I think Rod Devlin was beating Gwen."

At almost exactly the same time as I said that, Steve's voice came through the receiver, "We have a warrant out on Rod Devlin for the murder of his ex-wife."

"You do?"

"What sort of evidence do you have?" asked Steve.

I told him about the transpositions in the text of the essay and about the scene with Tom and Myrtle where he slapped her in company. Steve was muttering on the other end in agreement sounding noises.

"Well, we've got enough evidence gathered from Fort McMurray and from the crime scene to tie him to it. They're off to pick him up now. Randy, the reason I am calling is personal. I don't think there is too much likelihood, but I want to make sure you're safe. Are you locked in at the House?"

I smiled in spite of myself. It was so nice being worried about. I promised that I would go and deadbolt the front door of the House as soon as I hung up the phone. Steve figured he wouldn't be too much later than we'd originally planned, even with the paperwork and fielding the press that would ensue. I told him I'd expect him for ten p.m. at my place, and then after a smooch into the telephone receiver, I went down to check the lock on the front door.

Rod Devlin. Just as the statistics said, the most likely suspect was the spouse. The problem with that was, if he had killed Gwen, then someone else was in charge of all the rest of the stuff. Try as I might, I just couldn't see Devlin defacing office doors, or inciting riots, or burning feminist magazines. He might have used the published letter as a way to cover his own tracks, but he was an opportunist, not a mastermind. A Malvolio, not a Machiavelli.

So, if we erased Gwen's murder from the equation, who profited from all the events that had occurred? Someone who hated women, obviously. Or was that the common denominator at all? Maybe it was someone who stood to make a reputation from all of this. That let out Steve, since he'd been voluntarily taken off the case. I blinked, realizing that I'd actually had him on a mental list, even briefly. Well, Mark Paulson was making a name for himself reporting on all this. Both Grace's reputation as a strong feminist and *HYSTERICAL*'s advertising potential had increased, but that was beyond contemplating. No one would set fire to her own office. A little voice whispered "insurance fraud" to me, and I realized that people do that particular stunt all the time. Leo and Arno and Julian were all still likely suspects, if Steve's reasoning was anything to go by. Young men of a certain age being refused jobs or tenure because of employment equity considerations might come to a boiling point sooner or later. I doodled a bit more on my list of names, realizing that most of these people had fairly easy access to me, should they want to do me damage. The thought hovered like a darkling shadow for about two seconds, and then Jane's voice cut through my fears. I wasn't a victim, except of marking. If I was going to be home by ten I had better stop playing Trixie Belden and get back to it.

I'd got into a rhythm with the marking and was fairly sailing through the set. Every once in a while I'd click through the remaining pile on the left side of the desk to see how many more there were to go. I was almost through the first class and had dreams of getting a crack on the afternoon group before I pooped out. If that were possible, I might manage to see some of tomorrow afternoon if I started first thing in the morning.

I was just totaling up the marks on the third last paper of

the first class when something made me look up. Nothing weird, just a noise, like a floorboard downstairs. The only thing that made it unusual was that I had been completely alone all afternoon. The House had been so still that even the slightest noise made the difference. I stopped for a moment to hear more. Maybe, from the sound of the footstep, I could tell who had come to their office. Nothing.

I looked at my watch. It was six-thirty, not the witching hour by a long chalk. I shrugged and rolled my shoulders once more. Old houses make noises, especially in the winter months.

Halfway through the second last exam, the lights went out. Since the sun had set at approximately four forty-five, the lights really went out. I hate to think what my red pen did to the paper it had been resting on. I backed my chair away from my desk, and stood up. I could see from the window that the street lights were still on, so the power loss was just isolated to the House. I would have to make my way downstairs in the dark to find the fuse box. It was on the kitchen wall behind the basement door. I'd made sure I knew where it was after I blew the fuses in my apartment one winter and had to feel my way around for mine. I'd eventually found it behind the clothes in my closet. Cleaning up after myself had taken an hour, so I now checked for fuse boxes the way Elvis probably looked for side exits.

For a split second I thought of calling Campus Security to get them to come and trip the fuse for me, but discarded the idea as embarrassing. I remembered Jane's statement earlier in the day about there being no victim in my character. She was right, I guess, but although I wasn't about to cower in my office while the rent-a-cop came to my rescue, it didn't mean I wasn't a little nerved up.

I felt about my desk for a weapon. Where are those handy Inuit sculptures when you really need them? I found the mug where I kept pens, stamps and Linda Hutcheon's business card (she'd given it to me at a conference and I'd kept it as a talisman), and dumped the contents on the desk surface. Now that I was armed, I edged my way around the desk to my office door. I put my ear to the door, but could hear nothing. I turned the knob and made my way gingerly across the landing, holding out my free arm to find the standing banister.

How many stairs were there? I must have been up and down them a bazillion times and had never bothered to count. I could name you all seven Brothers for the Brides, every last one of Deerslayer's names, and sing all the words to the "Wreck of the Edmund Fitzgerald," but useful trivia like the stair count was nowhere in my brain. I felt my way down, riser by riser, and still did that stupid thump step at the bottom.

This is the point in any good slasher flick where the teenaged girl rushes into her baby-doll pajamas and heads down the basement stairs. Well, I was fully clothed, and aiming only for the kitchen, but I felt just as stupid. I gave myself an internal chiding. It was just previous events that had me spooked. A stupid blown fuse wasn't going to turn me into a sniveling wreck. Leo, if I ever felt the need for humiliation enough to tell him, would have a good laugh.

All the members of the House had tacitly agreed to keep the door to the basement closed since my "unfortunate incarceration" in the downstairs biffy, so I wasn't worried about taking an unwarranted tumble. I reached the doorway to the kitchen and reached out an arm to feel for the wall that should lead to the fuse box. My instincts hadn't been heightened any since my last sojourn in the dark, and I felt only empty space where there should have been seventeen layers of high gloss industrial paint. I took another step forward and was slightly off-balance to start with when I felt a thudding slam in the center of my back.

I used to have nightmares about falling down stairs. They'd begin with a flying dream, which everyone touts as such a liberating and glorious experience, but my flying dreams were always indoors, and I would usually be dogpaddling around the ceiling area trying to get away from someone. I'd find myself in a stairwell, and the task of flying downward would usually throw off my levitating abilities and my stomach would burble up the way it does on giant slides, toboggans, and moguls my skis weren't prepared for, and I would find myself tumbling downward, but never quite landing.

The stomach bit was the same, but my uncompromising connection with the floor probably made up for all those missed dream sequence landings. At some point, mid-flight, it occurred to me that whoever had opened the basement door was probably the same person who had pushed me. Since my life didn't pass in front of me on the way down, it was probably safe to pass out. So I did.

I'm not sure how long I lay at the bottom of the basement stairs. When I did wake up, it was because an inadvertent movement caused a searing pain to travel up my body from my toes to my shoulders. Trying not to move my lower body, I let my right hand feel downward, hoping not to find myself eviscerated. My clothes seemed intact, so I concentrated on my legs. Wiggling my left toes was no problem. Even shifting to try to wiggle the matching set made me nauseous. I was pretty sure my leg was broken.

Normally some natural light might have found its way into the basement, but the snowdrifts against the tiny, grimy windows were so high and solid that it took quite a while before my night vision could kick in at all. I checked my wrist in a Pavlovian way, and managed to hit myself in the chest with the mug I was still clutching in my hand. At least I was pretty sure it was the mug, since I couldn't really see it, or my stupid watch. Sure, a coffee mug can withstand a fall down the stairs, but not a bone encased in far more avoirdupois than really necessary. It made one wonder about the efficacy of all those engineering drop-the-egg contests. I set

the mug on the floor beside me, and sighed. I had no idea
how long I'd wasted lying in a heap, or when the cavalry
would show up.

Thank goodness I had a ten o'clock date with Steve.
Someone knew I was supposed to be somewhere. I thought of
those little beeping necklaces they used to advertise during
Coronation Street. The poor lady calling out, "I've fallen and I
can't get up." I laughed, which made my leg throb. I stopped
laughing.

Visualizing my path to aid took some time. I could imagine myself hauling my screaming leg up the stairs, but had a
hard time figuring out my plans from there. Was Rod Devlin
up there waiting for me? Part of my remaining intellect told
me that a murderer could just as easily have followed me
down the stairs and finished the job, so I wasn't as panicked
as I might have been. For some reason, I didn't think Rod
Devlin had done this to me. For one thing, I was sure I'd have
sensed a presence as big as his, even in a pitch black kitchen.
Whoever had pushed me didn't command that sort of field of
energy. Whenever the pain ebbed enough, I could see this as
akin to the graffiti and bathroom incidents. If Devlin was
responsible for Gwen's murder, then there were definitely two
parties at work; I would have to tell Steve.

Steve. Just the thought of him looking for me and trying to
find a way to get into the House made me tired. Or maybe it
was the pain from my leg. I think I passed out a second time.

When I came to, I was thinking a bit clearer. I couldn't hear
anything happening upstairs, so I figured that the bad guy or
guys were gone and that I'd be safe to appear in the kitchen if
I could make it up the stairs.

"Nothing ventured, nothing gained." I realized with a
shock that I'd spoken aloud. I also realized from the sound of
my voice that I was crying. I gritted my teeth and pulled
myself around toward the bottom step. I managed to haul
myself up two risers before the pain took over. I waited,

shivering from the cooling sweat pouring off my body, and then tried for two more steps.

I made it up seven steps before I could go no farther. Part of my loss of strength came from the sudden comprehension that making the kitchen wouldn't help much, since the only phone in the House I could get to would be the one in my office, and I knew I didn't have enough energy for another set of stairs. Besides, what if yanking a broken leg up seven steps had already done irreparable harm and I'd forever have to sport those same brown orthopedic shoes my mother had made me wear as a child to avoid knock knees?

I was shivering so much I could hear my teeth chattering.

"Well, it's probably half shock and half being stuck in a chilly basement in a condemned house in the middle of December," I said out loud.

I hooked an arm through the eighth step and tried to make myself comfortable. This thought made me laugh again, not a pretty sound. I was trying to tally up the current time, based on time I knew had elapsed. The lights had gone out at six-thirty; I'd probably made it to the kitchen by twenty to seven. Give or take a few seconds to tumble down the stairs, where did that leave me? Just how long had I been unconscious either time? How long did it take to get to this perch?

I figured it was either seven-thirty and I would die from shock, hypothermia, and internal hemorrhaging before anyone thought to look for me; or it was nearing ten and Steve would soon know I was missing. Either way, I should try to stay awake in order to shout when I heard any sign of rescue.

I should also try to stay awake in order not to fall and break the other leg.

Thank the Lord for Stephen Sondheim. I bounced right past trying to remember Shakespeare and started into musical theater. I'd managed to sing my way through *West Side Story* (noting that the enforced tremolo in my voice made "One Hand, One Heart" particularly moving) and was trying to belt out "If Mama Got Married" from *Gypsy* when I heard a lot of stomping upstairs from the vicinity of the front hall.

I kept singing, afraid that if I stopped my voice would dry up totally and I wouldn't be able to let anyone know where I was. The footsteps came directly overhead. I prayed they were wearing police uniforms instead of Nixon masks, and yodeled "Let me Entertain You" in my best Baby June.

The lights came on, the basement door opened, and Steve rushed halfway down the stairs. If I hadn't been linked onto the riser, he'd have probably sent me flying. I stopped singing as his hand reached down to wipe the moisture from my face. Tears and sweat; I was hoping against blood.

He was shouting for an ambulance, but didn't leave me. Instead he hunkered down on the ninth riser until more stomping occurred. I drifted in and out, humming "You'll Never Get Away from Me." Steve moved to allow two guys with a stretcher to sidle down the stairs and attempt to strap me to it at a ninety-degree angle without allowing me to slide back down. I could hear them muttering at the awkwardness of it all, but didn't feel particularly apologetic.

I saw Steve again as the kitchen came into view. After negotiating both the kitchen and front doorways, he walked beside the stretcher to the street, much taller than I remembered him until I noticed he'd been stomping on top of the snow pile next to the sidewalk. He climbed into the ambulance and sat beside me. No one argued, especially me.

I tried to smile.

"Everything's Coming up Roses," I warbled. And that's all I remember.

A T THE RISK OF SOUNDING LIKE SERGEANT RENFREW from the
Royal Canadian Air Farce, "when I regained conscious-
ness," I discovered that I'd been through surgery. Both
bones in my ankle had snapped in the fall, and I was now the
proud possessor of some hardware that should make airport
and library portals buzz through eternity.

Steve was waiting for me as they wheeled me out of the
recovery room and into a two-bed hospital room. Thank
goodness there was no one in the other bed. I'm very picky
about who is allowed to see me at my drooling, disoriented
best. They transferred me gently to the bed, with Steve hovering, ready to arrest anyone who made me wince. Frankly, I
think someone could have sat on my foot at that moment
and I wouldn't have felt a thing.

"You look like hell," said my prince.

And to think he'd probably stayed up all night to tell me
that. I tried to smile, which must have been a frightening
thing, since he moved closer and took my hand.

"How are you feeling? The doctor says you should be able
to move around in a couple of days."

"Really?" Having never broken anything more serious than
a fingernail previous to this, I was completely in the dark as
to recovery rates. Curiosity made me look down the bed to
my foot, which was encased in a large thing resembling an

oven mitt with Velcro straps. Steve began to convey the information he'd probably coerced out of the surgeon.

"They figure you'll have to keep weight off it for about six weeks, but they're happy with the way they've reset it. Some rest, some physio and you'll eventually only notice the occasional twinge on rainy days."

Maybe it was the reassurance that I'd be okay, or the thought of clomping about on crutches for six weeks, but I suddenly felt the first spurt of anger since I'd taken the godawful tumble.

"And?" I asked Steve.

He looked disconcerted.

"And what?"

"Any ideas about who pushed me? Or have you been just sitting here waiting to tell me how awful I looked?" It was unfair, but I wasn't feeling particularly beatific at the moment.

"Actually, I've been sitting here waiting to get a statement from you. All we got out of you last night was Broadway tunes." He pulled his notebook out of his pocket. "You are sure you were pushed?"

"Positive."

"Well, the only thing I am positive about is that it wasn't Rod Devlin who pushed you. In a way, this is a relief, because it highlights what I've long thought, which is that Gwen Devlin's death and the other events weren't actually connected."

While that was debatable in my mind, I told him as clearly as I could remember the events leading to my plummet. He quizzed me about anything I could recall of the other person in the darkened kitchen, but all that came back to me was the feel of a hard hand in the middle of my back.

"Don't worry, the times help. We can narrow things down based on who was where when, and all that." He flicked closed the ubiquitous notebook and metamorphosed back into concerned boyfriend.

"Get some sleep, kiddo. I'll be back in to see you in the afternoon."

I heard him conferring with the nurse outside the door, and something about a police guard, but I was too close to the land of Nod to care. I drifted back into a sea of Demerol.

THE NEXT TIME I SURFACED, DENISE AND LEO were keeping vigil at my bedside.

"How long have you guys been here?"

"Just a few minutes," Denise answered, watching Leo arrange a bunch of Safeway flowers in my water jug.

"Yes, I was all for tweaking a toe, but Denise advised against it." Leo smiled.

I felt much more myself this time, and for the first time also felt some pain from my leg. As I shifted on the pillow, I grimaced with the slight movement.

"Long enough to discover you snore, though," continued Leo from the only chair in my area. Denise looked around and went to pull the other chair from the still unoccupied half over to the other side.

"I do not," I replied, "that was a code to higher aquatic mammals."

"Say hi to Flipper for me the next time you snooze," Leo snorted.

Denise got as comfortable as one could in a hospital room, a darned sight more comfortable than me, and started right into business. Thank goodness none of this had changed her.

"They've arrested Rod Devlin for murdering his ex-wife."

"I knew that," I said smugly.

"Well, did you know that they have dropped the inquiry

into the graffiti and fire and are pushing this to the fore-ground?" Denise was furious in her dead calm way.

"You're kidding, right? How did you hear that?" Then I stopped. Leo looked arch behind Denise's set shoulders. There was one way for sure that Denise got her news these days.

"Mark tried to get a statement from the police spokes-person yesterday, and they closed him down completely," she stated. "They're not going to do anything."

Maybe, I thought. Or maybe they had other things in mind for Mr. Paulson. How far would someone go to get a Pulitzer Prize? If you could manufacture an addicted little boy, why not paint a few doors and set a little fire? My mind, hazy as it was on the pain medication, was painting some pretty ugly pictures. Suddenly remembering my too obvious facial expressions, I refocused on my guests. Denise was examining the flowers, but Leo was giving me a funny look. I heaved myself upward, trying to sit, and collapsed immediately with a scream. Denise looked up, alarmed. Leo pressed the nursing button, and pretty soon a nurse bustled in with some codeine-laced Tylenols for me. It was a shame to be off Demerol, but what the heck. Into all this, Steve entered. I smiled wanly at my knight in leather jacket, and then grimaced afresh, when I realized he was carrying a pile of unmarked exams. There is no escape from some tortures.

Or maybe there was. The pills began to take effect, and without any concern for my company, I drifted back to Morphius.

When I next awoke, Leo and Denise had left and Steve was sitting at my bedside, reading a Robert J. Sawyer paperback. He looked up and smiled a smile that made me push back thoughts that I might look like the wreck of the Hesperus.

"Hey," he said softly.

I smiled back, trying to shift without moving my foot. He bounced to the end of my bed to raise the head. Soon I was feeling a bit more sociable. I spotted the exams on the side table to my left.

"Thanks for bringing those over. I'm going to need a couple of other things in order to post marks, if I can impose on you some more."

"No problem. It sounds as if you'll be here the better part of a week, so I figured you'd want these out of the way. If you want, I can help later."

"You never know." I grinned. "They might be happier I marked them while under the influence of codeine than if I'd been totally sober."

Steve laughed. It was good to hear his laughter. It reminded me that there was a sane world beyond all the crazy things that had been happening. Thinking that, my mind snapped back to the one question I'd been waiting for the others to leave to ask him.

"Denise says the police have dropped the investigation. Is that true, or are the police just no longer talking to Mark Paulson?"

Steve smiled wryly.

"Mr. Paulson has been making a bit of a nuisance of himself. I think my colleagues are just a bit tired of his wanting to broadcast every tendril of evidence that goes floating past his nose."

"He has been wanting to get hold of me these past few days, you know. He cornered me in HUB the other day. Was it yesterday? Hey, what day is it? Students are going to be freaking out over their mid-term grades not being posted."

"Relax, you've still got a day or so, and I'll be in after my shift to help you. So Paulson wants to talk with you, does he? Any idea what about?"

I shook my head. "I haven't a clue. In fact, I've been feeling a little creeped out by him all along. Am I being too paranoid, or do you think he could have staged all of this in order to make a name for himself reporting on it?"

"I think that might be a bit too Byzantine, but if it makes you feel any easier, I've got an officer posted on your ward. No one nasty is going to get near you, I promise."

"I wonder what he wants from me? Mind you, I wonder how I got caught up in any of this, beyond being Gwen's prof." Steve sighed and agreed that that was the sixty-four thousand dollar question.

"But we're on top of it, don't worry. And we've caught the one guy who actually killed someone. You rest now, and knit up, and we'll work on getting the rest of the bad guys behind bars, okay?"

Steve stood and made a pathetic attempt at smoothing my covers and plumping my pillows. I gritted my teeth and smiled as he inadvertently jostled the pillow my foot was resting on. Love hurts, after all.

"I'll be in after my shift. Take care, Randy."

"Not much else to do." I kissed him goodbye and faded away, probably before he'd even reached the doorway.

I WOULDN'T WANT TO BE HELD ACCOUNTABLE FOR the futures of the students whose papers I marked in the next two days. Objectivity was not my strong suit. I alternated between laisser-faire as the codeine swept through my system, and slash and burn as the effects of the pain pills wore off. As a result, my averages seemed satisfactory as I filled in the results list. Life is a crap shoot; if my students learned that out of four years of university they would be well educated.

Steve had said there would be nothing to worry about anymore, but had stationed a uniformed policeman near my door on the ward anyway. He even followed my wheelchair to physio, although he stayed discreetly in the anteroom as I made a fool of myself trying to climb and descend mock staircases with crutches.

Even though it made me scream in pain at times, I enjoyed physio just because of the continuity of faces. Louise, my therapist, was there every morning to put me through my paces. Up on the ward, I'd found a different nurse a day, due to the steep cutbacks the Klein government had made to health care. The continuing motif was the harried look they all displayed, rushing to do far more than they had the time or energy to perform.

One thing you had to say for the cutbacks, they impelled you to get well in a hurry. Hospitals, never my favorite places to begin with, had taken on a haunted aspect. I couldn't help thinking I'd be far healthier on the outside. So, after lunch and a nap, I would work on the arm-strengthening exercises Louise had given me from my bed. If they did anything to reduce underarm flab at the same time as they built up crutch-wielding muscles, I would remember Louise in my will.

So, about five or six days after I'd taken my fateful tumble, I was sweating away, pulling myself up on my little trapeze and lowering myself back to the mattress in slow counts of seven. I had made it through two repetitions when that weird feeling that "something is not right with the picture" occurred to me. I lay back, panting, and looked around. Everything seemed the same. I looked through the doorway to the ward beyond. There was something niggling . . . and then I had it. My sentry was gone.

A flashback of being pushed down the stairs ran through my mind. I hadn't realized until he was gone how secure that uniformed man had made me feel. The sweat on my upper body turned cold and made me shiver. I thought of ringing for the nurse, but then wondered if maybe I was over-reacting; maybe the policeman had just gone off for a moment to use the facilities.

I waited, listening to my heart beating much faster than it had been during my bout of exercise. I tried to think of when I'd noticed him last. Surely it had been a while, long enough for my torpid unconscious to finally notice his absence. While I knew he would likely be busy, I reached for the phone to call Steve.

No joy. Steve was apparently en route to Fort McMurray, getting the evidence against Rod Devlin all in order with what the Mounties had uncovered there. Well, I likely had used up more of his time than I was entitled to, anyhow. Maybe the police guard had gone off for a bite to eat. I tried to think if I had noticed some pattern to when a guard was there and when one wasn't. It struck me that I'd been protected around the clock, but maybe I was wrong.

I left a message on Steve's pager, anyway.

This was ridiculous. Rod Devlin was behind bars and I was in a busy hospital in the middle of the day. Nothing bad was going to happen to me. I reached for the exercise triangle, trying to recall how far I'd been when the panic had set in. Just as I was huffingly into the middle of my fourth set of reps, I felt my throat dry up.

Mark Paulson was standing inside my room, pulling the door closed with his left hand. He was holding his right arm awkwardly behind him. My earlier Gothic thoughts of him inciting Gwen's murder and torching Grace's office to ensure himself a Pulitzer raced through my head, and I was scrambling for the nursing button when he pulled his hand forward into my sights.

He held out a paper cornucopia of flowers.

My shoulders sagged.

"Hi, Randy. Do you mind a visitor?"

He came forward hesitantly, the way people frightened of hospitals tend to walk. I was mollified a bit, but still wary, as he came around to the chair side of the bed.

"Denise told me your room number. I hope you don't mind me bugging you at a time like this, but I still really need to talk to you."

"I don't know anything, honest. I'm just lying here, out of commission," I babbled.

Mark looked puzzled, and then laughed. "I'm not here to get an interview, if that's what you're thinking. Although, when you're feeling a bit better, I wouldn't mind getting your take on the events."

Mark sat down in the chair without being asked, still holding the flowers. I began to wonder if they were for me, or whether they were some sort of protective coloration he'd used to get through the front doors.

He looked up at me like a basset hound, and the tumblers started to fall into place. This wasn't a reporter nosing out a story. This was some sort of personal thing.

"Actually, I wanted to talk to you about Denise," Mark said.

"Denise? What about her?"

"Well, I thought, what with Christmas coming up," he paused, and I started to feel the corners of my mouth turning up in spite of myself. I felt as if I was being propelled back into junior high at the same speed as Michael J. Fox had used in his souped-up Delorean.

"Would you, as her friend, happen to know what sort of perfume she likes?"

I laughed, which wasn't kind, but completely unavoidable.

Mark looked a bit puzzled.

"I think you couldn't go wrong with *Obsession*, Mark," I giggled.

Mark began to nod, in all seriousness, and tried to pull his notebook from his inner breast pocket. He discovered, through this action, that he still held the flowers, which he presented to me with all the grace of a Beaver Scout to the Queen, and scribbled the name in his book.

I looked at the flowers, which weren't quite as nice an assortment as Leo had brought, but were well meant. All in all, I supposed Paulson had just been doing his job. I looked at him, so earnest in his attempt to please Denise, and realized that my antipathy had not been for him. It had been a sort of jealousy; I was in the middle of awful things, and he had taken away my confidante, Denise. It was playground politics, not some awareness of evil.

Mind you, it was his publishing of the letter to Gwen that had started all this. Or pushed it on, at any rate. That was a question that I'd wondered from the beginning.

"Did you meet Gwen Devlin before you published her letter?"

"Me? No. I never did. I tried to get hold of her on the

phone, but no luck. I heard she was really a super person, though. I spoke with several of the students on her floor in residence after the murder."

"How did you get the letter, then?"

"What?"

"Her letter from the Party Animals. How did you get it?"

"It arrived in a press package from a source at the university. That was why I wanted to speak with Ms Devlin, to ascertain that it was actually what was in her letter. One of the lawyers for some of the other girls verified it as a Party Animal letter, though, so we ran it."

"Who was sending you a press package? I thought the university was trying to keep things quiet? I know our chairman was really adamant about not spouting things to the papers for fear of making things worse, or the university look bad."

Mark shrugged. "Someone thought differently. It wasn't Denise, I know that. I asked her point blank, since so much of what it was doing was the same as she was advocating. But she swears it wasn't her, and I can't imagine why she'd lie about something like that."

"No, I can't imagine Denise lying about anything, to tell you the truth." I smiled, and Mark beamed in the way lovers have when they are talking about their objects all sublime. What he had told me was puzzling, though. Back when Denise and I had been positing the culpability of the press in reporting on the poison pen letters, neither of us had questioned how the press had received its information. Now that we knew Mark personally, Denise wasn't in a mood to be objective, and I was suddenly curious.

Part of me still blamed the printing of that letter for Gwen's death. If her husband hadn't read that letter, would he have been so moved to murder her? He'd hurt her before, but perhaps, with the letter out there he'd felt he could get away with it. Whoever had sent the letter, though, wouldn't have known it would trigger Rod Devlin's rage. That letter was a direct attack at Gwen, and if Devlin hadn't written it, then someone else had also had an ax to grind against his wife. I stared at my flowers, and then at the pile of exams I had just finished marking, and an idea began to form. Perhaps there was a way to flush out whoever had written that letter.

"It's funny, when you think of it, all this boils down to words in the wrong people's hands."

"What do you mean?" asked Mark. There was a glint in his eye. The boy was a born reporter; he could smell the story brewing before I was even sure I was going to spin it.

"Well, Gwen died because of that letter. The Party Animals, by writing that letter, and then whoever leaked it to you, signed her death warrant, even if they didn't know it. I wonder how much they did know. Whoever wrote that sure knew she had left her children, right? Surely, if they were trying to do the right thing, they wouldn't have used such a pointedly personal letter as Gwen's for your sample, right?"

Mark nodded. I was just warming up, but thinking on my feet—so to speak—had always been a strong suit and what made lecturing, even on those days when I was under-prepared, bearable.

"Well, my role in all this, I suppose, has been to do with written information, as well. First, I had Gwen's journal, which was helpful to the police in locating her therapist. Her essay pointed to issues with her ex-husband that the police here and in Fort McMurray looked into, since they had a probable cause to do so. And now," and here I took a deep breath before moving into uncharted territory, "there is more evidence of a sort in mid-session exams being written by people who lived on the Party Animal floor in residence."

Mark's ears were almost twitching, like a hunting dog on point.

"You have information on the case in your exams? What sort of information?"

I was ad libbing desperately, and I had honestly meant to discuss this with Steve before saying anything to anyone else, but there is nothing like talking to someone who really wants to hear a story to make the storyteller work up all the embroidered angles.

"One of the essay topics in the exam dealt with the subplot of an anonymous letter being written in Shakespeare's *Twelfth Night*. Let's just say certain students seem to have decided to use the exam as a form of confessional for their own involvement in that situation. One of the students even ponders whether the original note written as a joke hadn't been enhanced by a second party before it was discovered, to make the original pranksters seem more culpable. Now I can't imagine who in *Twelfth Night* would want Sir Toby Belch to look worse than he already appears, so it made me wonder if the student hadn't been transposing some real life event onto his reading of the play. In other words, perhaps the note you published wasn't the note he wrote."

Mark was starting to splutter. I had him; trouble was I wasn't sure how far to take this. I wished Steve had been around to talk this over with.

"Mark, I am not saying you screwed up the letter. I am saying you were screwed. Someone wanted that letter printed, rather than a more sophomoric rendition. The question is, why? As soon as the officer in charge gets back to me, I'm giving him these exams as evidence." I smiled, I hoped winsomely.

Paulson took the hint. Besides, he was already writing in his head, I could tell the look. It wasn't a look you saw very often in undergraduates, mind you.

"Thanks for the tip on Denise's gift, Randy. And thanks for the other tip, as well. I'll talk to you soon, okay?" He was already halfway out the door.

I waved. Maybe he wasn't so bad after all. But I didn't mind manipulating him to suit myself. The way I saw it, looking at my mangled leg, he owed me. Or someone did. And with any luck, I'd be meeting whoever that was soon. On my terms, this time.

I stretched my arm to its fullest length and snagged the telephone. By now, I had the number to Steve's precinct memorized. I called and asked if I could get a message through to him, only to be told he wasn't going to be back in town till the next day at noon. Damn. The newspapers hit the stands before six a.m. Gritting my teeth, and preparing myself for a lecture, I asked for Staff Superintendent Keller.

A FTER CHEWING ME OUT ROYALLY, KELLER AGREED to replace the officer (who had been off for lunch) with an undercover guard. Once I'd called the English department for some course numbers I wanted to check up on, I was set. Now, all I had to do was sit and wait for someone to rise to the bait of my pile of mid-terms. They sat there on the side table, silently accusing me of, well what, exactly? It wasn't perjury, or slander or plagiarism. What *did* one call manipulating the press? Self-preservation?

Whatever it was, I wasn't exactly proud of it, and I was more than a little nervous. I figured I had till the early morning before hell broke loose. That is, if things were going to play out the way I was beginning to think they might.

I could hardly sleep that night, which was just as well, since the nurses came in twice to see if I wanted anything to help me sleep. I decided against it, since I didn't know how long those pills stayed in one's system, and I wanted to be firing on all cylinders when the morning came.

If pain keeps your head clear, I was incredibly cogent by morning. I was doing a breathing exercise my physiotherapist Louise had taught me to get above the pain, sort of a "modified Lamaze" as she'd called it. Hell, if childbirth was anything like breaking a leg, I had no idea why there was a population explosion.

No one came into my room except the same nurses I'd seen for the last three-day shift. I had no idea if there really was a detective watching out for me. Steve had called me from Fort McMurray late the night before, and was really annoyed with what I'd done, even when I told him I'd spoken with Keller. I wasn't sure whether it was me putting myself in danger that bugged him, or me poking my nose back into the case. Oh well, there would be time enough later to sort all that out. I hoped.

I'd spent most of the night thinking who it was that would walk into my room in the morning. I had worked it out from piecing together things I'd been too involved to notice, coupled with things that Mark Paulson had told me the day before. When the door opened, I wasn't surprised but a frisson of fear went up my back anyway. After all, this was the person who had pushed me down a set of stairs and left me to rot, who had trashed my office, who had incited riots and hate-mongering, who had set a fire to an office, and set a student up to be murdered. I wasn't taking this lightly.

"Hi, Arno," I said with a false brightness even I could hear. "How nice of you to drop by."

He looked around the room, satisfying himself, I suppose, that there was no one waiting to ambush him. Eyeing all the equipment around, I suppose he realized that a microphone could have been hidden anywhere. He smiled condescendingly at me, and I wondered if he just thought me too stupid to have twigged to his involvement. How superior did he really think himself to mere women, anyhow?

"Denise and Grace and Leo have been reporting to us on your progress, Randy. I thought you might be getting sort of stir-crazy by now, though. It's a long time to be cooped up, isn't it?"

Maybe he did think me below deductive abilities. Whatever. We could play this scenario any way at all.

"Yeah, well, it's not the Ritz." I shrugged. "But they have five different flavors of Jell-O!"

Arno laughed. He sat on my visitor chair, and I felt as if I was looking into the python cage at the zoo. The same cold eyes were smiling back at me. Arno made a pretense of looking around at the various floral bouquets, and then his eyes fell on the exam box.

"Don't tell me you're actually marking while in this condition? Surely breaking your leg entitles you to a rest, no?"

"McNeely allowed me a few days' hiatus, but I have to get the marks posted, just like anyone else. When you're a term employee, you can't take any time off. Your next term's employment depends on your last term's record. Well, I guess you must feel much the same, with the tenure committee coming up, right?"

Arno wasn't smiling quite so brightly anymore, but his eyes were still fixed on me.

"Of course, your upcoming tenure review mixed things up for me for a while. Every time I saw you with a new group, I just jumped to the conclusion that you were campaigning for their support. It kept me from questioning why you were certain places with certain people. You helped out with the vigil so you would know how to disrupt it the most effectively. The time I saw you with those undergrads, you weren't trying to get them to nominate you for a teaching award, you were having an outing with your little cabal, right? Do they still call themselves the Party Animals, or was that just for pen pal purposes?"

Arno's lip had curled into a sneer by this time. I am sure he was considering the place to be bugged, so he was choosing his words very carefully.

"Randy? I'm not sure what you're alluding to. Perhaps your pain medication is playing games with your mind?"

I smiled through my fear, his arrogance giving me enough anger to rise above my pain and fear. Louise would have been proud of me.

"What really brought you here, Arno? Were you looking for the confessional exam? What would you do with it? Burn it?"

"I'm not sure what you're getting at, Randy, but I don't intend to sit here and be tarred and feathered for something that doesn't concern me in the least. Is this how you treat all your company? No wonder your policeman friend isn't around anymore."

"Yes, you're right. He got tired of me playing at getting myself killed. Not like Gwen, who really got herself killed. I can understand you hate women in general, Arno. But what did you have against Gwen in particular?"

"What? I didn't even know the woman. She was in your class, wasn't she? How would I know her?"

"That's what I was wondering, but then I remembered, she transferred into my class, and her reasons were that she'd been placed in a class where a few of her residence underlings were as well. Yesterday I had the secretaries check which class that was. Guess whose class that was, Arno?"

He shook his head, the way politicians do when they know you've caught them red-handed and they can't find a way to admit it.

"She was being diplomatic, wasn't she, Arno? She was really trying to get out of your class, right? She'd just left a marriage with a wife-beater; she probably had your number the minute she walked into the class."

"Who are you playing, Randy? Nancy Drew? All this is, of course, conjecture. You are building a huge house of cards on a very few disparate factoids. Yes, Ms Devlin was for a short time in my class. I had forgotten, to tell you the truth. I am sure you are correct, though, because I do know that several of those unfortunate boys who allowed their drunken sport to get out of hand are in my freshman class. Therefore, she likely was trying to remove herself from being too often in their presence. I can see that ringing true. However, there's one thing you may have to back down on; since several of those boys are in my class, how is it that the newspaper this morning reports that confessional exams are being written in your class? You can have the facts one way or another, Ms Craig, but not, I would suggest, both ways."

I couldn't bring myself to smile at him anymore. "Why did you change the letter to Gwen? Was it even a death threat before?"

"What, for argument's sake, makes you think the letter to the *Journal* was not the one Ms Devlin received?" Arno was still eyeing my exams; I was willing to bet he hadn't managed to corral all the Party Animals in his class. It made me shudder to think that I'd been teaching all term to someone who despised me for my gender. If I lived through this, I'd ferret out the little weasel and . . . what? Deprogram him.

"Well, for one thing, Paulson didn't receive the letter from Gwen herself, he got it in an anonymous press package. For another thing, the wording was nothing a freshman would be playing with. The other letters were pornographic, but in a pedestrian way." In a flash of insight that had nothing to do with proof, and everything to do with men and women, I crowed at him. "You asked her out, didn't you? After one of your rabble-rousing lectures against educating women? Or did she actually go out with you before figuring you out? Did you know you were setting her up to die, or were you just lashing out at her rejecting you?"

Arno had lost all semblance of civility by now, and I could tell it was all he could do to keep from screaming at me. Instead, he did something far worse. I am not sure what he intended to do, besides silence me. I shudder to think, now. His hand went for the pillow my leg was resting on; in one tug he yanked it out and had it halfway to my mouth. Maybe he was going to smother me while murmuring polite chit-chat for whatever microphone he deemed hidden in the room, and then let himself out and hope for a head start before the next nursing shift came to check on me. He needn't have bothered worrying; my throat was parched with fear. I couldn't make a sound as I watched the pillow come for my face.

He should have gone with *Macbeth* instead of *Othello*, because dislodging my broken foot was all it took for my lungs to regain power and then some. I screamed with all the terror and pain and sheer non-codeined agony that was bundled up inside. Arno was startled enough to stop, pillow raised. I kept screaming.

Just then both the door from the hall and the bathroom door burst open. My guard, dressed as a hospital janitor, was in the washroom doorway, gun pointed at Arno. Two more cops were coming in the hall door, screaming at him to freeze. I wish he'd listened. He pivoted on one foot, and lost his balance, falling backwards. Onto my broken foot.

ALL IN ALL, I WAS GETTING MIGHTILY TIRED OF HOSPITALS.

They had reset my foot, after pulling one of the mending pins out of a ligament where it had been sent piercing from the weight of Arno Maltzan. I was back in physio and at almost the same place I'd been healing-wise when he'd managed to drop in for his visit. Luckily, second term didn't start for another week.

Speaking of visits, I was bored. Christmas was over, and I was feeling melancholy for having missed it and petty for feeling melancholy. People had been very kind, but I'd been anticipating romance and eggnog, not visiting hours and IVs. All I had to look forward to was limping home to a dead tree, or maybe a stick in a bucket with a pile of needles at its base. A person can watch only so much daytime TV, and I had passed my limit at about the beginning of the week. On impulse, I picked up the phone and called Steve.

I could tell he was busy from the slightly distracted tone in his voice, but I figured that having been the actual bait in a major case gave me a bit of leeway.

"Will you have time to come over today?" Hospital stay had stripped me of any overt sense of pride; I was a sniveling whine when it came to visitors.

"I think I can be there just after lunch."

"Do you want me to save you my Jell-O?" I asked, trying to

sound light-hearted, although I still felt strange about the loss of the guard.

"Well, there's always room for Jell-O," Steve parried, and we left it at that. I clumped over to my locker in the corner of the room, and pulled on my grey sweat shorts and top, which did a bit to make me feel less vulnerable. While I was still upright, I hobbled down to the nursing station to ask if anyone had a newspaper. A nurse offered to carry it back for me, but I figured I'd have to start acclimatizing to my situation, and tucked it under my chin, which made me feel like a clumsy St. Bernard.

I scanned the paper when I got back to my room. There was another article about Arno Maltzan, written by Mark Paulson, tucked into the third page.

Paulson had done some background research on Maltzan, giving highlights from his CV which weren't too shabby, but not enough to grant him tenure, it seemed. There was a quote from McNeely about the dismay felt by the department and the responsibility for professors not to indoctrinate their students. It was obvious they were cutting Maltzan loose. I wondered how much of his exploits would stick to the department in the long run.

Lunch came and went. Steve didn't. Dr. Stelfox came by and pronounced me well enough to leave the next morning. I called Denise to see if she could pick me up. Although my apartment is only three blocks from the hospital, they're long blocks, and I didn't want to try out my crutching skills on slippery winter sidewalks.

It took the hospital until ten-thirty a.m. to finish the paper-work necessary to unleash me on the world. Denise wheeled me to the sub-basement, where she'd parked the car close enough for me to hobble from the sliding doors, leaving the wheelchair behind. Denise said all the right things about my prowess with the crutches, even though I almost managed to blacken her eye with the arm rest end of one when pulling them into her car.

Once we got to my place and Denise had done the

requisite fussing, she seemed to think invalidism required—which included setting me up with a foot stool and books and putting the tea on to boil—things began to start to feel back to normal. As soon as we were equipped with tea, the conversation turned immediately to Arno Maltzan and the buzz around the department.

While I had thought he should be charged for accessory to murder for the letter incident, he was getting attempted murder for pushing me down the stairs. His fingerprints had been discovered on a fuse tossed into the backyard of the House. How they found it in the snowdrift was beyond me, but I have the greatest respect for our police force.

It was common knowledge that Arno had goaded his Party Animals, a disaffected group of freshman in General Studies, into writing the initial letters and disrupting the vigil. They had also been charged for the graffiti incident, since an examination of their wardrobes had discovered some red paint on clothing—in the lining of a jacket pocket, and on the tongue of a track shoe, just under the lace holes.

The biggest question, which still hadn't been answered to my satisfaction, was why Maltzan had targeted me and my office. Denise had some ideas on that score.

"Now that he's been arrested, and it's no longer cool to know him, a few of the kids he was Svengali-ing have begun to come forward. Apparently, it was considered important to get a journal from your office, because you push journal writing in your classes. According to scuttlebutt, some of your students work on their journals after class time and get rather involved in the contents."

"I've never noticed it," I commented drily. "But I still can't figure out why Arno would target me for any of this. It's not as if I'm the most obvious threat."

"No, but you were Gwen's teacher; you were discussing anonymous letters in *Twelfth Night*; and you spent some class time discussing the graffiti? Did McNeely know about that one?"

"No," I answered, "And I hope he doesn't hear about it, either."

"Well, anyhow, Arno likely decided to check out how much Gwen might have said about him in that journal. You were right, by the way, he did date her at least once. Mark found his name in the registration book at Fraser linked to hers as her guest. According to Mark, Arno's not saying too much, but I'm betting he was under the impression that you knew something. He probably had your office trashed to find anything you might have written. You do go on about the power of journals, you know." Denise grinned and poured us some more tea.

"Steve told me that they found her journal in his office. The exam was likely grabbed to cover tracks. You know, that's almost as irritating as him breaking my leg twice. I had to create a whole new exam."

"Well, he's going to get punished a lot more for breaking your leg than for lifting your exam, or for setting up Gwen, or for any of the other shit he stirred up.

"To use your position as a lecturer to proselytize is unconscionable," Denise went on. "He should be held responsible for all the actions of hatred regardless of who actually performed the deeds. I take it he was the phone caller, though."

I sank back on my pillows to think about Maltzan and his manifest hatred. I agreed with Denise and have always striven to keep my politics and personal biases out of my in-class discussions. But how much of my own biases had I disseminated to my students along with Austen's *Pride and Prejudice*? How did one keep personal feelings out of presentation?

What Maltzan had done was horrific. He deserved everything the law threw at him. It was funny, in a way. He'd probably be punished more severely for pushing me down the stairs than for any of the malevolence he'd stirred up on campus, and yet I was of the mind that his physical actions were less problematic.

That's why I've always maintained that Lady MacBeth and Iago are far worse villains in Shakespeare than, say Goneril or Caliban. Insidious manipulation frightens me. It's so hard to pinpoint or prove, and yet it shimmers all around, like glossy oil puddles in the alley.

Denise broke into my reverie with more tea, and chocolate biscotti. "Grace can't believe it. Apparently Arno had done some editing for *HYSTERICAL* in the past. He helped out in organizing the vigil, too; probably to get inside information for the hooligans. She won't listen to that, though. Grace is so ready to believe the best in everybody. Leo tried to point out to her that Arno had probably personally started the fire in her office, and she just shut down on him."

"She's in denial," I offered, thinking we probably all were.

Denise nodded. "It's certainly making me look twice at people, and think twice before I say anything. The safety has gone out of the ivory tower, that's for sure."

"Maybe that's not such a bad thing. Perhaps we've been too complacent, thinking that just because we're smart enough to disseminate literature, we're clever enough to see through all human foibles? Isn't that the work for the writers of literature, rather than the teachers of literature?"

Denise stretched out her legs, making me wish I could. It was getting to be time for my pills.

"Could be," she said, "although it hurts to think that human beings can't operate at a higher level given the proper stimulus and environment."

"So Arno was supposed to be a saint just because he was well-read? I disagree, not that I in any way want to exonerate Arno's actions. What he did was horrid and unforgivable, but not necessarily unbelievable."

Our conversation eventually moved on to other things, and after agreeing to drop by the next morning on her way into the department, Denise finally left me to myself.

It was just as well. I had some thinking of my own to do.

I T WAS PROBABLY EXACERBATED BY THE PAIN PILLS coursing through my system, but my mind was going a mile a minute in tangential directions. Sure, it was wonderful to think that the bad guys, both Arno and Rod Devlin, had been caught. It was also terrifying to think I'd been so close to being killed. What was really bothering me, though, was the feeling that I'd somehow screwed things up between Steve and me.

Although his boss, Staff Superintendent Keller, had been scathing in the talking-to he had given me after the fact and had made some snide comments about "women's intuition" which had me on a slow burn, it was Steve's silence that really was scaring me. It wasn't as if I'd been acting behind his back, which he somehow seemed to think. He had been out of town, and I had acted on impulse. Heck, how many times had he told me that he wasn't on the case, anyhow?

Perhaps he was feeling a bit threatened by me having even a peripheral part to play in his world. I wasn't willing to push the theory to the extreme; I didn't want to paint him in the same boat as a creep like Arno Maltzan. I just wasn't able to be so open emotionally with someone who could compartmentalize his job from his personal life—especially as I had been involved, albeit peripherally, in that job. If he could shut me out there, where else might I find a locked door?

Furthermore, was I really important to him, or merely useful to him as bait for bad guys? That wasn't actually fair, since I had placed myself in the trap without any help or encouragement from Steve, but I was not feeling logical. I was feeling wounded. I'd worked myself up into a proper funk by the time he knocked at my door.

I had to give him points for sensitivity. It took him all of a minute to gauge my mood. He helped me back to my chair and pulled up the edge of the coffee table to sit on, holding my hand.

"You're pissed at me," he acknowledged.

I shook my head ruefully. "I don't even know if I have a right to be."

"You do. I've been thinking about it all day. You have every right to doubt my reaction. I can't believe it myself. I thought I was a sensitive New Age kind of guy, but when I knew you were in danger, I went sort of caveman. I am ninety percent certain that I reacted because I was worried about you, and not because you were poking your nose in a police investigation where you had no business."

I had to laugh. At last we could turn the lanterns off in daylight, Diogenes. I had found an honest man.

"Is that what you're worried about?" I asked. "That I want to horn in on all your cases? Don't worry about that, honestly; I have no desire to be subjected to pain, and I'm not out to change the world."

Steve sighed, and pushed back some loose hair from my face with a fingertip. "Randy, you and I both know that your curiosity and sense of fair play are a terrifying combination. But you're right. I do have to keep some things from you, and anyone for that fact. I can't tell you things about an ongoing investigation. It's in the rules, and besides you wouldn't want to know. I know you're ticked off at me for keeping you in the dark about some things, just as much as I'm ticked off at you for putting yourself into such a potentially dangerous situation. There was nothing I could do about it, though. For instance, most of the work on this murder case was done in conjunction with the Fort McMurray RCMP, who have a record of violence on Devlin a half-inch thick. Everything from hockey fights to neighbors reporting a few black eyes for Gwen. We found a copy of the newspaper article on the letter-writing, along with her "Dear John" letter to him, and some uglified photos in his house. It took a bit to get the warrant, but we managed to justify probable cause. Your comments on Gwen's essay were on the money, but that wasn't going to cinch it. We had enough circumstantial evidence to make Gwen's therapist open her files, and after that it didn't take much to tie up the time sequence of Devlin taking time off work and the mileage on his truck. We even found someone on 117th St. who complained about his truck being parked in front of her house without a neighborhood parking pass."

"But you'd never have found Jane without my help!" I couldn't help interjecting.

"We'd have got the journal a whole lot sooner if you and I hadn't been mixing up romance with a case, though. That journal is what put you in far too much danger for my liking."

"Well, I feel as if you're trying to excuse yourself for keeping things from me at the same time as you're scolding me for being involved in the first place. It hurts not to be trusted, Steve."

"I wasn't keeping things from you because I thought you'd blab or screw things up. Randy, the world I see is so damn ugly, do you think I want to see it all over again when I look in your eyes?"

The man was good, and I was relenting. He noticed this, and pressed his advantage.

"I value your insights and I love you, but I want a relationship, not a work partnership. Is that all right with you?"

I shook my head, marveling at his ability to see through me.

"I guess I was reading too much Tommy and Tuppence, or Nick and Nora into all this," I admitted. "It's not as if I really wanted that, either, I guess I just don't know what to expect from this particular volume. If I'm going to live in a sub-literary genre novel, I at least want to be the intrepid girl detective, not the victim."

"There is nothing sub-literary about you, my dear. And besides, fiction is only that," Steve agreed. "Sometimes you have to fly without a script." He leaned forward to kiss me.

I kissed him back, releasing myself momentarily to a world without words. Ironic really, since it had been words that had begun it all. Words that stung, words that killed, words that destroyed. Regardless of how good it felt just now to have lips on mine, keeping them still, I wasn't going to underestimate the potency of words. But for now, I would bow to a greater mind, a much better writer. "The rest is silence . . ."